Elizur Wright

Myron Holley : and what he did for liberty and true religion

Elizur Wright

Myron Holley : and what he did for liberty and true religion

ISBN/EAN: 9783337261740

Printed in Europe, USA, Canada, Australia, Japan

Cover: Foto ©Andreas Hilbeck / pixelio.de

More available books at **www.hansebooks.com**

ith great respect and affection
yours
Myron Holley

MYRON HOLLEY;

AND

WHAT HE DID FOR

LIBERTY

AND

TRUE RELIGION.

———————

He knew to lead and to provide,
Who showed us how to DO and died.

———————

1882:
PRINTED FOR THE AUTHOR.
P. O. Box 109, Boston.

A copy of this book, which three leading publishers, though guaranteed against loss, have declined to publish, either with the author's name or without it, will be sent postpaid on the receipt of $1.50 addressed to Elizur Wright, Box 109, Boston. Or ten copies will be sent, free of freight, on the receipt of $10.00.

If any profit should accrue from the sale, it will all be paid to the descendants of Myron Holley, till such time as the State of New York shall have paid the just debt it owes them.

CONTENTS.

CHAPTER V.

CHAPTER VI.

CHAPTER VII.

CHAPTER VIII.

CHAPTER IX.

CHAPTER X.

CHAPTER XI.

CHAPTER XII.

CHAPTER XIII.

CHAPTER XIV.

CHAPTER XV.

CHAPTER XVI.

CHAPTER XVII.

CHAPTER XVIII.

CHAPTER XIX.

CHAPTER XX.

CHAPTER XXI.

CHAPTER XXII.

CHAPTER XXIII.

INTRODUCTORY.

SIXTY years ago the interior of this vast, well-knit republic was a wilderness, the home of wild beasts, hunted by almost wilder men. Seemingly interminable rivers traversed interminable forests; but no railroad, no canal; no common wagon-road which did not end at some forlorn-looking log hut. Scattered along the Atlantic coast were states almost strangers to each other, differing widely in manners and customs. At the north was close-fisted, hard-drudging industry, with an insatiable appetite for traffic, and getting the best of a bargain. At the south was prodigality, indolence, and chattel slavery. The only bond of union was, that all had together rebelled against the dominion of a mother-country, and achieved by common effort and suffering a costly independence. That such a string of states would long

hold together there was almost no reason to expect. Morally, geographically, ethnographi ally,
everything was against it, except the storms of the
Atlantic and the absence of steam-power, which
had made independence possible. The infancy
of the national republic had been precarious,
stormy, and full of narrow escapes from inglorious
wreck. It emerged from the war of 1812 pretty
evenly divided into two political parties, bitterly
hostile to each other on some comparatively unimportant questions, but both about equally under
the domination of the slave-holders of the south
on the vital question of personal liberty. Anything then more unlikely to happen than that the
shores of the great lakes and the northern valley
of the Mississippi would be peopled in thirty years,
or that slavery would be abolished in sixty, could
not well be conceived.

Among the moving forces which have conspired
to bring about the wonderful events we have lived
to see, there must be many men and women whose
lives are worthy of the most precise history and
careful preservation for the benefit of posterity.

Not always the men who get the highest place in the cotemporary record have the best right to be there. The most prominent at the time are not always the most effective. Some are inscribing their names, while others are quietly doing the work. It is of the utmost moment to posterity to know what manner of men they were who did the best work, whether in giving direction to the physical or the moral forces of the people. These forces, always intimately related to each other, must conspire and act in a certain concert to produce any great nation, any upward movement of the race.

It is the ambition of this slight monograph to point my countrymen, and especially my countrywomen, of this generation, to one who died before most of them were born, and whose memory deserves to be forever decked with the greenest wreaths and the loveliest flowers; to a man whose modesty never allowed him to spend a thought on the place he was to occupy in history, but who yet did more perhaps than any other one man to convert our great central forest into a garden, and then gave his life to make the continent one nation in which justice should reign.

Christianity in paying divine honors to its alleged founder traces, or pretends to trace, his lineage back to a remarkable king of antiquity, so the purpose of this sketch cannot be most effectively accomplished without going back to a very royal personage in the history of science, a genealogy which can be easily verified by any one who doubts.

CHAPTER I.

ANCESTRY.

IN 1656 there was born in London, as son to a wealthy citizen, one who, before the age of nineteen, had provided himself with Gallileo's instruments to watch the stars. Newton, a posthumous baby, born so small that a "quart mug would have contained him," was 14 years his senior. This youth of nineteen who was questioning the heavens with his own telescope nine years after Newton had conceived the idea of the law of gravity, and eleven years before that abnormal man published his immortal PRINCIPIA, was named EDMUND HALLEY, a name which his descendants in this country spell Holley. Edmund Halley was a stalwart, scholarly, profound, self-sacrificing, comprehensive philosopher, who filled with his labors a life of 86 years, for 29 of which he was secretary of the Royal Society. Determined from the start to know what was going on, and by what law, among the "fixed" stars and planets, he first delved into the dim records of the ancient astronomers to find the relative positions of heavenly bodies in their days, and then by the most laborious application to his telescope, discovered that these bodies were none of them "fixed." He discovered those motions of the star-suns, and those perturbations of the planets and their satellites, which Newton, Leibnitz, La Grange, La Place, and other mathematicians, have since gained immortality by explaining. His genius laid the foundation of modern astronomical discoveries. He gave his name to a comet which had for thousands of years been frightening mankind at intervals, by so carefully observing it in 1681 as to successfully predict its return in 1759. It came back again according to prediction in 1835, and will probably make another appearance about 1913. Halley's discovery of the "fixed" stars in motion, and the perturbation of the planets at first frightened even philosophers for the stability of our system. It might be crushed by and by. Even the genial and hopeful poet, Dr. Erasmus Darwin, grandfather of the immortal evolutionist, wrote, probably about 1760, —

"Star after star from heaven's high arch shall rush,
Suns sink on Suns, and systems systems crush,
Headlong, extinct, to one dark centre fall,
And Death and Night and Chaos mingle all!

Till o'er the wreck, emerging from the storm,
Immortal Nature lifts her changeful form,
Mounts from her funeral pyre on wings of flame
And soars and shines, another and the same."

La Grange and La Place had not then mathematically demonstrated the stability of the heavens, a demonstration which subsequent observations have confirmed to the extent of showing that our moon, even, is not approaching the earth, if at all, at an average rate of more than one fourteenth of an inch a month. Halley himself seems to have kept perfectly calm regarding the sublime motions and perturbations he had discovered as nothing but an orderly dance, or as a French mathematician has expressed it, nothing but the swinging of "the pendulums of eternity, which beat ages while ours beat seconds."

Edmund Halley was not a mere star-gazer, but a warm-blooded man of the world, who looked shrewdly into the life of our own planet, traversing oceans in two long voyages to find the magnetic poles. To him we owe it, that the mild, contemplative, absent-minded, and rather superstitious Newton, was encouraged, or almost compelled, to publish his *Principia*, rather than to waste all his time in interpreting the scriptural prophecies.

CHAPTER II.

BIRTH AND EDUCATION.

MYRON HOLLEY, a lineal descendant of the great Royal Astronomer of the previous chapter, was born in Salisbury, Connecticut, April 29, 1779, and died in Rochester, N. Y., March 4, 1841. He had the advantage of spending his early years in one of the loveliest spots on this or any continent, where the cloud-capped Tahkannuc and its gaily wooded attendant mountains see themselves in many embowered lakes, and listen to the unceasing farewell of a river that has lingered, lovingly, in the intervening valley till it is obliged to overleap its marble barrier and make haste to the sea. It was here that Nature had done her best, and she found a true worshipper in young Myron. It was in the groves of this paradise that he saw the choicest birds build their nests. It was from its rock-ribbed mountain walls that he saw marble hauled slowly away by oxen to build great cities. It was from the glowing furnaces and forges where the evergrowing wood of the mountains met the red ore from underneath the hills, that he saw go the great anchors to hold our ships in every harbor of the world. And his father, Luther Holley, had before the revolution been one of the woodchoppers to feed these furnaces.

It is at the mention of this LUTHER HOLLEY, that one feels almost irresistibly tempted to stop and write a book. He was a model American, not only for his own but for future ages. A man with no nonsense about him. An independent, self-centred man, who despised no church, and belonged to none. A man always of the laboring class, too wide for anything narrow, and charitable equally to the poor and the rich.

Luther's great-grandfather, coming from England, settled first at Stratford and then at Stamford, Ct. His grandfather came up the Housatonic into the wilderness as one of the first settlers of Sharon, adjoining Salisbury. His father, John, was a prosperous farmer there, till a fire consumed his house and all its contents, reducing him to poverty, which was followed by the total loss of his health. Two older brothers having already left home to make their way in the world, the whole burden of the farm and support of a sick father fell upon Luther, a lad of sixteen, aided only by his mother and sisters. In this lad's old age he wrote to his distinguished son Horace, a very graphic sketch of his early life, in which he says : — " I worked hard during the day, and at night had to go after doctors and medicine. As doctors were then scarce, I had often to go eight or nine miles, when I was so weary that I have fallen asleep on my horse and rode for miles without knowing where I was, contriving to balance, however, so as to keep my seat."

In mending a plough he inflicted a cut on his knee, by which he lost twelve weeks of time and narrowly escaped losing his leg. While disabled from work by this accident he qualified himself to teach school, having never attended school but five days himself. In this he was successful, earning seven dollars a month by teaching in the winter, and working on the farm in summer as well as his stiff leg would permit. Bad crops and the death of a horse, for which he was partly in debt, did not discourage him, and he finally achieved the highest proof of honest manhood in paying for that horse in full. And at the same time he naively writes to his son, "I was, notwithstanding, actually negotiating with your mother, and in the following October we were married." This mother was Sarah Dakin, the daughter of a Calvinistic Baptist preacher, a very religious woman, but of whom it is recorded, that " she never could be persuaded to believe that her own child would suffer endless torments on account of a point of faith." * By fair dealing and industry, which seems never to have given him time more than to take a little rest in a church, the husband became a man of comparative wealth in Salisbury, and the wife the mother of a large family, of whom John Milton, Myron, Horace and Orville L. made their marks in the world. The first owed his name to his father's admiration for the poet of Paradise Lost, a work which he could repeat from memory, and which with a universal History composed most of his library.

Like most self-educated men, this Luther Holley no sooner found himself possessed of sons and means than he was disposed to devote a good deal of the latter to what is called the liberal education of the former. Three of his sons, Myron, the subject of this memoir, Horace, the

* Notice the importance of that fact in regard to the education of her son.

President of Transylvania University, and Orville
L., were college graduates, — Myron, like the late
James A. Garfield, graduating at Williams College in 1799, Horace at Yale in 1803, and
Orville Luther at Harvard. But the father by no
means entrusted the education of his sons wholly
to the colleges, as the letters from him which
they preserved abundantly show. One of them,
addressed to Horace, in 1802, makes one wish
this rustic Luther had been president of a college
himself. It is a nugget of native gold, and
worthy of a place in the Bible of Humanity whenever that book comes to be canonized. It must
be quoted nearly entire before entering on the
life of the greatest of the three college-bred sons.

SALISBURY, March 21st, 1802.

DEAR HORACE :— After several attempts, which have
been interrupted, I hope soon to be able to finish and
send you a letter. There would be no difficulty in
writing if I had nothing to say out of the common way.
But without further preface, I shall proceed to the subject which will occupy the principal part of this sheet.
I have long since viewed you as possessing talents
above the common level, and several pieces of your own
composition, which you read when last at home, more
fully confirmed my opinion ; yet with all your activity
and good sense, I feel some degree of anxiety on your
account. Are you not too much inclined to domination,

and, though honest and upright in disposition, prone
to consider the common class of mankind with too
little attention? I have not time to be very particular,
but would not a fair and candid investigation give you
different ideas, and be of use to you in your future
course?

Look round, my son, and carefully examine the
causes by which the United States are thus rapidly
increasing in wealth and improvement. Is it not
because we are habituated to, and not ashamed of
labor?

When you view the highly-cultivated fields, the towns
and villages, the useful as well as the more elegant
arts; nay, when you are conveniently dressed, and
comfortably fed, are you not led to say: These are the
productions of labor; and for these am I beholden to
the hard hand of industry? Why then should we not
say, The laboring class, though less informed in science,
and perhaps less entertaining in conversation, are yet
the most meritorious citizens?

If we look for men most necessary in times of immi-
nent danger, where are we better furnished than by
applying to those who are inured to hardship, like Cin-
cinnatus and Gideon of old, the former called from the
plough, the latter from the threshing-floor. General
Lincoln, I am told, cultivated his farm with his own
hands. General Greene was not only a farmer, but a
forger of iron. General Putnam, we all know, was a
laborious man, and, although rough in manner, was a
good commander. Once more, I am informed that the
battle of Bennington, which first checked the victorious
army of Burgoyne, was fought by an intrepid band of
farmers. Many people think that the time is approach-

ing when the great cities and commercial towns of the
United States will be ingulfed in luxury ; and inevitable
ruin must ensue, but for the yeomanry, who, scattered
over the country, simple in their manners and living,
bold and hardy from the habits of labor, will, it is
hoped, form a wall of defence.

My intention, however, in writing, is not to damp the
ardor of your mind, or to discourage in you that laudable ambition, which you so handsomely and ingeniously
distinguish and describe in your letter to Milton, but so
to direct you that your conduct may not only be dignified, but tempered with that becoming modesty which
helps much to regulate the entrance into life, and to
assist in placing a just value on every object.   The
most pleasing thing in nature must be, to be able to
converse with the wise, to inform the ignorant, to pity
and despise the intriguing villain, and to compassionate
and assist the poor and unfortunate.*

If this could be treasured in the mind and heart
of every young man, in college and out, the world
would owe more to Luther Holley than to Martin
Luther.   Such was the father of Myron Holley.
The son lived what this excellent father taught.

A picture of the childhood and boyhood of Myron Holley, as they passed blithely away in the

---

* In 1798 Luther Holley resided in Dutchess County, N. Y.,
and it is much to the credit of his fellow-citizens there that
they elected him to represent them that year in the General
Assembly of their state.

valley of the lovely Housatonic and among the green hills, with their singing brooks, that stretch over to the Hudson, would be grateful to the reader. But time has left no record of his early morning. We only see it beaming still in his sweet, manly face, as painted by Aimes. Yet a remarkable reflection of it has been preserved by one of his daughters in a number of letters written to him by four or five of his boyish friends before he went to college, while he was at college in Williamstown, at the law-school in New Haven, and in the office of Judge Kent in Cooperstown. Never was a young man so worshipped by his boy friends. They were in love with him. His father had lived a while at Red Hook, and afterwards at Dover, N. Y., while Myron was fitting for college, at the age of sixteen. Addressed to him at the latter place, a letter from a boy friend in Red Hook is a fair sample of the way he was worshipped. It is written in a strong, bold hand, and signed "Birch."

RED HOOK, 20th Oct., '95.

DEAR MYRON, — We had quite a dance of the first magnitude last night at a Mr. Holmes's, who has lately put up a public house in this town. There were Ladies and Gentlemen from forty and fifty miles distance, and all of the *Beau Monde*. I heard of its having been determined to be a very genteel one, and so I thought I would just walk over to Mons. Holmes's to learn politeness. There were a good many of them : the Ladies were dressed very rich, and the Gentlemen tolerably so. But you may poultice my eye with a turnip, if I thought I saw anything terrible in their manœuvres. I thought them nothing but mortals, and that perhaps one of them did not know the sweets of friendship ; so I walked home again, with as little satisfaction as you please. Believe me, Myron, I had rather have one squeeze by your hand than to dance fifty times with all the high-lifed things in the world.

Make my love to your brothers. Forgive the maiming of this thing, as the man is a waiting who is to carry it.

God bless you !

BIRCH.

After his graduation at Williams College in 1799, Myron seems to have directed his studies towards the law. I find a letter addressed to him by a classmate, Peter Starr, Jr., from Westfield, Mass., as " law student in the office of Judge Kent, Cooperstown, State of New York," and dated June 23, 1800. This long letter of personal friendship winds up with a glimpse of the politics of that period, which will have some interest to those who know what has been the political history of Westfield ever since. " Politicks," says Mr. Starr, " are very little talked of here, the people being generally united. While the federalists in this quarter stand in awful dread for the event of the approaching election of President and Vice President, the Jacobins triumph in the assurance of having Mr. Jefferson for the supreme magistrate of our nation. Certain it is, that the industrious and influential Jacobins, in this quarter, as well as in other parts of the United States, have succeeded to an unparalleled degree in corrupting the public mind. Their success has indeed been proportionate to their endeavors; which can be measured by nothing but the industry of the devil in working the destruction of the original parents of mankind." It is not to be supposed that young Holley, whatever his political bias may have been, shared this intensity of prejudice. Possibly he may not have been studying law at Cooperstown in 1800, for he says in a letter to his son Samuel, in 1834, speaking of New Haven: "I was delighted with seeing it, after an absence of thirty-three years; for perhaps you know that in my early manhood I lived a year at that place, studying law, and was admitted to the bar there in 1801." One of his fellow law-students there was Professor Benjamin Silliman. In 1802 he seems to have essayed the practice of law in Salisbury, his native place. But there he could not long have remained, for he is recorded as having settled in Canandaigua, N. Y., in 1803, and as having been married to Sally House of that village in 1804.

CHAPTER III.

CANANDAIGUA.

A more fortunate selection of locality he could not have made. For though Canandaigua, or Canadarque, as it was then called, was but an insignificant village in the bosom of a vast wilderness, it had among its inhabitants a number of men of transcendent ability and the highest culture in the country, who seem to have conspired to select for themselves the best and most beautiful spot in the Empire State. It was from the start the focus of intellect, enterprise and wealth for Western New York, and though but ten years from its first log hut,* sat, already looking forth from its fair gardens over its crystal lake, like the queen it is ever to be. But in

* When Myron Holley settled in Canandaigua before his marriage, he, together with Peter B. Porter, Augustus Porter and Judge Howell, boarded with a Mrs. Sanbourn, who nearly ten years earlier had traversed the wilderness between Utica and that place on horseback, following an Indian trail, with no company but her infant, which she carried tied up in her apron, when she had occasion to use both hands.

acquiring young Holley, the place was even more fortunate than the man. As long as that great home of gardens lasts, the spot on its broad, grandly shaded, main street, where his unpretentious home stood, will be pointed out with pride by every citizen to every admiring stranger. The house, directly opposite the old Ontario Bank, is still the same as that in which he lived, though its exterior has been a little brushed up. Other homes in Canandaigua, as of the Greigs and Grangers, had an air of magnificence without as well as within, as they still have, but that of Myron Holley was all glorious within, in the intellectual hospitality of the man and the charming presence of his beautiful wife and happy children. The grey-headed men of the place, and of many others, recount with delight how they spent an evening with Myron Holley and listened to his wonderful reading and conversation. He was, in fact, the pet artist of Canandaigua in that line. Without knowing it, he seems to have been the founder of the "Parlor" as the school of civilization.

CHAPTER IV.

CHOICE OF PURSUIT.

THE question arises why a young man full of natural eloquence, carefully educated to the law under the best masters, and not specially enamored of literature as a profession, should not have devoted himself to the practice of law. That he would have become a great ornament of the bar, and still more of the bench, is quite certain from the fact that he was always resorted to as an arbitrator, and generally proved satisfactory to both parties. His commanding presence, wonderful equanimity and ready flow of words, seemed to fix his destiny for the legal profession, but happily for his country, he never entered beyond the threshhold. A tradition, given by one of his sons, seems to let in some light on the question; indeed, so much that I endeavored in vain to verify it by searching the records of the Court. It may nevertheless be correct, for the custodian of these records was of opinion that such a fact would not have been noticed in those very meagre

minutes if it had occurred. The story is, that
Mr. Holley was, for his first brief in Canandaigua,
assigned by the Court to defend a man indicted
for murder. He visited and conferred with his
client in the jail, and becoming thoroughly convinced of his guilt, immediately on coming into
court next morning resigned his brief, and never
after appeared as an advocate. However this
may be, certain it is from his after life, no man
ever cherished a profounder regard for truth and
justice. He had an instinctive aversion to all
crookedness. Whether he held that this disquali-
fied him for a profession in which nothing is more
indispensable to pecuniary success than a faculty
of suppressing the truth and making the worse
appear the better side, I find no record. One
success, as a lawyer, he had achieved in his native
town of Salisbury, Ct., which is well worthy of
record as showing the character of the man and
the age. On a mountain over which passes the
road leading from the iron mines to the furnaces,
lived in a hut by himself a solitary wood-chopper
who had acquired the reputation, not so uncommon in that day, of a wizard. He was supposed
to have power over the teams that hauled the ore
across the mountain. Heavy loads and bad roads

were not sufficient in the minds of the drivers to
account for the balkiness of the horses, and the
poor old wood-chopper had to bear the blame and
the curses. One day a stalwart Dutchman, whose
team stopped half-way up and refused to stir,
determined to try what he had heard to be a sovereign charm or exorcism in such cases, to wit, to
draw blood on the wizard. So ascending the
mountain he seized the poor man and with his
jack-knife cut a frightful gash across his fore-
head, and left him bleeding. . Returning to his
horses, which by this time had rested themselves,
he was confirmed in his superstition by their
readily taking the load up the hill. Young lawyer Holley brought an action for damages against
the Dutchman and obtained judgment in favor of
the innocent wood-chopper.

Having given up the practice of the law, without
much loss of time he married, bought the stock
of a bookseller named Bemis, became the literary
purveyor of the county town and surrounding
country, and devoted himself to the creation of a
happy home. His books, his garden and his
children occupied his time. For about four years,
between 1810 and 1814, he was County Clerk,
and the voluminous records of the titles of real

estate in his faultless manuscript attest his industry. The years 1812 and 1813 were very
gloomy for the people of the lake frontier, for the
war had burst upon them entirely unprepared.
What they suffered is well set forth in a letter
addressed to DeWitt Clinton, then mayor of the
city of New York, and to Col. Robert Troup,
Gen. Clarkson, John B. Coles, Thos. Morris,
Moses Rogers, Robert Bowne and Thos. Eddy,
distinguished citizens. It was written by Myron
Holley, and because it is highly characteristic of
him, and of the situation of the country immediately before his grand public life commenced, I
give it here entire. It had an immediate effect,
not only in calling forth large private donations,
but $3,000 from the city, and $50,000 from the
state.

CANANDAIGUA, 8th January, 1814.

GENTLEMEN, — Niagara county, and that part of
Genesee which lies west of Batavia, are completely de-
populated. All the settlements, in a section of country
forty miles square, and which contained more than
twelve thousand souls, are effectually broken up. These
facts you are undoubtedly acquainted with, but the distresses they have produced, none but an eye-witness can
thoroughly appreciate. Our roads are filled with people, many of whom have been reduced from a state of
competence and good prospects to the last degree of
want and sorrow. So sudden was the blow by which

they have been crushed. that no provision could be made either to elude or to meet it. The fugitives from Niagara county especially were dispersed under circumstances of so much terror. that, in some cases, mothers find themselves wandering with strange children. and children are seen accompanied by such as have no other sympathies with them than those of common sufferings. Of the families thus separated all the members can never again meet in this life. for the same violence which has made them beggars, has deprived some of their heads and others of their branches. Afflictions of the mind, so deep as have been allotted to these unhappy people, we cannot cure. They can probably be subdued only by His power who can wipe away all tears. But shall we not endeavor to assuage them? To their bodily wants we can certainly administer. The inhabitants of Canandaigua have made large contributions for their relief, in provisions. clothing, and money. And we have been appointed. among other things, to solicit further relief for them from our wealthy and liberal-minded fellow-citizens. In pursuance of this appointment. may we ask you. gentlemen, to interest yourselves particularly in their behalf? We believe that no occasion has ever occurred in our country which presented stronger claims upon individual benevolence. and we humbly trust that whoever is willing to answer these claims will always entitle himself to the precious rewards of active charity.

Signed,   Wm. Shepard.   Thad. Chapin,
           Moses Atwater,   N. Gorham.
           Z. Seymour,   Thos. Beals,
           Myron Holley,   Phineas P. Bates.

           Committee of Safety and Relief.

In 1816 his fellow-citizens had the wisdom to discover his fitness for vastly more difficult duties, and from that date the materials for his biography are only too abundant, for they include a great deal of the history of the country for thirty-five years.

Of the previous twelve years of his life, there would not have been left a vestige at this day, but for the remarkable fact that in his long absences from home, while on public business, he carried his family in his heart, and at a time when mails were few and expensive, deluged his children with letters, many of which a heroic daughter has piously preserved. A man of extensive reading, excellent taste, and the most fascinating conversational powers, he was by no means an artistic writer. Like all other natural orators, his eloquence on paper is rather long-winded, or at any rate, its wit does not consist in its brevity. There is clear daylight, no clouds, no lightning, no fog. He is all the while turning his soul wrong side out, and there is a vast deal of it. He is never ambitious to make you admire himself, but to make you understand his subject. He is no iconoclast, no grumbler, no detractor, but wide, genial, hopefully progressive, sympathetic with all, yet marching in the front rank with the best. The front rank at that day, it must be remembered, was not far in advance of the mass. Where he stood almost alone in 1840, millions stand now.

CHAPTER V.

MARRIAGE.

It was on the 4th of December, 1804, that Mr. Holley, then twenty-five years and eight months of age, was married by Rev. Timothy Field, the first Congregational minister of Canandaigua, to Sally House, the daughter of Capt. John House, one of the earlier settlers of the place. She was a remarkably comely and well-developed person, eighteen years and four months of age, having been born in Schenectady in 1786. Her father was one of the patriots who volunteered to serve his country in the war of 1812, and fell at last in the battle of New Orleans, fighting under General Jackson. She was a Methodist in her religious faith, and so continued till she died at Buffalo in 1868, aged 82. That Mr. Holley had no reason to regret his choice, is quite certain, for she made him the father of six daughters and six sons, and in the darkest hour of his adversity, twenty years after their marriage, he addressed to her the following lines on the occasion of his leaving home for Albany. It is almost the only time we find him indulging in versé, and as it was only for her, the critic has no business with it. But here is the heart of the man at a time when he had given the Empire State its Erie Canal, and made himself poor by it :—

> " For thee, dear wife, as age advances,
>   Affection's light still cheers my heart,
> And twenty years with thee enhances
>   My bosom's pain whene'er we part.
> When first in youth thy pleasing form
>   Filled all my soul with fond desire,
> And holiest vows had lent their charm
>   To cherish love's unceasing fire,
> 'Twas then the joy that filled thine eye,
>   The roseate hue upon thy cheek,
> The auburn curls that waving high
>   Thy polished forehead did bedeck,—
> 'Twas thy soft smile and winning air,
>   The dance alert and figure's grace
> Which made me hold thee dearer far
>   Than all things else in time's long race.
> But all these charms may fade away,
>   Thy eye may sink, thy cheek turn pale,
> Thy locks may bleach, thy limbs decay,
>   And age thy figure's graces steal.
> Still thou wilt be more dear to me
>   Than all these causes e'er would prove thee,
> For all thy truth, from youth to age,
>   Compels me more and more to love thee."

The beauty of Miss House had, in fact, turned the heads of most of the young men in Canan-

daigua and thereabout, and it was a very happy
thing for her that she found a husband who could
see and appreciate the sterling worth that lay
beneath it, and by his own abundant culture
supply her lack of it.

CHAPTER VI.

CHURCH CONNECTION.

Myron Holley, without a particle of bigotry, was always religious, in the higher and better sense of that word. He had a profound reverence for human nature, and an intense desire to promote the dignity and happiness of the race. Socially attractive, he seems to have drawn the religious people of his day in Cananduigua up to himself rather than to have been drawn down to them. By the records of the First Congregational Church, I find that he, with his mother-in-law, Elizabeth House, joined that body April 30, 1815, and that they with six of his children were baptized that day. Some of the present members of that church, when inquired of as to his religious views, said he was a Unitarian, and others said he was a Universalist, but all expressed their surprise at the fact above stated, and some their incredulity. The sequel will explain this curious phenomenon.

Religious or rather denominational prejudices
fade with exceeding slowness, but they do fade.
Religious tolerance was considered almost a crime
by most people in the first two decades of this
century, no matter how religious or useful the person might be who indulged in it. Elkanah Wat-
son, the founder of the Berkshire Agricultural
Society, and who began agricultural shows in 1807
by exhibiting two merino sheep, shocked a great
many good people and earned hard epithets, by
the following passage in his agricultural address,
delivered Sept. 24, 1811 :

"It is as ridiculous, as impertinent, for a man to
quarrel with another for not thinking as *he thinks*, as for
not looking as *he looks*. Two centuries ago Europe
was deluged in blood, on the score of religious intoler-
ance.

In these enlightened days, as we are pleased to call
them, we look back with astonishment and disgust at
the folly of men in those days. Will not our descendants have equal cause to regret the folly of the present
age? How can we Americans boast of our freedom,
when we are all combined to enslave each other's opinions, — whereas the freedom of the mind is the most
powerful attribute of *freemen*, and the most valuable
prerogative of human nature."

CHAPTER VII.

ERIE CANAL.

Thus in accord with the influential society in which he lived, and in reality its favorite, when Canandaigua wished to do its utmost to promote the great enterprise of connecting Lake Erie with the Hudson River by a canal, it sent him, then in the prime of his manhood, at the age of 37, to represent it in the General Assembly at Albany, in 1816.

With the present means of locomotion and transportation, the Erie Canal has almost dropped out of sight. If you spin through the State of New York in an express train, by daylight, you see large barges, seeming stationary, in a meadow. Otherwise you see nothing of an achievement which half a century ago was the pride of America, and the envy of Europe. But to appreciate the triumph of its accomplishment you must conceive of the American wilderness as it existed up to 1816; you must conceive of the general poverty and bit-

ter political strife of that era, and in fact you must
have traversed the State of New York in a canal
packet after having made the journey repeatedly
through mud so execrable as to make the prehis-
toric *corduroy* bridges of round logs laid side by
side in the mud, a relief. In those days there
were but two ways for New Englanders to get into
the great wilderness of Ohio. One was over the
Pennsylvania mountains, by the most ridiculous
apology for a road, the other was through the
swamps of New York and along the southern
shore of Lake Erie. Either took a pilgrimage of
about forty days, and never a family but had accidents by precipice, mud or flood to recount for
years afterward in its log cabin. In comparison
with this, either as to danger, toil, or expense,
emigration to the states west of the Mississippi
to-day is nothing. Then all the roads in the new
countries were Indian trails without bridges.
Emigrants with wagons had often to cut their way
through the woods, by the pocket compass for the
last day or two. At the rate the great wilderness
was settling previous to the opening of the canal,
it would have been mostly a wilderness to this day,
for as soon as his new farm yielded a surplus, the
farmer discovered the impossibility of getting it to

market. The vast region of the upper lakes was cut off from the sea coast by the sublime cataract of Niagara, and Mr. Geddes, the first canal surveyor, incredible as it may seem, found no wagon-road from one lake to the other on American soil.

Up to 1816 the 353 miles between the Hudson and Lake Erie, stretched through a wilderness largely of swamps, with only here and there a village. Where the great and splendid cities of Syracuse and Rochester are now, bears and wolves were more at home than men. Emigrant families were toiling laboriously with ox-teams along the rough, miry, and wild roads, bound for the country south of Lake Erie, in the face of remigrants, shaking with ague, and looking like ghosts.

Doubtless enthusiastic travelers had dreamed, even before the revolution, of peopling the interior of the continent. But the beginnings were exceedingly small, and the progress hardly exceeded the regress. As long ago as 1784 one Christopher Colles memorialized the New York legislature for the removal of obstructions to the navigation of the Mohawk. A committee to which his memorial was referred reported that if Colles

would undertake it himself, he and his assigns
should be allowed to take toll, but the State
should be at no expense. No Act passed. Colles
applied again in 1785 and got an appropriation of
$125 (!) to enable him to make an " essay " and
report his success to the next legislature. He reported in 1786, but nothing was done and Colles
subsided. After a silence of five years Gov. Clinton [not De Witt, but his uncle,] brought up the
subject, and an appropriation of $250 was made,
and the Land Commissioners were authorized and
instructed to make surveys of the Mohawk and
Wood Creek. From this resulted a company
which slightly improved the navigation of the
Mohawk, locking around Little Falls and connecting that river with Wood Creek by a canal,
through which boats could pass into Oneida Lake,
and down its outlet to the Oswego River which
falls into Lake Ontario, but is too rapid for navigation. The improvement enabled the boats to
ascend the Seneca River into Cayuga and Seneca
Lakes.

With this improvement the great idea of connecting Erie with the Hudson,* if it existed at all,

---

* The dream of a river running from Lake Erie to the Hudson is said to have existed in the brain of Gouverneur Morris,

slept in embryo till 1807 or 8, when Jesse Hawley, an enterprising Yankee, who as the fashion was in that day had contrived to get himself into jail in Ontario County as a debtor, and lived out on the "jail limits," very distinctly set it forth in a stirring pamphlet and communications to the newspapers. The grand idea, coming from such a source, perhaps aroused more prejudice than favor. But it pleased Gouverneur Morris, and possibly awakened De Witt Clinton. The former, with great political ability, was a magnificent dreamer, and among his dreams was that of connecting Lake Erie with the sea-board by an artificial river, running down a gently inclined plane, without a lock! The latter was a born politician of the most pronounced type, an aristocratic democrat. Inheriting wealth and distinction he hated the federalists of his day with a perfect hatred. And yet he was destined to come in conflict, practically, with his own party in its

even in his waking moments, as early as 1802. It can hardly be called an idea. He was a very pleasant gentleman and a fine scholar, dressing also in powdered wig, small-clothes and knee-buckles, and probably thought it as easy for water to run up hill as down, or at any rate that labor enough could keep it from running to Montreal. When the canal is again enlarged it will be as good as a "river."

hour of victory. Neither side ever gave him a support suited to his ambition. This caused him to retire from politics in disgust, and he is said to have fallen almost a hopeless victim to the god of the vineyard, when some of his personal friends, in the hope of rousing him to manhood, suggested that he should make himself the leader of the great scheme so attractively set forth by the impecunious debtor of Ontario County. Exceedingly fortunate this for New York on many accounts. With talents and culture fit to have made him one of the grandest Presidents of the United States, De Witt Clinton was reserved for something more important. He seized the new opportunity. The great State of New York began now, as if an inspiration had struck it, to act in earnest, though it relied almost wholly on the Federal Government to provide the requisite funds. It is needless to detail the efforts it made to interest Congress in the matter. Nothing could have been more hopeless. Besides the natural jealousy of rival states, there was the bitter feud of factions and the struggle for sailors' rights which was soon to culminate in the war of 1812. The nation was then poorer than any state, and to have helped the richest of the old states to an advantage over the

rest, would have been a miracle of magnanimity.
If there had been any national action then, it
would have been exactly in the wrong direction.
The same opposing forces, only a little less intense, existed in the State of New York itself, so
that all that could be done before the war came to
suspend action altogether, was to appropriate
$600 for a survey in 1808, and appoint a board of
commissioners to make more thorough exploration in 1810.   Mr. James Geddes, a very thorough
and painstaking engineer, went over the route in
1808 and made so favorable a report to Simeon
De Witt, the Surveyor General, that he was
allowed 75 dollars beyond the appropriation for
his labor, all of which he certainly earned and
much more.   Mr. Geddes of course did not find
any such state of the surface as would allow the
dream of Gouverneur Morris to be realized, but he
did find, to his intense delight, a singular provision of nature to aid in carrying the intended canal
over the deep valley of the Irondequot without
locking down, only to lock up again.   An enormous natural embankment, almost complete and
just where it was needed, he looked upon as an interposition of Divine Providence in favor of the
undertaking, though he confessed that when he

made the discovery he little expected to live to
see boats running on the top of that embankment.
It was as if he had discovered the ruins of an
ancient canal which was waiting to be repaired.

CHAPTER VIII.

EXPLORATION OF 1810.

The Board of Commissioners appointed in 1810 consisted of Gouverneur Morris, Stephen Van Rensselaer, De Witt Clinton, Simeon De Witt, William North, Thomas Eddy and Peter B. Porter. They were instructed to explore the route from the Hudson to Lake Erie, examine the navigation and make such surveys as they should think proper, and report in regard to further improvements. Nothing beyond exploration resulted, and the war so set everything back that even the exploration had to be done over in 1816. But of this first exploration De Witt Clinton kept a careful private diary, which was not published till 1849. It gives a better idea of the nature of the enterprise and the situation when Myron Holley devoted himself to its practical accomplishment, than can be found elsewhere.

It is impossible to set forth the work done by any great man of the past without taking into view the obstacles he overcame and the people among whom he worked, so I shall make no excuse for quoting largely from Mr. Clinton's racy diary of this exploring expedition. His brief and pithy notes, jotted down as he went along, do great credit to him as a careful and comprehensive observer, and it is a pity he did not in his lifetime publish in full all that he saw and thought on that interesting trip.

On Saturday, June 30, 1810, Mr. Clinton left New York city on board a steamboat — of which there were then only six in North America — and arrived in Albany Monday morning, July 2. The Commissioners met there that day. Morris and Van Rensselaer concluded to go by land; the other four as much as possible by water.

Under date of July 2 the journal says: — "We employed ourselves in laying up the necessary stores for our voyage, having previously drawn from the Treasury $1,500 in favor of Mr. Eddy. A mattrass, blanket and pillow were purchased for each Commissioner; but we unfortunately neglected to provide ourselves with marquees and camp-stools, the want of which was sensibly felt."

The following extracts from the 178 pages of this journal, covering the time to Aug. 23, when

Mr. Clinton returned to New York, will serve, perhaps, better than any condensation of it, to show the character of the country and its population at that period :

"On the 3d July we set out in carriages for Schenectady, and put up at Powell's hotel. We found that Mr. Eddy had neglected to give directions about providing boats, and that Mr. Walton, the undertaker, who is extensively engaged in transporting commodities and merchandise up and down the river, had notice of our wishes only yesterday. He was very busy in making the requisite preparations. He had purchased a batteaux [what French!] and had hired another for our baggage. It being necessary to caulk and new paint the boats, — to erect an awning against the rain and sun, and to prepare a new set of sails, we had no very sanguine hope of gratifying our earnest desire to depart in the morning, although we exerted every nerve to effect it.

"*July 4th.* On consulting with Mr. Walton about our departure, he informed us that this being a day of great festivity. it would be almost impracticable to drag the men away. We saw some of them and found them willing to embark as soon as the boats were ready, and we therefore pressed the workmen with great assiduity.

"The true reason of this anxiety, was the dulness of the place. Imagine yourself in a large country village, without any particular acquaintance, and destitute of books, and you will appreciate our situation. Schenactady, although dignified with the name of a city, is a place of little business. It has a Bank, a

College, and a Court House, and a considerable deal of
trade is carried on through the Mohawk; and all the
roads which pass to the westward on the banks of that
river necessarily go through this place. A great portion
of the crowd that visit the mineral springs at Ballston
and Saratoga also visit Schenactady. With all these
advantages it does not appear pleasing, and we en-
deavoured to fill up the gloomy interval between this
time and our departure, by viewing the pageantry which
generally attends this day.

"There were two celebrations and two sets of
orators — one by the city and one by the college.
The feuds between the burghers of Oxford and Cam-
bridge, and the students of those Universities, appear
to be acted over here. In the procession of the students, we saw a *Washington Benevolent Society*, remarkable neither for numbers nor respectability. The
President was a Scotchman, of the name of Murdoch,
and certainly not a warm Whig during the war."

"On receiving information that our batteaux were
ready, we embarked at 4 o'clock in the afternoon. Our
boat was covered with a handsome awning and curtains
and well provided with seats. The Commissioners who
embarked in it, were De Witt, Eddy, Porter and myself;
and the three young gentlemen before mentioned also
accompanied us. The Captain's name was Thomas B.
Clench, and we were provided with three men, Freeman, Van Ingen, and Van Slyck. In our consort were
the captain, named Clark, three hands, three servants
and about a ton and a half of baggage and provisions.
We called, ludicrously at first, our vessel the *Eddy*, and
the baggage boat the *Morris*. What was jest became
serious, and when our batteaux were painted at Utica,

these names were doubly inscribed on the sterns in legible characters.

" A crowd of people attended us at our embarkation, who gave us three parting cheers. The wind was fair, and with our handsome awning, flag flying, and large sail, followed by another boat, we made no disreputable appearance. We discovered that our mast was too high, and our boat being without much ballast, we were not well calculated to encounter heavy and sudden gusts. These boats are not sufficiently safe for lake navigation, although they frequently venture. A boat went 'from this place to the Missouri in six weeks. The river was uncommonly low. Goods to the value of $50,000 were detained in Walton's warehouses, on account of the difficulty of transportation. After sailing a couple of miles a bend of the river brought the wind in our faces. Our men took to their poles, and pushed us up against a rapid current with great dexterity, and great muscular exertion. The approach of evening, and the necessity of sending back to Schenactady for some things that were left, induced us to come to for the night at Willard's tavern, on the south bank of the river, and three miles from the place of departure.

" This tavern is in the 3d ward of the city of Schenactady. In the election of 1809, the first after the establishment of the county, a great disproportion was discovered between the Senatorial and Assembly votes, which could not be accounted for on fair principles. A greater number of persons testified that they had voted for the Republican candidates, than there were ballots in the box ; and there could not be the least doubt, but that Republican tickets had been taken from the box, and Federal ones substituted. This tavern was located

as the scene of the fraud. The boxes were kept here
one night, and, it is said, locked up in a bureau, left
there for the express purpose, as is supposed. The
tavern-keeper and some other accomplices perpetrated
the atrocious deed. The present incumbent looks as if
he were capable of any iniquity of the kind."

"The south road leads in front of the house. While
here, we had an opportunity of seeing the pernicious
effects of these festivals, in the crowds of drunken,
quarrelsome people, who passed by. Among other disgusting scenes, we saw several young men riding Jehu-
like to the tavern, in a high state of intoxication, and
their leader swinging his hat, and shouting 'Success to
Federalism.' A simple fellow handed me a hand-bill
containing the arrangements for the procession, and
was progressing in his familiarities with the rest of the
company, when he was called off by the landlord, who,
in a stern voice, said, 'Come away, Dickup;' and poor
Dickup, alias *thick head*, immediately obeyed."

So this charming explorer and representative
American goes on, giving bits of history on every
old house he passed, noticing the larvæ of bees in
the dried mullen stalks, and the muscle shells on
the banks of the river. Under date of July 7th
he gives a glimpse of the literature of the day,
just springing up under freedom of the press.
They started that morning at five o'clock, and to
facilitate the passage of their boats up a difficult
rapid, they *walked* on shore a mile and a half.
After getting on board he says : —

" In order to furnish as much amusement as possible, we put our books into a common stock, or rather into a trunk, and appointed one of the young gentlemen keeper of the library. The books, which were most extraordinary, were a Treatise on Magic, by Quitman (this I purchased at Albany), and a pamphlet on Religion, by Mr. D. L. Dodge, a respectable merchant in New York, with an answer by a Clergyman (these were furnished by Mr. Eddy.) Quitman's Treatise is a labored argument against magicians, and to disprove their existence. Dodge's work is principally levelled against war, breathes a fanatical spirit, and is completely refuted by the adversary's pamphlet. As a specimen of his reasoning take the following : — ' If a good man does not resist an assailant and submits to be killed, he will go to heaven. On the contrary, if he kills the assailant, he may probably send a soul to hell, which if spared, may be converted and saved to life everlasting.' Dodge's pamphlet, weak as it is, has given him a great name among the Quakers ; and, through their recommendation, he is now a trustee of the New York Free School."

This honest confession by De Witt Clinton of the weakness of "Dodge's pamphlet" reads strangely by the side of his own Address at the Anniversary of the Bible Society in 1823. In that address, to be sure, he only hypothetically admits that the Bible is a revelation from God. But with all the eloquence of which he was master — and he was master of much — he contends that the belief of the future heaven and hell is the foundation of good government. For example, he says : —

"'The codes of men and the laws of opinion derive a great portion of their weight from the influence of a future world. Justice cannot be administered without the sanctity of truth, and the great security against perjury is the amenability of another state. The sanctions of religion compose the foundations of good government; and the ethics, doctrines, and examples furnished by Christianity exhibit the best models for the laws of opinion."

Mr. Clinton here plainly assumes the "ethics" and "doctrines" of Christianity to be inseparable, and unless his views of the latter had changed since 1810, he was telling the Bible Society that false doctrines are essential to good government. If he had lived till to-day, he would probably have discovered that the doctrines which contradict the ethics had better not be relied on as a bulwark against perjury; that a future heaven and hell depending not wholly on personal character and conduct, but on faith in vicarious obedience and imputed righteousness as well, are destructive of the sense of moral obligation, rather than otherwise.

The navigators of the mighty Mohawk reached Little Falls on the 8th July, a village "built upon rocks of granite, containing about thirty or forty houses and stores, and a church, together with mills." Here their "batteaux" were lifted through the rude locks of the "Inland Lock Navigation Company," incorporated in 1792; and he notices that its tolls there, from 1803 to July, 1810, had been $62,789.23, and that in the previous three months 242 boats had passed. Here says our prudent explorer, "The rainy weather induced me to procure thicker stockings; for a pair of coarse worsted I paid 11s., and for two pair of cotton half stockings, 6s. 6d. each." [Probably $1.37½ for the worsted, and 81¼ cents each for the cotton, in Federal money.] An old style of reckoning money changes almost as slowly as an old style of theology.

Another laborious day brought the voyagers to Utica, at ten o'clock in the night, and the journal says: —

"Morris and Van Rensselaer having pre-occupied Baggs' tavern, where we intended to quarter, we put up at Billinger's tavern in Utica."

That bag has grown bigger since two travellers could pre-occupy it. "Utica," continues the journal, "is a flourishing village on the south side of the Mohawk; it arrogates to itself being the capital of the Western District. Twenty-two years ago there was but one house; there are now three hundred. * * By the census now taking, it contains 1,650 inhabitants. Two newspapers are printed here."

Morris and Van Rensselaer, the two aristocratic Commissioners, continued to journey by land, and the navigators overtaking them at Rome, a meeting of the Commission was held there on the 12th, of which Mr. Clinton is so cruel as to place this on record: — "At this meeting the Senior Commissioner was for breaking down the mound of Lake Erie, and letting out the waters to follow the level of the country, so as to form a sloop navigation with the Hudson, and without any aid from any other water." Every party politician should know that his absurdities will be enjoyed by the opposite party.

The Commissioners adjourned to meet in Geneva, and the navigators proceeded on their voyage by a canal of one mile and three-fourths, connecting the Mohawk with Wood Creek, an affluent of Oneida Lake. While on the latter the journalist mentions dining "on a salmon caught at Fish Creek, about eight miles from Rome."

De Witt Clinton, as a worthy pioneer of civilization and "internal improvements," had a sharp eye for both the beauties and utilities of nature, as the following extracts will show. What a pity it is that those who have followed him should have made so much waste both of the utilities and the beauties!

"The Mohawk is barren of fish. It formerly contained great plenty of trout — it now has none. The largest fish is the pike, which have been caught weighing fourteen pounds. Since the canal at Rome, chubb, a species of dace, have come into the Mohawk through Wood Creek, and are said to be plenty. A salmon and black bass have also been speared in this river, which came into it through the canal. It would not be a little singular if the Hudson should be supplied with salmon through that channel. The falls of the Cohoes oppose a great impediment to the passage of fish; but the Hudson is like the Mohawk, a very sterile river in that respect.

"We saw great numbers of bitterns, blackbirds, robins, and bank swallows, which perforate the banks of the river. Also, some wood-ducks, gulls, shell drakes, bob-linklins, king-birds, crows, kildares, small snipe, woodpeckers, woodcock, wrens, yellow birds, phebes, blue jays, highholes, pigeons, thrushes, and larks. We also saw several kingfishers, which denote the presence

of fish. We shot several bitterns, the same as found
on the salt marsh. The only shell fish were the
snapping turtle and muscle.

"We saw a bright red bird about the size of a blue-
bird. Its wings were tipped with black, and the bird
uncommonly beautiful. It appeared to have no song,
and no one present seemed to know its name. I saw
but three besides in the whole course of my tour, one
on the Ridge Road west of the Genesee River. It is
therefore a *rara avis*."

De Witt Clinton was a subscriber to Alexander
Wilson's great work on ornithology, but as the
second volume in which the *Scarlet Tanager* is
described was only published in 1810, he probably had not seen it. But from Clinton's description it was doubtless that bird. "Among all the
birds that inhabit our woods," says Wilson,
"there is none that strikes the eye of a stranger,
or even a native, with so much brilliancy as this.
The depth of the woods is his favorite abode.
There among the thick foliage of the tallest trees,
his simple and almost monotonous notes *chip*,
churr, repeated at short intervals, in a pensive
tone, may be occasionally heard ; which appear to
proceed from a considerable distance, though the
bird be immediately above you ; a faculty bestowed on him by the beneficent Author of

Nature, no doubt for his protection, to compensate in a degree for the danger to which his glowing color would often expose him."

" On the banks of the creek," proceeds the journal, " was plenty of boneset, the Canada shrub, said to be useful in medicine, and a great variety of beautiful flowering plants. Wild gooseberry bushes, wild currants, and wild hops were also to be seen. The gooseberries were not good ; the hops were said to be as good as the domestic ones. In the long weeds and thick underwood we were at first apprehensive of rattlesnakes, of which we were told that there are three kinds — the large and the small, and the dark rattlesnakes. But neither here nor in any part of our tour did we see this venomous reptile. The only animals we saw on this stream were the black squirrel and the hare, as it is called in Albany, a creature white in winter, of the rabbit kind, although much larger."

As descriptive of the country through which the Erie Canal was to pass, and in which Mr. Holley was to be occupied in all sorts of weather for seven years, nothing can be truer to life than the account Mr. Clinton gives of his observation and experience along Wood Creek.

" We passed, on the north side of the creek, the appearance of an old fortification, called Fort Bull. The remains of an old dam, to impede the passage of a hostile fleet, and to assist the operations of the fort, were also

to be seen. Although there is now a road on that side
of the creek, yet in those days there could have been
no marching by land with an army. The transportation of provisions must have been impracticable by land ;
and, indeed, the general appearance of the country
exhibits a sunken morass or swamp, overgrown with
timber and formed from the retreat of the lake. . . .

  " We rose early in the morning and breakfasted at
the Oak Orchard, six miles from Gilbert's, on the south
side of the river. The ground was miry, and in step-
ping into the boat my foot slipped, and I was partly
immersed in the creek. The Captain assisted me in
getting out. The dampness of the weather, and the
sun being hardly risen, induced me, for greater precau-
tion, to change my clothes. This trifling incident was
afterwards magnified by the papers into a serious
affair."

  The exploring party descended the outlet of
Oneida Lake to Lake Ontario, and returning ascended the Seneca, through the Cayuga marshes,
as far as Geneva, hauling their boats around the
falls and rapids. The effect of such a damp wilderness on human health could not well escape so
close an observer and frank describer as De Witt
Clinton, and we get a very correct view of the
perils of supervising the construction of a canal
through that region in what he says at the completion of their voyage, under date of July 24th.

"Having now concluded our voyage and intending to proceed from this place by land, it may not be amiss to look back and reflect upon the means which we took to guard against sickness during a voyage of twenty-one days, through the most insalubrious waters, exposed to the alternations of heat and rain, the miasmata of marshes, the exhalation of swamps, the fogs of rivers, the want of sleep, and frequently of good water.

"In the first place, we were well provided with good victuals. Our appetites were generally good, and our principal drink was port wine, which was recommended to us by the Senior Commissioner.

"In the second place we took medicines when we found ourselves indisposed. Dr. Hosack had provided us with James's Fever Powders, Elixir Proprietatis, Bark and Emetics; and we had got at Albany Lee's Anti-bilious Pills—pills recommended by Mr. G. Morris, and some mentioned by Ellicott, when he was Commissioner to run the boundary line between the United States and the Floridas. He says in his Journal that it was given to him by Dr. Rush, and that as long as his stock lasted he was free from fever, but as soon as he quit the use of it he was seriously attacked. The receipt is as follows: 'Two grains of calomel with half a grain of gamboge, combined by a little soap.' These pills we used liberally, and found them very efficacious.

"In the third place: although we passed through places where people were taken down with fever, and although one of our captains was seriously sick, and from the aspect of the land and water it appeared to be impossible for a stranger to escape their deleterious influence, yet we maintained a uniform flow of good spirits. The song and the flute, the jest and *vive la bagatelle*, more than our most powerful medicines, were the best antidotes to sickness."

How high the party kept up their "good spirits" is indicated by a number of practical jokes set down in the journal. For example: "We dined in the woods, ten miles from Columbia, on the north side, and at the head of Cross Lake. Visiting an adjacent house, and seeing three lusty women at the washtub, none of whom was older than forty, we thought we would involve the Commodore (Eddy) in a scrape, through the medium of his curiosity, and told him there was a woman at the house 100 years old, with grey eyebrows, and that her faculties were remarkably good. He immediately left the boat in a great hurry, and passed with uncommon rapidity through a hot sun, to the house, and inquired with great earnestness for a sight of the old woman. Instead of meeting the fate of Orpheus, he was received with laughter, and returned completely hoaxed."

The residue of the exploration to Buffalo having to be performed by wagons, gained very little information of the swampy route which the canal was destined to pursue; indeed the commissioners do not seem to have added anything of practical

value to the report previously made by Mr.
Geddes. They simply had an interesting trip,
and their report gives us a graphic view of a rich
wild country and the condition of its sparse and
uncultured people. A few extracts from the last
pages of the journal will give glimpses of the
character of the early population. Here is his
account of a

CAMP MEETING.

" On our return, a mile from Lyons, and a mile from
the road in a thick wood, we stopped to see a camp
meeting of Methodists. The ground was somewhat
elevated; the woods were cleared, and a circle was
made capable of containing several thousand. The
circle was formed of wooden cabins, tents, covered
wagons, and other vehicles. At one end of the circle
a rostrum was erected, capable of containing several
persons, and below the rostrum or pulpit was an
orchestra fenced in. We arrived at this place before
the meeting was opened, and we found it excessively
damp and disagreeable from the heavy rains. Here
eating and drinking was going on; there people were
drying themselves by a fire. In one place, a man had
a crowd around him, to listen to his psalm-singing; in
another, a person was vociferating his prayer. And
again, a person had his arm around the neck of another,
looking him full in the face, and admonishing him
of the necessity of repentance; and the poor object of
his solicitude listening to his exhortations with tear-
suffused eyes. At length four preachers ascended the

pulpit, and the orchestra was filled with forty more. The people, about two hundred in number, were called together by a trumpet, the women took the left and the men the right hand of the ministers. A good-looking man opened the service with prayer, during which groans followed every part of his orisons, decidedly emphatical. After prayer he commenced a sermon, the object of which was to prove the utility of preaching up the terrors of hell, as necessary to arrest the attention of the audience to the arguments of the ministers. And this was undoubtedly intended as a prelude to terrific discourses. Capt. Dorsey, who was a member of the Assembly last session, and who is a devout Methodist, was kind enough to show us seats, and to invite us to breakfast in the morning, at his house; but the dampness of the place and the approach of night compelled us to depart before the sermon was completed, which we did singly, so as to avoid interruption. We were mortified at the conduct of our drivers in turning the carriages, so as to draw off the attention of the people from the sermon. We sent our apology for it to Capt. Dorsey, they were expressly directed to do this on our arrival. As far as we could hear, the voice of the preacher, growing louder and louder, reached our ears as we departed, and we met crowds of people going to the sermon. On the margin of the road we saw persons with cakes, beer, and other refreshments for sale.— *Life and Writings of De Witt Clinton*, page 106.

The following observations from Clinton's journal, though having only a remote connection with the canal, are interesting :—

August 1 (at Ithaca).—" It was pleasing to see all over the country advertisements of machines for carding wool.

" Mr. Gere has finished, for $2.300 in stock of the Ithaca and Owego Turnpike Company, three miles of that turnpike, from the 10th April to the 10th July, with eight men, four yoke of oxen, and two teams of horses. Scrapers are a powerful engine in making roads. He is also building an elegant frame hotel, three stories high, and 50 by 40 feet, with suitable out-buildings and garden. The carpenter's work was con-tracted for at $1.500 : the whole will not cost more than $6.000. Travellers from New York, Philadelphia, etc., will find this a much nearer route to Geneva, Genesee, the Lakes and Upper Canada than by Albany, and the road very accommodating when the Ithaca and Geneva turnpike is made. Gere is a very enterprising man, and vastly superior to his brother-in-law, Judge B., who appears to have exhausted his genius in giving his children eccentric names, as Don Carlos, Julius Octa-vius, Joanna Almeria."

[Here we, perhaps, have the source of that eccentricity of names for which the State of New York is remark-able.]

" Fourteen miles from Ithaca, in the town of Spencer, Tioga County, is a settlement of Virginians called *Speed;* they are Federalists. An old man by the name of Hyde belonging to it, spent at least five hours in the tavern to-day, and went off so drunk that he could hardly balance himself on his horse. Behind him was a bag, containing on each side a keg of liquor, and his pockets were loaded with bottles. In the bar-room he abused Jefferson, Madison and a number of other leading Republicans.

"Does it make any essential difference to the community where its produce is sold if sold to profit? If a bushel of wheat can be carried to Baltimore for six shillings less expense than to Albany, ought not this to be encouraged? Here the profit to the farmer competes with that of the merchant. But the importing merchant is not injured; the money is carried to New York and expended in merchandise, and more is expended in consequence of the increased price of the commodity. How does this doctrine bear on the Montreal trade? This idea deserves further reflection."

De Witt Clinton had been ardently fostering the canal policy, partly in order to divert the Montreal trade to New York. Here he seems to have begun to doubt the validity of one of his arguments, and to let down a bar towards the doctrine of free trade.

CHAPTER IX.

EXPLORATION OF 1816.

THE war of 1812 was no sooner over than the project of the Erie Canal revived with some diminution of political if not physical obstacles. The need of easier communication with the west had been demonstrated at any rate. The powerful eloquence of Myron Holley in the Assembly of 1816 produced the appointment of another Board of Commissioners, on which Mr. Holley himself had a place.

He became, in fact, the executive power, without which the great enterprise would have proved a failure in more senses than one. It was his practical wisdom, energy and utter self-sacrifice that carried it through in eight years in the face of powerful and unrelenting opposition, with an economy quite unparalleled in the history of public works. Never was a republic prouder than New York when the cannon thundered from Buffalo to Albany to announce the wedding of Lake Erie to the Hudson; and, alas! never was one more un-

grateful. It remains for History to right the
enormous wrong, by showing posterity its true
benefactor, and shedding upon coming ages the
benign light of his glorious example. Posterity
will be enriched by his living in their hearts, and
that was his life's aim.

The first year's work on the canal was one of
survey and calculation. Competent engineers were
employed, and under the careful and constant personal supervision of Mr. Holley, nearly every
separate mile of the route was the subject of a
thorough and close estimate of the expense. The
report of this work, drawn up by Mr. Holley and
submitted to the legislature on the 17th of Feb.,
1817, is a model document of 74 pages, culmin-
ating in the following estimate of distances and
expense. Never was a work of such magnitude
so thoroughly laid out in so short a time, nor with
so close a prophecy of its actual cost.

| | DISTANCE. | | COST. |
	Miles.	Chains.	
From Lake Erie to 11 miles up Tonne-wanda,	27	–	$250.877
From Tonnewanda to Seneca,	136	2½	1,550,985
From Seneca to Rome,	77	–	853,186
From Rome to Scoharie,	71	27	1,090,603
From Scoharie to Albany,	42	–	1,106,087
General expenses,	–	–	75,000
Total,	353	29½	$4,926,738

As a preliminary of this survey Mr. Holley and
two other commissioners had visited and carefully
examined the Middlesex Canal in Massachusetts,
a water-way of 27 miles connecting the Merrimac
with Boston harbor and which, constructed by private hands, under a charter, had cost, with only
three-fourths of the depth, or a capacity to pass
a boat of 14 tons instead of one of 100, like the
Erie, the sum of $528,000. It had several wooden
aqueducts, which were beginning to rot in 1816.
Considering length and section, if the Erie Canal
had been as costly, it would have cost $13,000,000
instead of $5,000,000.

The Middlesex Canal was projected and char-
tered in 1789 by a few patriotic citizens of Boston
who do not seem to have expected to make it
very profitable. The stock was divided into 800
shares, to be assessed as money was needed for
the work. On 96 shares nothing seems to have
been paid. The first surveyors were ludicrously
incompetent, for they made the summit level, 22
miles from Boston, only 68½ feet above tide,
whereas it was 104 ; and 16½ feet above the Merrimac, while it was 32. The company suspected
the incompetence and sent to England for Mr.
Weston, an experienced engineer, who reported

in 1794, and a boat passed from the Merrimac to
Boston harbor in 1803, though the work was not
entirely completed.   In fact, assessments continued till one hundred had been paid, making the
outgo on each share, counting interest at six per
cent, $1,455.25 before any dividend was paid, the
whole income up to 1819 being expended in improving the navigation of the Concord and Merrimac rivers. Thus the property stood the proprietors
in $1,164,200 before it began to pay anything.
From 1819 to the opening of the Boston & Lowell
Railroad in 1835, the dividends were good, but
the income fell off one-third the first year after
that, and continued to go down till 1843, when
the company made a desperate effort to sell the
Concord River to the city of Boston as a water
supply for drinking purposes. At last the Railroad bought the franchise and the canal was abandoned.   In 1816 the tolls on that canal were
$30,000.   It cost 8 cents a cord to carry wood
through a single lock.

The Middlesex Canal perished before the railroad system, because the navigable capacity of the
Concord and Merrimac is nothing compared with
the Lakes beyond Buffalo. The Erie Canal sur-
vives, with a greatly enlarged channel, and will
long continue to if the State of New York is wise.

CHAPTER X.

THE FINANCIAL PROVISION.

In the face of this grand report the various interests opposed to the work were not strong
enough to defeat it. They only prevailed so far
as not to commit the state irrevocably to the completion of the whole line. The commissioners
were authorized by law to complete the section
from Rome to the Seneca River, and funds were
provided only sufficient for that purpose. This
satisfied those who thought their interests would
suffer if Lake Ontario were left out, and who denounced a ditch of nearly 200 miles through the
swamps, parallel with that lake, as a piece of
superfluous folly. The western landholders had
made large donations of land for the canal, and it
readily occurred to the legislature that the people
in the immediate neighborhood of the canal could
be specially taxed on the betterment of their
estates, but these resources were only prospective.
Ready money must be had, and for this recourse

was had to the banks, from which a loan of
$400,000 was authorized. The banks were will-
ing to loan at a lower interest, provided their
paper circulation might be extended by the disbursement of small bills to the workmen ; and by
accepting this condition the state saved, first and
last, over $80,000. But to Mr. Holley, who,
without any extra salary or compensation, acted
as Treasurer to the Canal Commissioners, this sti-
pulation worked a grievous woe, and all the more
so from the just, generous, and economical policy
he pursued with his contractors, whereby, beyond
doubt, the state saved some millions. It will be
apparent to any one who has the slightest acquaintance with business, that the disbursement of large
sums in small bills, to a multitude of contractors,
scattered through some hundreds of miles of unin-
habited wilderness, where numerous subordinates
must be trusted, and the accounting bureau must
be on wheels or horseback, camping in shanties or
the open air, must be exposed to chances of considerable loss. No man with his eyes open to these
chances, and to his own individual safety, would
have taken this responsibility without an extra
compensation or commission sufficient to secure
himself against loss. The very least would have

been as much as the state saved.   Mr. Holley, beyond doubt, understood the nature of the risk he
incurred, but so profound was his sense of the
value of his object, and so little in its presence
did he think of himself, that he would not for a
moment imperil it by insisting on his own security.
He silently took the additional labor and responsibility; and the result, considering all the circumstances, was as much of a financial success as
would have been the nautical one of crossing the
Atlantic in a dug-out, to be swamped in the breakers of the last mile.   But this will be explained in
its proper place.

By the Act of the legislature the sum of $75,000
was appropriated for the purchase of tools by the
commissioners, but Mr. Holley was wise enough
to see that it would be far more economical to
have his contractors use their own tools than those
of the state, even if the state had to advance
money to purchase them, and he acted accordingly.
In his report of Jan. 31, 1818, he thus describes
his master-stroke of policy in preferring small
contracts to large ones, — " It will be perceived
that the length of the line embraced in the several
contracts for excavation and embankment varies
from forty rods to three miles.   The contracts,

generally, were made to embrace less than would
otherwise have been necessary, in order that men
in moderate pecuniary circumstances might be
enabled to engage in the work, provided they
could procure the necessary security. And although this multiplication of the contracts created
much more trouble and labor for the Commissioners than a contrary course would have done, — as
on every job it was necessary not only to draw and
execute a contract, but also a counterpart thereof,
so that each party might have one in his possession,—yet this was obviously more just and equitable than, by a diminution of the number of
contracts, to have put it in the power of a few
wealthy individuals to have monopolized the whole,
and to have made sub-contracts at reduced prices
with the laboring part of the community." Fifty-
eight miles had been put under contract in this
way, before the formal and ceremonial commencement of the work, and the same just and enlightened policy was pursued throughout. It is plain
enough how much this enhanced the risks of the
disbursing commissioners.

CHAPTER XI.

THE DIGGING.

As considerable work had been done on the American revolution before July 4th, 1776, so there had probably been some *digging* on the canal before July 4th, 1817, but it was resolved to do some at Rome, solemnly and ceremoniously, on that auspicious day, and it was done. But it seems to have been an affair of only local interest, for I find no record of it in the leading newspapers of New York. DeWitt Clinton was not there to wield the spade, for he was that day escorted to the municipal celebration of the city of New York by the " *Washington Benevolent Society*," of which he wrote so disrespectfully in Schenectady in 1810.

But I do find some other things worth noting just here, and especially about a " peculiar institution" whose grave began to be dug that day.

It was " the era of good feeling," for President Monroe was then making his tour of New England, and was that day in Boston. The newspapers of the country were occupied with addresses to him, and his felicitous replies. Boston merchants, who had almost rebelled at the protection of sailors by the destruction of their trade, were now in exuberant good humor by the prospect of profits on cotton. Everything was lovely, at least on the outside.

A Cincinnati newspaper of July 4th, 1817, had the following curious piece of " ship news ":

SINGULAR ARRIVAL. — Arrived at this port on Monday morning last (June 30th), a small schooner-built boat of about six tons burthen. 30 days from Rome, on the Mohawk river. State of New York! The boat was conducted by Capt. Dean and four Indians; passengers, two squaws and an Indian boy. It was a handsome model, painted in neat style, with two masts, and sails, and an appropriate flag. They sailed hence on the afternoon of the same day for the Wabash. Their avowed object is to enter lands on behalf of their tribe, and then to ascend the Wabash to its source, cross over with the boat to the Miami, and return by the way of Lake Erie. This boat left Rome on the first of June, passed into Lake Ontario by way of Wood Creek, Oneida Lake, and Oswego river, and after navigating the greater part of the southern coast of the lake, was conveyed around the Falls of Niagara on wheels, eleven miles; then by way of Buffalo, across the end of Lake Erie, to the mouth of the Cataragus Creek, and up it to a portage of eight miles and an half, across to the head waters of the Alleghany river. It arrived at this place after passing two portages amounting to nineteen miles. During this time they were detained nearly ten days by h·a·l winds and rains.

These descendants of the forest, now wearing the habiliments and appearance of civilization and industry, manifested in their deportment that ingenuousness and dignity of mind which have characterized, in many instances, the savage of the forest, improved in a considerable degree by the hand of civilization. While gratifying the curiosity of several of our citizens, by taking them on board, and with a gentle breeze, sailing a considerable distance up and across the river, the following characteristic and appropriate toasts were given by one of the Indians, accompanied by the firing of his gun; while on the Kentucky side, " The patriotism and bravery of Kentucky ;" while on the Ohio side, " Free trade and no slavery."

This Indian seems to have remembered how some hundreds of Kentucky volunteers had to make foot-paths through the wilderness of Ohio, after Gen. Hull's surrender. And what a pity it was that he had not been in the convention that drew up our present Constitution, to advocate direct taxation, by which trade might have been made free, if not all men.

It is a little significant that the foregoing "ship news" was copied entire into the *N. Y. Commercial Advertiser* and *National Intelligencer.*

But the *Columbian Centinel*, of Boston, in copying it, left out the last sentence, the most interesting of all.

On the same day appeared in the *N. Y. Spectator* (the weekly issue of the *Daily Commercial Advertiser*) the following communication : —

NEGRO SLAVERY. — The kidnapping of a number of negroes the last week, with an intention of transporting them to Georgia, demands public attention. The extent to which this has been carried on from this and other middle States, exceeds the belief of many who have not made it a subject of inquiry. Particularly has this been the case within the last two years. The high price which the productions of the South have commanded since the peace, has induced many to engage in planting. This has made slaves in higher demand. Prime negroes have been sold for eight hundred dollars and upwards.

To give a better idea on this subject, the following is extracted from the journal of a young gentleman who visited the Southern States during the last winter : —

AUGUSTA, Feb. 3rd, 1817.

" Last night my attention was attracted by a number of fires on the opposite side of the river. On enquiring this morning, I found them to be at the stalls of negroes exposed for sale. A land that boasts its freedom ! A land of high-toned democracy, where human beings, like dumb brutes, are driven to market, and, instead of dying by the hand of the butcher, die a lingering death of slavery and bondage !

"Immediately after breakfast, I resolved to visit this camp of human misery. On my arrival I assumed the character of a planter's son wishing to purchase slaves. The camp consisted of nearly three hundred; and the keepers, thinking they had a good customer, exerted themselves to shew their property to the best advantage. They took me from tent to tent, until I had seen the whole. With more brutality than Turks they cracked their lashes, and ordered about these miserable beings to make them appear to the best advantage.

"These poor creatures, bought in the States of Maryland and Virginia, and driven across, in a few days, what would require for an army weeks to traverse, were beseeching some one to buy them, that they might have a home. Once I was addressed by a child, who could hardly speak, 'Master, won't you please buy me and my mamma, that we may have a home?' Looking round, a miserable object presented itself to view. A woman, with an infant not three days old, and which first saw the light on the ground, where it then lay, was the mother of the boy who so feelingly addressed me. In silence I turned away; astonishment made me dumb.

"The exportation of slaves from Virginia to Georgia, since the abolition of slave trade, and more especially since the peace, has yielded great profits. Wealth is power, and power is the object at which mankind aim. To acquire this what will not man attempt? What has he not attempted?

"More than twenty thousand slaves, if we may believe those who best know, have been imported into Georgia within the last two years. Legislatures have attempted to put a stop to this barbarous traffic; but

such is the debasement of many of the people where
slavery exists, that it will require the united efforts of
the virtuous in every country to stop this horrid practice.   Were I to make laws, death should be the punishment of him who sells a man."

Thus in the latter half of the summer of 1817 a
beginning had been made in the vast enterprise,
and such an enthusiasm enkindled in a large
body of contractors and workmen that the frost
and snow of winter could hardly stop them.   And
when it was no longer possible to dig, they took
advantage of the easier transportation through the
swamps when frozen to haul to the line the stores
that would be needed the next summer.   Unfortunately the next spring was so exceedingly
wet that no work could be done till June, and
then under great disadvantage.   But the system
and energy with which the work was pressed forward by Mr. Holley after it did begin, encouraged
Gov. Clinton to make his mightiest effort at the
session of 1819 to have the legislature commit itself to the completion of the whole work; and in
spite of able and determined opposition he succeeded.   In his message to the legislature he
stated a fact which now, sixty years later, seems
almost incredible, and serves to show the magni-

tude of the obstacles which stood in the way of what its opponents then called the "Quixotic canal policy." "At the present period," said Gov. Clinton, "a ton of commodities can be conveyed from Buffalo to Albany, by land, for one hundred dollars, and to Montreal, principally by water, for twenty-five." And he predicted that as soon as the canal was completed a ton could be carried from Buffalo to Albany for ten dollars. It is now carried for two!

In his report to the Assembly of 1819 Mr. Holley says: "The avidity with which great numbers of respectable citizens sought contracts was highly gratifying, and afforded a sure pledge of the energy which has since been displayed in their execution. Many applications for every section were always made immediately after and often before the returns of the engineer had been received, so as to render it proper to let them out. A very few of the contractors are foreigners, who have recently arrived in this country; but far the greatest part of them are native farmers, mechanics, merchants and professional men, residing in the vicinity of the line; and three fourths of all the laborers were born among us."

With such men, set to work to make the great

water-way through a dense forest, the giants of
which bound the earth with their interlacing roots, it
was to be expected that some mechanical ingenuity
would be evolved. The calculations of cost had
been very close. If the contractors were to be
held within them, and were to work only with
axes, mattocks and spades, they would make little
or no profit. And accordingly we find that new
implements and processes at once sprang into existence. Even the wheelbarrow was wonderfully
improved, so that its oldest friends hardly knew
it.* Trees had no longer the honor of being
chopped down. Living and breathing, they were
pulled up by the roots. When old stumps stood
in the way, they too were pulled up, with as little
ceremony as if the contractors had been dentists.
Oxen and scrapers made the excavations and
embankments.

In his report, Mr. Holley gave some glimpses
of the inventive talent which the grand enterprise
developed, exceedingly interesting as the first
skirmish line of the great battle which has trans-
formed a continent.

"Machinery has hitherto been used with most suc-

---

* The new one-wheeled vehicle was called the Brainard Wheelbarrow, in honor of Jeremiah Brainard, of Rome, the improver.

cess in the heavy business of grubbing and clearing. By means of an endless screw connected with a roller, a cable, a wheel and a crank, one man is able to bring down a tree of the largest size without any cutting about its roots. For this purpose the means are all, except the cable, combined in a small but very strong frame of wood and iron. This frame is immovably fastened on the ground, at a distance of perhaps one hundred feet from the foot of the tree, and to the trunk of which, fifty or sixty feet up, one end of the cable is secured, the other being connected with the roller. When this is done the man turns the crank, which successively moves the screw, the wheel and the roller, on which, as the cable winds up, the tree must gradually yield, until at length it is precipitated by the weight of its top."

Every one who has travelled much through American forests must have noticed how nature herself has sometimes made roads, everything but removing the prostrate trunks. She simply combined the force of the whirlwind with that of gravitation. Art, imitating the lateral force of wind, effected a vast economy of force over the use of the axe in making a road for the Erie Canal through the then almost unbroken forests of western New York. But wherever the land was already cleared, the stump of every departed tree at that period stood firm, and gravitation could afford no aid for its removal. Of this obstacle Mr. Holley said : —

" There is no grubbing so difficult and expensive by the common methods as that of sound green stumps ; and as our citizens west of Utica are every day multiplying these evidences of their industry, it was desirable to discover some easier method of eradicating them. Such means have been found ; but the cost of the machinery, in which they partly consist, would forbid the use of them in ordinary cases. Two strong wheels, sixteen feet in diameter, are made and connected together by a round axletree twenty inches thick and thirty feet long ; between these wheels, and with its spokes inseparably framed into this axletree, another wheel is placed, fourteen feet in diameter, round the rim of which a rope is several times passed, with one end fastened through the rim, and with the other end loose, but in such a condition as to produce a revolution of the wheel whenever it is pulled. This apparatus is so moved as to have the stump, on which it is intended to operate, midway between the largest wheels and nearly under the axletree ; and these wheels are so braced as to remain steady. A very strong chain is hooked, one end to the body of the stump, or its principal root, and the other to the axletree. The power of horses or oxen is applied to the loose end of the rope mentioned, and as they draw, a rotary motion is communicated through the smallest wheel to the axletree, on which as the chain hooked to the stump winds up, the stump itself is gradually disengaged from the earth in which it grew."

The cost of such a machine, he says, was $250. They had also invented a plough with a sharp-cutting edge of steel, which, running its long nose under the roots, with its razor edge turned upwards, and making a narrow furrow, so chopped them into small pieces that they were easily swept away by the scraper. Mr. Holley was remarkable for stating in his reports all the difficulties met with, so that his candor could never be impeached. He rather hoped than promised, and the public was never disappointed by him, except favorably.

The Act of April 7, 1819, authorized borrowing $600,000 and completing the canal from Seneca River to Lake Erie. But to gain this the friends of the canal policy were obliged to extend equal favor to the eastern end and the Champlain Canal. And now all its enemies combined their energies to defeat the western section, and to stop the great ditch at Oswego. The whole work as authorized by the legislature they said would ruin the state, and a ditch of 200 miles through a swamp parallel to a lake, was idiotic. As the hands of the commissioners were so full with work not completed, it was hoped that public sentiment might be aroused against it before anything was done on the western section, and to this end a very able writer was

employed, who, under the name of "Peter Ploughshare," stirred up the jealousy of the eastern farmers and all the people of the Ontario Lake ports.
The obstructive ability of this pamphlet can hardly
be realized at this day. It is probably well for
the writer, obviously a man of talents and culture,
that his real name, if it ever was known, has been
thoroughly forgotten in New York, for a more
despicable piece of demagogism was perhaps never
clothed in good English. It was addressed to the
Members elect of the Legislature of the State of
New York, and dated Jefferson County, July 20,
1819. It was printed in Utica and probably sent
to every farmer in the eastern part of the state.
It was entitled, "CONSIDERATIONS AGAINST CON-
TINUING THE GREAT CANAL WEST OF THE SEN-
ECA." "Facts are stubborn things" was its motto.
To the future legislators it said :

"As the representatives of the interests of a free,
great and growing people, it undoubtedly becomes you
to examine thoroughly before you decide a question of
such vital importance — to be morally certain, before
you strike a blow which must affect unborn ages, that
its effects are to be beneficial — &c., &c., and finally to
beware lest you load the present generation with a
grievous and real burden, for the sake of a distant and
problematical benefit to posterity."

Turning to the farmers, with a humility worthy of Uriah Heep, and which doubtless accounts for the occultation of the real name of the writer, the pamphlet proceeds : —

" With these impressions, a plain farmer — accustomed, as every farmer ought to be, to think for himself on subjects that concern his own interests and the interests of the community, but unused to the display of his thoughts in public — now takes the liberty to address you ; not with the presumptuous hope of being able to produce conviction by the powers of rhetoric or the wiles of sophistry ; but with the humble expectation, by a candid statement of facts, to excite inquiry, rend from a subject of immense public importance the veil of political intrigue and self-interested ambition in which it has been shrouded, and present to your consideration and the view of the public the naked question of expediency which it involves.

" I think, indeed, my brother farmers, east of the Seneca to the Hudson, thence down that noble river to the vicinity of New York — embracing at least a moiety of the farming interest of the whole State — may rationally doubt whether the completion of a work which has for its avowed object the bringing of the whole western world to compete with them at their own market, can be beneficial. That they will naturally ask themselves : Why should I be taxed to effect a plan, which, if effected, places the farmer at the head of Lake Michigan in a better situation than myself, and reduces the value of my surplus produce exactly in the same ratio in which it increases the quantity brought to my natural market? "

After working this vein sufficiently, the writer argues with great ingenuity, that transportation from the West would be cheaper by Lake Ontario than by the canal, trusting, doubtless, that his brother farmers would see that Western produce, once afloat on the lake, would be as likely to go somewhere else as to thread the canal into their "natural market."

But for the wisdom and energy of Mr. Holley, this astute pamphlet would have had a most disastrous effect. With such a man at the helm of the great enterprise, it defeated itself, for it stirred him up to get a large portion of the Western section under contract and in process of construction before the session of the legislature, which otherwise he would not have done. He saw that the best answer to such a pamphlet was to say to the legislature, "It is too late. You ordered the work; it is begun, and cannot be stopped without immense loss." How this mighty "Ploughshare" movement was defeated, Mr. Holley modestly tells in a letter to Henry O'Rielly, dated Rochester, Dec. 18, 1837.

From the beginning of our great system of canal improvements a strong party existed in the state, who favored the project of passing from the middle section to

Lake Erie, by way of Oswego and a lateral cut around the Falls of Niagara. This party offered no strenuous resistance to the opening of the canal from the Rome summit to Montezuma; but, after that portion of the line was contracted for and nearly finished, exerted itself with ingenuity to accomplish its object. Its views required that the Canal Commissioners should be restrained by the legislature from making contracts for work on the line west of the middle section. It was in the winter of 1820 that the crisis arrived between the party in question and the friends of the inland route.

At a late day of the session of the previous winter authority had been given to the commissioners to extend their operations over the entire lines not previously surveyed and let out, of both the Erie and Champlain Canals, under a limited but liberal appropriation. This extension of authority had been earnestly opposed, but not very vigorously, because full concert of action had not been secured between the opponents of the whole canal policy and the friends of the Oswego route; and because it was deemed impracticable by the public for the commissioners, during the season next after it was granted, to do much more than to complete the middle section and make some preliminary surveys on the other sections.

At this time Mr. Seymour and myself were acting commissioners on the Erie Canal. Early in the season we directed Engineer White to enter upon the surveys between the Seneca and Genesee Rivers. The facts previously understood, with the knowledge soon acquired by Mr. White, left no room for doubt or hesitation as to the general location of the line between Montezuma and

Rochester; and this latter place was perceived to be a necessary point on the line.

Under these circumstances, and with a special reference to the approaching crisis in legislative action, in July, I directed Mr. White to proceed to Rochester and ascertain carefully where the Genessee could best be crossed, and thence to lay out the line easterly as far as he could, marking its dimensions by stakes, and dividing it into suitable sections for actual contract. To these directions he industriously conformed.

In October, 1819, the Canal Commissioners held a meeting at Utica. Well aware of the progress of Mr. White, I moved the board at that meeting to pass a resolution that all the line east from Rochester, located and prepared, should be, as soon as practicable, let out to contractors and put in the course of actual construction. This motion was resisted by Mr. Seymour, but was adopted by the votes of Messrs. Clinton, Van Rensselaer and myself, Mr. Young not being present.

Under this resolution about twenty-six miles of canal, from Rochester to near Palmyra, were let out previously to the meeting of the legislature, and a large amount of money justly earned upon them.

In January, 1820, the legislature met. It soon appeared that the friends of the Oswego route were determined to prosecute their views with increased zeal and pertinacity. Both in the legislature and out of it, they were numerous and active. An intelligent canal committee was raised in the Assembly, with Gen. Huntington, of Oneida County, for its chairman; and to them were referred the canal interests for that branch of the legislature.

The doubters and opposers of the canal policy had

early proposed to lay a local tax from the vicinity of the
line adopted, to assist in defraying the cost of the works.
A resolution in favor of this proposition was introduced,
and referred to the committee. But the great measure
of the friends of the Oswego route was a resolution
introduced to confine all canal expenditures to the eastern
section of the Erie Canal and the Champlain Canal till
they should both be completed. This resolution was
also referred to the canal committee.

The adoption of the last resolution by the legislature,
it was plain, would constitute an essential modification
of the state policy. The subscriber was thoroughly persuaded that such a modification would be vitally mis-
chievous, and labored with much zeal to avert it. The
committee requested the views of the Canal Commissioners on the two resolutions. In answer to this request,
a letter was drawn up by me, with great labor of inquiry
and anxious consideration, and submitted to the
board. A majority of the board approved it, signed it,
and sent it to the committee. Messrs. Young and Seymour witheld their sanction from it. The committee
reported so in favor of the views presented in the letter
as to advise against interfering with the plans of the commissioners. Their report was opposed with much warmth
and persistency, but prevailed, and the legislature
upheld the policy, which led to the speedy completion
of the canals, and has already issued so happily for the
interests and honor of the state.

The motive under which Mr. Holley acted so
vigorously and efficiently was a vision of the
future, well expressed in a sentence of his subse-

quent answer to the cunningly hypocritical "Peter Ploughshare."

"When they [the canals] are complete, the wealth of every island and every lake, of every continent and every ocean which is visited by the light of heaven, will contribute to weary their waters with commerce."

The facts as stated by Mr. Holley in regard to this decisive blow were never questioned by the opponents of the canal.

About two years after this grand practical victory, De Witt Clinton, under the pseudonym of Tacitus, brought forth in pamphlet form probably the ablest production of his pen, under the title,

"The Canal Policy of the State of New York, delineated in a letter to Robt. Troup, Esq.

"'Nothing extenuate,
Nor set down aught in malice.'—*Shakespeare*.

"Albany: Printed and published by E. & E. Hosford, 1821."

On page 45, he says:

"Mr. Holley and Mr. Young were authorized to make contracts, and to the judicious and indefatigable efforts of those gentlemen, too much credit cannot be ascribed."

And it is greatly to the credit of De Witt Clinton himself that he did not content himself, so far as Mr. Holley was concerned, with this sentence, but adds in a note on the same page : —

" Mr. Holley was a member of the legislature when the initiatory canal law was passed, which he advocated with the whole force of his talents. This gentleman is a member of a numerous family distinguished for genius. His mind is improved by reading, reflection and conversation, and is distinguished for extensive research, and acute discrimination. He has devoted his whole time and attention, mind and body, to the canal ; and some of the most luminous reports and communications have proceeded from his pen. Whatever he touches he adorns, and whenever he speaks or writes he instructs. His mild and conciliatory manners, his elevated character, his spotless integrity, and his indefatigable business talents, have rendered his services as an acting Canal Commissioner invaluable."

Every year of Mr. Holley's after life confirmed and emphasized this noble testimony to his character. The way in which he pushed the great work forward, shouldering responsibility himself when the state failed to meet the contracts it had authorized him to make ; the way he bore himself when this self-sacrifice had thrown him into embarrassment ; his uncomplaining sedateness of temper when he met the cold ingratitude of a republic enriched by his sublime foresight and toil; the power, dignity and wisdom with which he administered his part of that rebuke which taught secret societies their place in the republic; his opposition to fanatical revivalism; and, above all, his grand and practical energy in making the ballot-box the safeguard of human liberty, all established his title to be remembered, as an example of virtuous manhood, by the remotest ages of the future.

CHAPTER XII.

ECONOMY, PUBLIC AND PRIVATE.

THIS is the proper place to notice a trait of
Myron Holley's character to which he owed the
suffering which he bore with a heroism more uncommon than the suffering. It is not uncommon
for men who are enthusiastically engaged in public
service to forget their own individual interests ; but
they are apt, at the same time, to be rather care-
less of economy for the public. In Mr. Holley's
management of the public business his economy
was most exemplary. His fault was that he
guarded its interests more carefully than he did his
own. This cannot be better illustrated than by
the report in regard to canal expenses.

The Act of April 17, 1816, appropriated $20,-
000 for preliminary expenses. The comptroller at
the call of the Assembly, reported April 2, 1817,
that the expenses under this appropriation up to
that date were $16,930.29. The Commissioners at
the same date reported their expenses, included in

the above, as $2,478.17.   This report, signed by Clinton, Holley, and Young, is exceedingly interesting as showing the economy of public service at that period.

After an apology for not making the report earlier, the document proceeds :

" The expenses of the commissioners include the expenses of travelling at various periods — of their visit to the Middlesex Canal — and of their superintendence of the whole route of both canals — of their meetings at various times, and are brought up to their first meeting, the present session of the legislature.

They consist of the following sums : —

Expenses of commissioners' meeting, 17 May, 1816, in New York, including the expense of going there, of stay there, of two commissioners, with two engineers, going to view the Middlesex canal, stay there, and return home, . . . $515 00
Expenses of commissioners in meeting at Utica on the 15th July, while there, while exploring the route of the western canal, and returning home, ... $1,080 12
Expenses of the commissioners in exploring the northern canal, and directing operations thereon, ... $679 19
Expenses of commissioners in meeting at Albany in November last, and returning home, ... $193 86

The whole of the items amount to . $2,468 17

Considering that upwards of 313 miles on the western
canal, besides that part of the route south of the mountain ridge and west of Genesee River, and more than 60
miles on the northern canal, have been explored, surveyed and levelled; that the routes of the canals have
been actually laid out, that perspicuous maps and pro-
files have been made, and that full reports have been
presented, it is believed that no operation so extensive,
so complicated and so important, has ever been performed with more economy of expenditure.

A sum not exceeding $4.000 will be required in
addition to that part of the appropriation which is
unexpended, to complete the payment of the engineers
for their services; to defray the expenses of printing,
engraving and stationery, to pay the expenses of the
meeting of the commissioners and their attendance on
their duties during the present session of the legislature;
to satisfy some demands not yet presented, and also to
make a reasonable compensation to the secretary and
treasurer of the board, whose time since the first meeting in May has been almost exclusively engrossed in
discharging these trusts, and in attending to their general
duties as commissioners."

The report might well boast that so much and
so important work had never been done for $24,-
000.   And the credit of it was mainly due to Mr.
Holley, who himself was treasurer of the board,
for which extra service from 1816 to 1824 inclu-
sive he never received a cent of pay.

During that year Holley and Young were the

only *acting* commissioners, the former acting as
treasurer, and the latter as secretary. They were
allowed by the Board $2,500 a year and expenses.
The other commissioners were only allowed expenses. In 1819 the state fixed their salary at
$2,500 and expenses, which in 1820 was reduced
to $2,000.

CHAPTER XIII.

EMBARRASSMENT.

Out of this exceedingly meagre compensation — meagre even at that time for a labor and responsibility so vastly important — Mr. Holley managed, in company with two friends, to secure a small tract of land at Lyons, on the line of the canal, where he built a plain, substantial and convenient house, planted fruit trees, and made himself a home. A man of his calibre, looking out for himself, could easily have secured territory, which, by the inevitable rise of real estate in favored spots on such a work, would have made him rich. He no more did that than he thought of fortifying himself against the extra risks of having to disburse such large sums of money for the state.

Hence it was, that after the success of the great work had become triumphantly assured, after boats were traversing 280 miles of it, and it was certain that it would be completed without much

exceeding the original estimate, with aqueducts
of stone where wood had been contemplated, Mr.
Holley, on his own motion and to the astonishment of friends and enemies, reported to the
legislature that he found a deficiency of vouchers
of about $30,000 to account for the two and a half
millions of the public money which he had had to
disburse, and he most reasonably asked the
legislature to allow him a commission on that
sum, which would, at least, make him square.
Inasmuch as, by the dilatoriness of the state, he
had often, to keep contractors at work, been
obliged to raise funds on his own credit, which
had enhanced the risk of his treasurership, and
considering what the state had saved by obliging
him to circulate small bank bills instead of paying
his multitude of contractors by check, this seemed
to many then, and must to all now, a reasonable
request. The legislature's refusal to allow this
commission, obliging him to make good the
deficiency out of his slender property, is perhaps
the meanest piece of ingratitude ever chargeable
against a republic. The State of New York is
convicted of this by its own documents. For an
investigating committee, representing Mr. Holley's
enemies as well as his friends, unanimously

acquitted him of having applied a single dollar of that deficiency to his own use. With the exception of the ignorant, there was not one of his opponents base enough to make that charge against him publicly till, when, years after, he was a candidate of a party which grew out of the murder of William Morgan.

The request which Mr. Holley made to the legislature on the 30th of March, 1824, is too characteristic of him to be omitted here. His words were:

" To the performance of my official duties I have now, for eight years, devoted the best faculties of body and mind, under all vicissitudes and apprehensions, with constant, persevering and lively zeal. I have been withdrawn from the education of my children, have relinquished the enjoyments of domestic life, have encountered, without flinching, all the dangers of sickness, in seasons and situations eminently unhealthy, whenever and wherever my duties have required, and have labored with effect in promoting the object of my appointment. * * * At the first meeting of the Canal

Board, on the 17th of May, 1816, I was
appointed treasurer of the Canal Commissioners, and have ever since performed the
duties of that office, and have always
thought myself entitled to a reasonable and
adequate compensation therefor. This compensation I have not asked of the Canal
Commissioners, because a majority of that
Board are so situated as to render preferring such a claim to them for decision,
indelicate. But I perceive no such indeli-
cacy in preferring it to the legislature.
And of you I ask to be paid one per cent.
upon the amount of monies received and
disbursed by me towards the construction
of the canals. With the aid of this allow-
ance I can immediately make arrangements
to pay up fully my accounts with the
Comptroller. And this claim commends
itself to my sense of justice, in consideration
of the extra expense, service and hazard,
which the receipt and payment of this
money has involved."

Why he did not prefer this claim to the legislature earlier, need hardly be said. His patriotic zeal to avoid giving the watchful enemies of the great work any pretext for stopping it, outran his personal discretion. He sacrificed himself for the future of his race, trusting it would do him justice. It is not too late for this generation to do it. What he told the legislature of his exposure to the danger of sickness, " in seasons and situations eminently unhealthy," was no idle boast. In 1820, between the months of July and October, not less than one thousand men employed upon the canal between Salina and Seneca River were prostrated by malaria. To the sick, Holley was always a ministering angel, a friend in need, and as such he was long gratefully remembered by individuals who had experienced his kindness. The writer received the following illustration of this trait in his character from his daughter Sallie, so well known as a teacher in the colored school in Lottsburgh, Va.

" My father's benevolence was like an overflowing fountain, especially toward the poor and helpless. One of the very earliest illustrations of his kind nature, outside of our own family (that I can remember) occurred in 1832. A solitary case of Asiatic cholera in Lyons, our village, resulted in the death of the poor woman, living near the canal locks. The panic-stricken neighbors all fled. Nobody could be found who dared to go near to bury the body. As soon as my father heard it, he at once volunteered his services, and asked the next prominent citizen to aid him in carrying the body to the grave, which they did, to the wonder of the villagers. Such an example did more to restore tranquillity to the excited community than medicine or preaching."

Though Mr. Holley had conducted this arduous and dangerous business of constructing the canal through a region of deadly malaria, with an unselfish devotion and a democratic spirit which attached to him the humblest laborers, as will be touchingly shown by and by, the moment he had so honorably confessed this comparatively slight deficiency in his accounts, some of the bitter and defeated enemies of the canal policy anonymously raised a howl against him through the press as a criminal defaulter. This howl even terrified his political friends of the Whig party, so that they dared not do what they knew to be just. And the Democrats, who in spite of their leader, Martin Van Buren, had mostly opposed the canal, made all the political capital they could out of the humiliation of a man who had enriched his state by being a genuine democrat. As the legislature did not see fit to grant his most reasonable request, Mr. Holley resigned his commissionership and made over his property to the state to satisfy a deficiency which arose from no fault of his. This property was appraised at $18,000, though its prospective value was doubtless considerably more. Its alienation left Mr. Holley with a large family and no resources outside of himself. His little property was finally restored to him by the state, not as a gratuity, but as a debt — interest and costs not included.

Mr. Holley's temper and patience during the four years in which, for his family's sake, he was seeking this simple act of justice, while he had such an overwhelming claim on the generosity and gratitude of not only the state but the whole world, is something more to be admired than any miracle recorded in history. Whether Hercules went through any such experience after the valuable labors for which he was deified, history does not inform us. It is of more importance to the people of our great republic to know how our modern Hercules bore the ingratitude of the Empire State than how he led the pathway of commerce through her Serbonian bogs.

It has already been detailed how, on the 20th of

October, 1819, Mr. Holley struck the decisive
blow which gave his great enterprise its assured
success and New York her glory as the leader of
our mighty march of internal improvement. We
can better realize what the whole country owed
him by considering what Thomas Jefferson wrote
to De Witt Clinton, Dec. 12, 1822.

" New York," said the Sage of Monticello, " has an-
ticipated by a full century the ordinary progress of
improvement. This great work suggests a question,
both curious and difficult, as to the comparative capa-
bility of nations to execute great enterprises. It is
not from greater surplus of produce, after supplying
their own wants, for in this New York is not beyond
some other States ; is it from other sources of industry
additional to her produce? This may be ;—or is it
a moral superiority? — a sounder calculating mind,
as to the most profitable employment of surplus,
by improvement of capital, instead of useless consump-
tion? I should lean to this latter hypothesis, were I
disposed to puzzle myself with such investigations."—
Dr. Hosack's Life of Clinton, page 348.

Whoever will weigh the facts, and especially
those that immediately follow, will see that the
" moral superiority " of a single individual had a
great deal to do in solving the riddle which puzzled
Mr. Jefferson.

Immediately on Mr. Holley's calling the atten-

tion of the legislature to the deficiency in his
accounts, about one-half of which consisted in
outstanding notes signed by himself, on which contractors had drawn money from the banks, the
other active commissioners, Seymour, Young,
and Bouck, who had disbursed money from the
state, demanded that their accounts should be
examined, so that their own party, the democratic, should not suffer from the storm apparently
rising against Mr. Holley. The same committee
which vindicated them in 1824 * did not thoroughly

---

* Though Mr. Holley was treasurer of the Canal Commissioners, by their own appointment, neither they nor the state
seem to have recognized him as such, for they individually
received money of the state which was entrusted to and
charged to them individually, without regard to their treasurer. Hence it may have happened that packages of paper
money, charged and transmitted to Mr. Holley for the use of
the canal, fell into the hands of some other commissioner
engaged in disbursement. The fact that every other commissioner could show vouchers of disbursement for every
dollar charged to him individually, was no proof that this
did not happen. When one of the commissioners,—by no
means on account of poverty,—some years after shot himself
in his own back-yard, the defect in the financial arrangements
between the state and the Canal Commissioners became apparent to some thoughtful persons. The mistake of Mr.
Holley was, that being treasurer of the Canal Commissioners,
he did not oblige them and the state to recognize him as such,
and so keep his accounts that he could not be held responsible for money which he did not receive. It is not safe to
trust even a state.

vindicate Mr. Holley, but reported that his property in Lyons was worth only $16,000 or $18,000,
and said : " It appears that it was made a condition in the canal loans that the bills of the banks
that made the loan should be circulated on the line
of the canal, and this consideration, as appears by
a statement of the cashiers of the State and Mechanics' Banks, has caused a saving to the state
in the negotiation of certain loans."

A committee was ordered to investigate further
during the recess. It did not find Mr. Holley
guilty of any embezzlement whatever, and so reported. As the bondsmen could not be held
responsible, the legislature passed an act, March 7,
1825, to pay the notes, amounting to $15,808.58,
and April 21, 1825, and an act authorizing the Canal
Commissioners to settle with Mr. Holley and take
the real estate conveyed by him, *but not to pay
any percentage* on his disbursements. This action
was by no means up to the report of the committee, which set forth that by reason of Mr. Holley's
meritorious and valuable services as Canal Commissioner, the great difficulties by which he had been
surrounded in disbursing moneys in one, three and
five-dollar bills, amidst woods, swamps, and new
settlements, constantly exposed to mistakes, some

of which had been ascertained, and others rendered highly probable, &c., &c., the committee recommended that the state accept a conveyance of Mr. Holley's real estate (reserving thereout Mr. Holley's house, lot, and improvements, in Lyons. worth $3,000), and discharge him and his sureties altogether. The bill to this effect was considered as making Mr. Holley a donation of $3,000, and by a rule of the Assembly must have a two-thirds vote. It passed the Assembly 72 to 38, thus wanting two votes to become a law, to the disgrace of the state. Hardly anything could be conceived more pitiful. A man who could command his temper under such provocation, who could appeal his cause to future intelligence, from a legislature so besotted with stupidity and meanness, must be no ordinary mortal. But Mr. Holley's faith in human nature did not fail, for total depravity was no part of his creed.

Myron Holley knew that his services would be appreciated in time, and whether they were or not, he knew he was the benefactor of those who most railed at him. As he was an advocate of free speech and the equal representation of all classes, he could listen with composure to the unjust judgments of the ignorant, or even be amused at them. His daughter relates how he used to laugh at the speech of a partially intoxicated democrat in the Assembly, who said he had " frequently rode by Mrs. Myron Holley's bleach-yard in Lyons and seen three thousand yards of linen lace bleaching, — that the family bought oranges by the bushel — made no more of 'em than he did of praties — and drove about in the most elegant coach of the country," — alluding to an old stage-coach which Mr. Holley had taken for a debt. His daughter also says of this period : " I have often heard my father speak with emotion of a little circumstance that occurred in Albany at the height of his accusation. One day as he was walking by Gourley's, the hotel where all members of the legislature and many other gentlemen stopped, the front piazza was thronged with a great crowd of these gentlemen, when the Presbyterian minister came out from among them all, and most cordially and warmly seized my father's hand in both of his, and in the tenderest tone possible remarked : ' Mr. Holley, I know you are an innocent man, for no one else could wear the look of your countenance ! I ask you to be my friend, as I am truly yours.'"

Mr. Holley had a most charming and lovely family, — sons and daughters, blooming and bud-

ding ;— and conscious of his own honest and tri-
umphant service of the public, his heart turned to
them with all the fervor of health and hope. The
black cloud gathering over his affairs and threaten-
ing to leave him houseless, only intensified his
affection for those he loved best, and for his whole
country as well. His grand old father, Luther
Holley, was still living in Salisbury, Connecticut. Released from the canal service, previous to
the legislative action already related, he visited
the place of his birth. And now, instead of the
rumbling old stage coach, was the delightful canal
packet,—which, even in these days of parlor cars,
old people look back to with some regret. Here
are, in full, two of the letters he wrote on this
trip, one to the second of his daughters, and the
other to his father at Salisbury, after his return
from that place.

THREE MILES BELOW UTICA,
ON BOARD THE PACKET SAMUEL YOUNG,
13th August, 1824.

MY DEAR CLARISSA,— Our passage thus far has
been altogether convenient and agreeable, the boats
having been not overcrowded. and the passengers
having been many of them intelligent and agreeable.
There have come on board the boat, from Utica to
Schenactady, six young ladies and gentlemen, who
have been on a tour of curiosity and pleasure, to visit

the Falls of Niagara, the Falls of Trenton, and several other places between New York and Niagara River. They seemed to have belonged to two parties, who separated at Utica on their way out, and have met at the same place on their return. And the gratification of witnessing their cordiality, and hearing their gay and animated remarks on the several occurrences which have interested them since their separation, is lively. They have been well educated and accustomed to genteel association, and feeling and exhibiting, as they do, the ardor and liveliness natural to young and happy travellers through a country abounding with many beautiful, novel and magnificent objects, their conversation is not only charming to themselves, but to all who listen to it. One of the most interesting associations which necessarily connects itself with it in my mind, belongs to my own dear daughters and sons. I hope one day to see you more accomplished than either of them, and happy as they appear to be. And I know you will not lose the opportunity, offered to you at Geneva, of qualifying yourself to sustain the elegant and interesting part which the young ladies above alluded to are playing here, but also to discharge with propriety and self-satisfaction, the more important part belonging to the most serious duties of life.

I know that you and Elizabeth will approve yourselves good scholars, and obtain the applause and respect of your teacher. But with the literary acquisitions and other accomplishments which you will not fail to have, I am desirous of impressing upon you most earnestly the importance of cultivating and preserving an equal temper.

After long experience of life, nothing is more effec-

tually established in my mind than the indispensable
necessity of good temper to enjoyment, if not to respectability. No situation in which you have ever been
placed was calculated to affect your future happiness so
much as that in which you will find yourself at Geneva.
With your sister, who is very lively, sensitive and even
irritable, you will find it sometimes difficult to maintain
that even, affectionate and amiable intercourse, which
it is of great importance that you and she should always
hold together, and as you are the oldest and the most
sedate. the responsibility of keeping up such intercourse
will chiefly devolve on you. Elizabeth is tender, affectionate and grateful naturally. And if she sees you
overlooking some provocations. and determined to live
with her on the footing of an amiable elder sister, I am
persuaded she will determine not to be outdone in the
good offices which will so peculiarly become you both,
in all your associations, and harmony between you will
recommend not less than literary attainments. Before
you will have been long at Geneva I hope to visit you,
and to provide, as far as I shall be able, all that may be
wanting to make your studies and your life useful and
pleasant.

In the meantime and ever be assured that you and
Elizabeth are now, and will always be, objects of my
strongest affection.

MYRON HOLLEY.

ALBANY, 31st August, 1824.

DEAR FATHER, — Robert and I arrived here yesterday,
a little before 5 o'clock P.M., having come from
Hudson on a return post coach. My travelling has
probably been beneficial to my health, for I now feel

entirely recovered, with reasonable appetite, and for
the two last nights have slept sufficiently without any
medicinal aid.

You have learned from Alexander that Edward and
his family were well, and that no news existed at
Hudson of any interest. Our ride from Salisbury was
pleasant, but from Hudson here, in consequence of the
roads being very dusty and wind being with us, we
were very much annoyed and thoroughly covered with
dust.

I have found no letter here from home, from which I
infer that all is well there. This city is alive with the
expectation of soon being honored with the presence of
La Fayette. Great preparations are making to do him
honor, and he is expected here on Thursday. Gen.
Stephen Van Rensselaer is to meet him, by order of
the governor, at the line of the state bordering on
Massachusetts, with a detachment of horse, for the
purpose of escorting him to Albany, where, in front of
the Capitol within the public green, an arch is erected
for the occasion. In front of the Capitol, at the second
story above the piazza or vestibule, a gallery is erected,
as I understand, to be filled by ladies who mean to aid
in giving a public welcome to " the nation's guest."
Perhaps from this place, some one of them, to be
selected for her beauty and accomplishments, may
bestow upon the head of the hero of the occasion, and
one of the most disinterested and constant asserters of
liberty in the world, a wreath of flowers, or some other
emblems of praise and gratitude, suitable to the sim-
plicity and sincerity of republican manners. Such a
wreath, on such an occasion, and so bestowed, would
be more dear to a gallant and feeling heart than all

the rewards of chivalry, and would make La Fayette the happiest man in the world.

If La Fayette returns to France, what effect upon his situation there will the voluntary honors he is receiving in this country have? Will they not make the adherents of arbitrary rule envious of him, and induce them to traduce, villify and injure him? All men of sense will perceive that he is receiving in this country a higher and more illustrious distinction than can, or ever could, be conferred by kings or emperors, with all their generosity and magnificence; because this distinction proceeds from the unbought, sincere, deep-felt, universal love of a reflecting, intelligent, sober-minded people, without art or hypocrisy, in the ingenuous, straightforward exercise of their feelings. In my opinion, the state of the general feeling in this country towards La Fayette is creditable to our People, and argues well for the interests of humanity. The great distinction and advantage of this age over all preceding ages, is, that public sympathy and public opinion are much more controlling and imperative than they ever were before; and that they should be manifested in a manner so spontaneous, and so lively, and so universal, in our country, and in behalf of one so disinterested and so worthy, will have a tendency to give them a wider influence and a still more thorough control. And it is self-evident that public sympathy and public opinion must always be in favor of the rights of man, and of whatever will advance the dignity and happiness of the human race; that is, they will be in favor of the mass of men, and not in favor of exceptions.

It is probable that we shall remain here two or three days, by which time I expect to be able to get through with my necessary business here, and then return to Lyons, where I shall cherish some expectations of seeing you in the course of the fall. •

Please give my best love to mother and Caroline and other friends.

With great respect and affection,

Yours,

MYRON HOLLEY.

LUTHER HOLLEY, ESQ.

On reading this allusion to Lafayette, one cannot help thinking of what was just then going on in the royal household of Louis XVIII. That arbitrary monarch, restored to his throne by the allied despots of Europe, had been endeavoring for ten years to pacify his subjects by swearing to a charter which promised to secure their rights, but did not, and was now on his deathbed. The Jesuits had gained complete control over him for the last four years by means of the beautiful Madame du Cayla, such a tool as they always knew how to use. But the dying king, who really had no faith in the church, had honestly made up his mind that he would die outside of its pale, and without touching its sacraments. He doubtless remembered, with natural disgust, how, when in 1815, he had hardly stepped one foot on his throne, it came near being upset by the priests outraging public feeling by refusing to receive into the church of St. Roch, or say prayers over the body of Mademoiselle Rancourt, a popular actress. He had to quiet the tumult by sending his own priest to read the service. He also remembered the religious murders at Nismes, and like a sensible man, king though he was, he thought he would die without adding his kingly sanction to such priestly nonsense. The ultramontanes and Jesuits stood aghast at his resolution. Cardinals and prelates did their best to shake it, but in vain. Nothing could overcome it till they called Madame Du Cayla from her religious retirement at St. Ouen's, who by her beauty and tears prevailed on him to take the final sacraments. No doubt the corrupt power that ruined the Bourbons, vilified Lafayette all it could. It vilifies everything good within its pale as well as without. Both Lafayette and Thomas Paine, with the profoundest reverence for human liberty, did all they could to prevent the cause they reverenced from being stained by the murder of either priest or king. They were, both, the best and wisest friends kings ever had.

CHAPTER XIV.

AT HOME WITH HIS FAMILY.

MR. HOLLEY having retired with dignity and a good conscience from the office of Canal Commissioner, in the spring of 1824, spent much of the next summer in conference with his successors in the great work, and with the legislative committee of investigation whose report, as we have seen, was far more favorable to him than the legislative action resulting from it. In the mean time let us look at him in the bosom of his family in Lyons. His oldest daughter Caroline had just been married to Graham H. Chapin, a lawyer, and afterwards a member of Congress, and Clarissa and Elizabeth were at a boarding-school in Geneva. In a letter to the former he gives a picture of the family and of himself, which cannot be reduced to a smaller compass without injury to the coloring.

LYONS, 5th December, 1824.

MY DEAR CLARISSA, — Behold me, with your mind's eye, seated in the upper kitchen, by the side of a good

hickory fire, one side of which is occupied by your
mother singing Cornelia to sleep, just beginning to
carry into effect the gratifying purpose of conversing
a little with you. And as I know all our household are
dear to you, I will complete the description of our
present domestic condition, by telling you that Sam
and Sally, and Myron and Cuyler are engaged in very
good natured but noisy intercommunication with Viny
in the lower kitchen. Your aunt Betsey and Caroline
have gone to take leave of Mrs. Church, who starts
with her family this evening in a boat, to take up their
residence in Syracuse. Robert and William have
walked down to the store to spend their evening, and
Mr. Chapin is over at his new house watching the fires,
which have been kept up there in all the fire places
since yesterday morning, for the purpose of drying the
recently plastered walls and ceilings. After considerable delays Mr. Chapin's house is now completed, with
the exception of the inside painting, and that will be
a job of no great length, so that Caroline expects to
commence house-keeping in about one week from this
time. Yesterday the process of cleaning the joiner's
work for the reception of the paint was commenced,
and to-morrow it is to be renewed with energy. It is
impossible to tell yet, whether the chimneys will draw
smoke well, or not, and from all the opportunities of
judging thus far furnished, there is some diversity of
opinion upon that very interesting subject. The house
will be found, we all think, very convenient, and sufficiently roomy, being built nearly upon the plan of our
house in Canandaigua, though a little larger. But,
while we have lately all been anxious, in our different
modes, to do everything in our power to aid Caroline

to start fair in her new character of mistress of an independent establishment, we have not neglected to cherish, in our hearts, the liveliest affection for you and Elizabeth, who are equally dear to us with your elder sister. And as the cold weather seems now to have set in, in sober earnest, we anticipate great happiness, in your good company at the approaching Christmas. Perhaps we may some of us see you before that time, but whether we do or not, we shall not forget the promised boon of a visit then from yourselves, and several of your interesting friends.

I have just concluded the reading aloud to your mother and aunt of the novel of the Abbot, which you know derives its chief interest from the exhibition which it gives of the character, embarrassments and friends and enemies of the celebrated Mary, queen of Scotland. The impression left upon our minds by the beauty, accomplishments, virtues, vices, distresses and sufferings of that unhappy lady, is quite gloomy, though a candid view of her conduct and its results is decidedly favorable to virtue. Her character attracts all the complacent interest which can possibly belong to the most amiable dispositions, elegant figure, charming countenance and gracious behaviour, united in a female well educated, and moving in a sphere so conspicuous as to impart an important influence through every heart in several of the leading nations of Christendom, until after her unfortunate marriage with the foolish, licentious, and ridiculous dandy, Lord Darnley. Her very reasonable disgust with him seems first to have opened her mind to intrusions of the vile, and it must be confessed that in reference to him and the contemptible musician Rizzio and the profligate Bothness, she degraded herself to the commission of crimes of the grossest dye. But if she greatly sinned, she greatly suffered, and at last, after nineteen years of close and rigorous captivity, she met the death prepared for her by her inhuman enemies, with the greatest fortitude, and even piety, leaving upon the whole a stronger claim to the sympathies of posterity than any female sovereign of modern Europe.

Your aunt and Caroline have now returned, and their conversation with your mother has become so lively, as to break off this long letter in midway, which I am afraid you will find so dull as to leave it uncertain whether I ought to apologize for continuing it so long, or for breaking it off.

With great affection for you and Elizabeth,

Your very obt.,

MYRON HOLLEY.

Miss CLARISSA HOLLEY.

Please give our love to Mrs. Plumb and her amiable family.

A man never enjoyed his family more, or was more faithful to it. He also enjoyed, in spite of the loss and calumny it had cost him, the great public blessing which his labors had conferred upon mankind, though he was to see the glory of it transferred, for the present, from himself to others.

CHAPTER XV.

THE WEDDING OF THE WATERS.

It was in the fall of 1825 that the waters of Erie met those of the Hudson, and the great wedding festival was celebrated from the 26th of October to the 4th of November, beginning at Buffalo and ending in a blaze of glory and gush at New York. A great amount of the sublime was mixed with plenty of the ridiculous. But the whole people were really glad, and no man was gladder of that than Myron Holley, who honored the great wedding cortege with his presence from Lyons to New York. The people of this generation can hardly conceive the delight experienced by those of that, from one end of the land to the other, when it was telephoned by cannon from Buffalo to New York and back in three hours, that the great lakes were, in a commercial sense, level with the ocean. Every one saw how this laid the foundations of thousands of fortunes, and made every industrious man and woman richer.

Whoever will dig into the files of New York, Boston or Philadelphia papers of that date will find them, dry and barren as they then were on most topics, perfectly luxuriant, blooming and flamboyant on the canal celebration. Eloquence, and even poetry sprang up as by magic, where they were least expected. The old jokes about "Clinton's big ditch" gave place to millions of fond anticipations of a voyage in a splendid packet-boat on the "raging canawl."

The ceremonies had of course been carefully arranged and formulated beforehand, so as to satisfy everybody, especially those most ambitious to send their names by water to posterity. In Buffalo, then a scattering and inconsiderable village, more notable for an enterprising hotel keeper and stage proprietor than anything else, there was a vast concourse of people from the surrounding country, who moved in solemn procession to the head of the canal, where a canal-boat, named the "SENECA CHIEF," splendidly and appropriately decorated, and bearing kegs of Lake Erie water destined to be poured into the ocean by Dr. Samuel L. Mitchell, below the narrows of New York harbor, received on board Gov. Clinton, the Lieutenant-Governor, and New York and other delegations. This boat was drawn by four horses, and was followed by three others, gaily dressed, and bearing distinguished citizens. Jesse Hawley, now a citizen of Rochester, instead of the jail limits of Geneva, addressed the crowd in behalf of the visitors, and was replied to by Judge Forward of Buffalo. Then started the horse-drawn boats on their slow way, greeting on the banks of the canal, as they passed the sparse clearings, nearly the whole population of many square miles of territory on each side. In every smart village or incipient city the aquatic pageant was received with shouts, music and cannon; speeches of welcome and speeches of reply; dinners and balls. The progress was not rapid. That was not the fast age. It was Wednesday when the " Seneca Chief " started from Buffalo. It was noon the next " Sabbath day " when it arrived in Utica. The Governor and party attended church there in the afternoon, and it does not appear that any legal measures were taken in regard to the fracture of the Jewish law, — perhaps it is less liable to fracture on water than on land.

Monday morning the processions, cannon firing, music, and speech-making began again, and grew more and more intense as the pageant passed Little

Falls, Amsterdam, Schenectady, till, at half past 10 o'clock on Thursday, Nov. 3, the "Seneca Chief" unhitched its team of horses and floated into the Albany basin, through which it was towed by yawls manned by twenty-four masters of sailing vessels, between lines of canal boats vocal with huzzas and hallelujahs.

As soon as the Governor's party landed, it was escorted to the state capitol, where Philip Hone tendered the congratulations of the New York Corporation, and William Jones, of Albany, those of the capital city. Three hundred and fifty persons sat down to a feast under a double arcade upon the capitol lawn, presided over by John Tayler and Ambrose Spencer, assisted by Martin Van Buren and seven other vice-presidents. One of the regular toasts was worthy of a proud state:

"A generous competition among all the states of the Union in promoting our common prosperity. New York has led out with steamboats and canals."

Gov. Clinton's volunteer was still worthier of memory:

"The love of country — may it ever rise superior to the spirit of party and personal consideration."

Steam lost no time in towing to New York not

only the "Seneca Chief," but a whole fleet of canal boats, for the next day was to be the great one there — a demonstration of all the trades and arts, on land and water, to be followed in the evening by the largest and most magnificent ball ever danced on this or any other continent.

Charles King, editor of the "New York American," must sum up the story of that day, the details of which would fill a larger volume than this. I quote his editorial of the 5th.

The celebration of yesterday was everything that heart could desire. It was the appropriate expression by a great and free people of their joy at the completion of a work alike useful and magnificent, achieved by their own unaided means, industry, and self-denial, and of which the influence, moral and political, will extend to the remotest times, and to the most distant quarters of our Union.

The heavens, too, smiled on the happiness of man. A more beautiful day never dawned. It was the very atmosphere which a painter would have chosen to give effect to the brilliant, the unrivalled water scene. A warm light mist hovered over the bay, and served to magnify without obscuring the numberless and various vessels that floated on its tranquil bosom. It was to the reality what poetry is to truth, a beautiful amplification. When the gaily decorated steam and canal boats, with their countless passengers, were drawn up off the battery, at about half-past nine o'clock, in preparation for their departure towards the ocean, a spectacle was presented which not only has never been equalled, but which no other place in the world has the means of equalling. Twenty-one steam-boats, besides canal and pilot boats, barges, and a ship, all dressed out with flags, and alive with happy human beings, brought within the distinct view of tens of thousands of delighted spectators, and surrounded with a scenery of which the beauty is nowhere to be surpassed. It was a glorious sight, and on a most glorious occasion.

To those who were not present yesterday in the city, it is quite impossible to convey anything like an idea of the scene. It was altogether the most impressive we have ever witnessed; and the conduct particularly of both actors and spectators, was orderly and decorous, not only beyond all former example, but beyond, we are bold to say, anything that was ever seen anywhere amidst such an immense mass of people. There were, independently of about five thousand persons who walked in the procession, probably over one hundred thousand lookers-on, of every age and description, and degree, from puling infancy to spectacled old age, countrymen and citizens, gentle and simple; and among them all,—and at some time in the day they almost all fell under our observation,—we saw not a single instance of drunkenness, no quarrel, no riot, no confusion. We make this remark with even greater pride than that with which we record the celebration itself, or the great cause of it, for it speaks most emphatically in praise of the moral character and conscious dignity of a free people.

CHAPTER XVI.

THE STRUGGLE FOR JUSTICE.

Yet the man whose wisdom, energy, and self-sacrifice had achieved this glory, more than any other one man's, whose integrity had been certified by the most rigid examination, who had conveyed his whole property to the state to save harmless his bondsmen, after all this rejoicing, did not find enough of love-thy-neighbor-as-thyself in the State of New York, to restore to him his small property till March, 1828. Till then, with a stout heart and a placid temper, he most courteously pleaded with the legislature for justice, year after year, backed by such friends * as dared

---

* That DeWitt Clinton was one of those friends, the following grateful letter testifies :

ALBANY, 21st April, 1825.

GOVERNOR CLINTON, — I beg leave to tender to you, and to Mrs. Clinton, my most grateful thanks for the repeated and effective expressions of your favorable opinions of my claim, presented to the legislature during the present session. The bill, which has passed the Senate and Assembly, will, I trust, lead to the entire discharge of my bail, and leave me in posto stand by him, without heeding the hoarse cries of " defaulter," " defaulter," coming from the dens of political knavery, and from religious bigotry too, no doubt; for, though Mr. Holley was born religious, and grew more and more religious till he died, whatever bigotry he may ever have had had been all washed out by his canal experience. But the struggle with prejudice was long and dubious, as letters to one of his daughters in 1827 will show : —

ALBANY, 24th March, 1827.

DEAR CLARISSA, — I was very happy to receive your good letter yesterday, with the postscript of Elizabeth, and I thank God that you are able to write so good a letter, and that you are all so well. I have help and hopes here, but must not be too sanguine. The committee of the Senate, to whom my memorial was re-

session of a shelter for my family. It may, and I think it ought, to do more. But whatever may be the determination of the commissioners, it can never impair the just admiration with which I regard the conduct of yourself and your lady in my behalf. To remit provocation bespeaks an elevated and honorable mind; to cure the disposition, from which it may be supposed to proceed, by active beneficence, is a sure index of that enlarged and precious charity, which is better even than faith and hope. That the perfect reward of these, and of every other christian virtue, may belong to you and Mrs. Clinton, both in this life and forever, is the earnest prayer of, Sir,

With the highest respect and most grateful affection,
Your very ob't.,
MYRON HOLLEY.

ferred, have reported favorably, and the bill for reconveying my lands to me, which they introduced, is made the order of the day for Wednesday next, when I hope it will pass. I have a package for Mr. Chapin, which Mr. Forbes, of your neighborhood, told me he would soon call for. This contains my memorial and the report of the committee.

I hope, my dear, that neither you nor any of the rest of the family, go to the night meetings, as I look upon the awakenings which take place there as, on the whole, not promotive of religion or virtue. In the young and innocent they are the result of high and unsafe excitement, and in those of mature years, they are sometimes hypocritical, and sometimes the evidence of remorse for misconduct, which produces no permanent good. There is no evidence of real religion like that which is afforded by a sedulous devotion to useful actions, and a constant cultivation of amiable affections; and the best and safest place for the display of the actions and affections for my family, in my present situation, is at home.

Do not show this, nor let its contents get out of the family, because it would wound the feelings of some of my friends unnecessarily, and would be misunderstood; but do not go to any of the night meetings.

Give my love to all. Kiss Bolivar.

Yours, in haste,

M. HOLLEY.

LYONS, 1st. Sep., 1827.

MY DEAR CLARISSA. — You will be very welcome home as soon as it may be safe and convenient for you to return.

I have not at present the money to pay your expenses; but if Robert cannot let you have it, write me soon after the receipt of this, and I will raise it for you. It is not proper that you should incur much obligation to your aunt or uncle, and I have for some time felt considerable solicitude lest you should incur more than you ought. Believe me in this, as I speak out of nothing but love to you, and have had larger opportunities of knowing human nature and character than you have. The reverse of circumstances which I have experienced has been the means of testing the sincerity and strength of that sympathy, which many persons professed for me, and perhaps not unfortunately, for we are often much benefitted by knowing the truth of professions. A large proportion, some even of my blood relations, have not borne the test so well as I could have wished. But I cannot consent for a moment to suppose, that my own children are any of them in the smallest degree alienated by my reverse. It would give me inexpressible pain if my dear Clarissa should give me any reason to think her affections could be at all influenced by it. I believe few parents have taken more delight in providing for the happiness of their children than I have. And there is nothing, even in my anticipations of heaven, which gives me more intense enjoyment than the hopes which I cherish of their useful, respectable and happy progress in life. I know not by what company you are surrounded, but I have much, that is, all reasonable confidence in your discretion, and I count too on Robert's judgment in that concern, and fully on his affection towards you. And I have no doubt that your uncle and aunt would prevent you from all harm, which they might think menaced you, from that source. Still I have some fears that at your susceptible age, and possibly with your mortified prospects and diminished hopes, you may suffer yourself to contract ties which may not be most happy. Clarissa, be not mortified, be not at all disposed to abate one jot of hope or of expectation for yourself or your connections by my reverse; for I do think it will not long oppress me or hinder me from doing all that parental affection and propriety may suggest for the education of all my children, and for their advancement in the world. Your mother and I were, a short time ago, at Canandaigua, where we were treated with great and very friendly attentions by Mr. and Mrs. Greig, who, among other instances of regard, offered to send you to school at Troy for a year at their expense, with many expressions of kindness toward you as well as us. Mrs. Pawling, I believe, had written to them on the subject, and they wished to have you home and ready to set out for the school with Miss Lavinia Porter, who is to go there very soon. Your mother and I declined the offer of Mr. and Mrs. Greig, not without the most grateful thanks for the generous sympathy with which it was made, and not without much reluctance, for we very much wish that you should enjoy the advantages of more school teaching. Our reasons for declining are, that it would take some time to prepare you for going there: you are absent from home, where we hope you are happy and useful. Within six months we hope to have my claims upon the state allowed, which will enable me to send you and Elizabeth to a boarding school together; and your age will not be such as to make you six months hence an unfit inmate of a boarding school; and we do not like altogether Mrs. Willard; and if my property is restored, it would be sordid and unbecoming for me to lay under such deep obligations for the education of my children or any one of them to another. I intend, and want you should remember it. if my prosperity is restored. as I think it will be next winter, to send you and Elizabeth abroad to school for one year. perhaps at New Haven.

I have not refrained from writing to you from any diminution of affection, or because you were not every day in my thoughts, but for reasons altogether different. and which. I think, you may easily imagine.

We have heard but few particulars of the most melancholy fate of your uncle Horace, whose death I cannot help deploring as a public calamity, and who was one of the truest and dearest of my earthly friends.

We have heard by letter from Alexander to John that the ship in which he died was the Louisiana. That he and Mary were both sick together, he being in a cabin below. and she being in one above him on deck ; that they could not help each other. and had little or no assistance either from nurse or physician. We are all anxious to hear more. Give my love to Robert.

Most affectionately yours,

MYRON HOLLEY.

These letters reveal a spirit of stern integrity, independence and self-help, along with an absence of cunning, or what is sometimes called shrewdness. which accounts for the suffering which grew out of a deficiency comparatively so trifling, and the long delay in obtaining a partial reparation so obviously just. Had Mr. Holley possessed the cunning of the ordinary politician, he would not

have told the legislature of that deficiency of $30,-
000, and would have kept square with the comptroller by means of his friends — "making friends"
as the scripture says, "of the mammon of un-
righteousness " if necessary.   If he had had the
shrewdness of an ordinary detective, he would
probably have found out who robbed him and have
laid the odium on the shoulders that deserved to
bear it.   But he was too grandly proud to make
the most of his friends, and never stooped to court
friendship either by flattery or promises of favor.
Genial as the sunshine, he spoke evil of none,
whatever he might think.   Almost any conceivable
man in his position, and doing what he did, would
have taken care that the person who wrote under
the pseudonym of "*Peter Ploughshare*" should
be consigned to the eternal infamy due to hypo-
crites.   Mr. Holley undoubtedly knew who he was,
but he let him pass quietly into oblivion, where it
is difficult to find him to-day.   *Stat nominis umbra*
only.   We know that it was no farmer who thus
disgraced the most honorable of tools and occupations.

But justice and dignity finally prevail, and their
success is worth far more than any which ever
crowns the work of political cunning.   Mr. Holley

thus announces to his wife the close of his four years siege at Albany.

ALBANY, 20th March, 1828.

MY DEAR SALLY. — My bill has this day passed the Senate by a large majority, 20 for it and four against it. It wants only the signature of the acting Governor Pitcher to become a law, and he has told a friend of mine this morning that he will sign it as soon as it is presented. The bill provides for restoring to me all the property which I conveyed to the state, and thus affords the authority of the legislature in favor of the great truth, that while I was Canal Commissioner I used no money but what I had a right to use. The bill has passed both houses as a majority bill, not as a two-thirds bill; that is, it is regarded not as a charity or gift, but an act of justice, requiring the legislature to pass it as a duty of moral and legal obligation. I announce this good news to you first, because there is none to whom the annunciation will give more pleasure, and, my dear Sally, I do hope and trust that we and our lovely family of children, who have been somewhat in the shade of adversity, may now be able to enjoy and improve our lives in the healthy sunshine of prosperity.

Most affectionately yours,

MYRON HOLLEY.

I shall start for home in two or three days, if by that time I can get the proper conveyances of my property executed.

This modicum of justice must have rejoiced many hearts outside of Mr. Holley's family circle, and especially his neighbors and acquaintances in

Lyons and Canandaigua. Mr. John Greig, one
of the earliest and most distinguished citizens of
that place, writing to Col. Troup on the 21st of
May, 1828, says: "To Mr. Holley, more than
any one else, are we indebted for that meeting [in
Canandaigua, Jan. 8, 1817], and the popularity
which the canal policy immediately afterwards
acquired in the western part of the state. Indeed,
I have always been satisfied that his intelligence and
zeal and unwearied exertions both of mind and body
on the subject, from the moment of his appointment as Canal Commissioner, essentially con-
tributed to bring the Erie Canal to a successful
completion."

The bill, whose passage caused Mr. Holley, his
family and particular friends so much joy, was
unanimously reported in the Assembly pretty
early in the session of 1828, but action on it was
considerably delayed by the

DEATH OF GOV. CLINTON

on the 11th of February. As Mr. Holley was
on terms of respectful intimacy with that great
man, during the greatest work of his life, and
well knew his character and his aspirations, the
notice he takes of him in his correspondence with

his daughters is of peculiar interest. In his letter to Clarissa, afterwards Mrs. Dr. Beaumont, written the next day, he says, "Perhaps, before this reaches you, you will have heard the news of the death of Gov. Clinton. He died at 7 o'clock last evening, suddenly of, as is supposed, a disorganized condition of the heart. He was sitting in his study with two of his sons, to whom he remarked, putting his hand to his breast, that he felt a stricture there. His eldest son said, 'Perhaps you had better walk a little,' being at the same time preparing a paper to hand to his father, who had not yet got up, when the son perceived that his father's head dropped a little forward, and coming to him found him incapable of speech or motion. A physician was called in in ten minutes, and much pains were taken to restore him, without success. The Governor had been well enough to write letters during the afternoon, though his health has not been good for some time past. This morning at the meeting of the Assembly, the Governor's death was solemnly announced," — and the letter proceeds to detail the action taken to honor his memory. Writing the next day to his younger daughter Elizabeth, afterwards Mrs. Kingman, Mr. Holley says : "His funeral will take place tomorrow at 2 o'clock in the afternoon, and the legislature and citizens are taking measures to have it conducted with all possible honor to the deceased. Mrs. Clinton was abroad at Judge Duer's, when the death of her husband occurred. A messenger came to Judge Duer's with the news and communicated it to the Judge, who immediately informed Mrs. Clinton that the Governor was taken ill, and wished her to come home. She immediately exclaimed that he was dead, and started for home, having fainted before she reached there. When she reached home she became frantic with hysterical affection, and though much pains were taken for her relief, they were ineffectual till last evening, when she fell asleep, and is now probably better. Yesterday she remained all day unconscious of her situation, dressed for company, went to the corpse of her husband, told him to get up and comb his hair, and warm himself, for he was cold. Her condition is one of great distress and excites universal sympathy. During the last season, though it is not known to the public, he had a paralytic shock, which it was very much feared, for an hour, would terminate his life, and then she was affected in some degree.

as she has been by his actual departure. It is certain that not only her private and personal affections have been most violently wrought upon by this sudden separation from her husband, but that the prospects she must have cherished most dearly are blasted by it. The distinguished character and station of her husband ever since their marriage must have kept her almost constantly engaged in the elegant and splendid courtesies of the most distinguished social circles, she herself being for the most part the graceful, dignified and accomplished mistress of those courtesies. And no doubt her ambition was excited and directed to the anticipation of all the pleasures and gratifications of the still larger and more brilliant circles supplied at the capital of the United States, where she might have hoped to see her husband occupying the highest station of honor which can be conferred by earthly agency. It is not therefore surprising that her affliction is overwhelming. Mrs. Clinton is a woman of amiable dispositions and good principles, and will probably recover her senses and her composure, and lead a useful life for years to come. But how different must it be from that which her probable hopes and expectations had depicted for her?"

It is quite true that at the very time when
Myron Holley threw himself into the great labor
of constructing a canal through three hundred
miles of forests and swamps to open the valley of
the Mississippi and the upper lakes to the ocean,
George Stephenson, a younger man by two years
and forty days, made real the idea of an iron horse
on iron rails. And by the time the Erie Canal
was completed, and the pæans were echoing from
Buffalo to New York, he had fairly made the rail-
way system of the world a fixed fact. The canal
is now put out of sight by it, as the moon is by
the sun in the daytime. But how soon would
railroads have pervaded the Mississippi valley, or
how fast would they have spread over Europe, if
the canal had not existed, pouring the food of that
valley into the stomachs of the iron-workers
wherever they worked? The canal was slow but
sure. It created the wealth and inspired the
enterprise* which gave us the railroads. Though

---

* Work had hardly commenced on the New York canal before the State of Ohio began seriously to consider how she
should take advantage of its completion. Lines of canal
connecting the Ohio river with Lake Erie were projected, and
surveys made, long before the completion of the New York
enterprise. Throughout that vast wilderness were then scattered stumpy farms whose surplus produce would not pay for
transportation over the execrable roads of mud and corduroy.

"water" in the latter is not so useful as in the
canal, they have been to the great body of the
people an incalculable blessing. They are giving us a country freer in both muscle and mind,
and better worth loving.

The first requisite for abolishing poverty is the
easy interchange of the products of labor. This
effected, the thing becomes in some degree possible. For it opens a possibility of universal education. This tends to enlarge a middle class of
people, leaving the excessively rich and the excessively poor in a minority of no great account.

The people turned out voluntarily to assist the surveying
parties. The writer well remembers how proud he felt, when
an ambitious stripling, to "carry chain" a little while for
Mr. Geddes along the banks of the Cuyahoga. It was previous to 1822.

CHAPTER XVII.

HORTICULTURE.

It has already been mentioned that Myron Holley had a beautiful garden in Canandaigua. He was naturally a gardener, which means that he was a lover and improver of nature. At Lyons he reserved for his own home two acres which became a wonderful garden under the slight opportunities which his constant and weighty cares on the canal allowed him. No sooner was he released from his embarrassments by the tardy justice of the legislature, than he returned to this garden home with delight. But he was not content with cultivating his garden and enjoying its flowers and fruits himself. His delight was to induce others to enjoy the same pleasures. If he made any improvement in flowers or fruit, and he made many, he wished all others to have the benefit of it. A letter to one of his friends soon after his return from Albany in the spring of 1828 illustrates this trait in his character.

DEAR SIR, — This day I have taken up six, from among the best of my little quince trees. and addressed them to you, to the care of Joy, Bruce & Co., agents for the Pilot Line of canal boats, at Albany. And I hope they will come to your hands in good condition. If they shall live and flourish in your grounds, as similar trees have in mine, they will bear the year after next. from twelve to twenty quinces each, and in five years, from one hundred and fifty to two hundred and fifty each. The fruit of them will be yellow, tender and fragrant.

In commencing the cultivation of my garden and other grounds this spring, I feel that the establishment of my just claims to the absolute title of them, by the legislature, has given a new impulse to my taste for rural pursuits. And there is no employment, not immediately connected with the successful introduction of my children into life, and the welfare of my family, from which I anticipate, for my declining years, so many useful and interesting results. For a long time some of the most valuable sources of human enjoyment, as it respects myself, have been too much dependent upon the caprice, prejudice and passion of others. This dependence is now happily removed. And for my remaining days, I intend to adopt a course of exertion in my opinion equally characterized by philosophy and benevolence ; in short, sir, I am ambitious of emulating your example, by retiring from the bustle and storm of life to the occupation of the garden and the field, with nothing like the feelings or motives of an ascetic — but in perfect charity with all mankind. and because such occupations afford the best means of improving the mind and heart of intelligent men who are truly devoted to them, and at the same time secure the most desirable advantages of peace, useful employment and true dignity.

With grateful respects for Mrs. Buel, I am, with much esteem, sir,

Your very obt.

MYRON HOLLEY.

JESSE BUEL.

As we shall see, by and by, there were human interests ready to appeal to his heart, which could not allow him to end his days in a garden. The last thirteen years of his life were to leave him hardly more leisure for that delightful occupation than the previous ones. That others might have better gardens, he had to neglect his own. Still it is to be recorded that Central and Western New York, so conspicuous for useful and elegant gardening, owe as much to Myron Holley as, perhaps, to any other man. He was a very grand pioneer. In all horticultural literature, the useful and the sweet are, perhaps, nowhere better mingled than in his "INITIATORY DISCOURSE, delivered at Geneva, 27th November, 1828, before an assembly from which, on that day, was formed the DOMESTIC HORTICULTURAL SOCIETY of the western parts of the State of New York."

After describing, as no one could better than he, the hardships and perils endured by the earliest settlers in the great valley which his own labors had done so much to open to the world, he swept over the history of gardens from the mythic Eden downwards, culling gems from the poets as he went, and making his path blooming and fragrant. After quoting Homer's grand compliment to the garden of King Alcinous in the 7th book of the Odyssey, he grandly wipes prejudice away from the memory of the much-abused Nebuchadnezzar as follows :—

"But the hanging gardens of Babylon, if they were not more fruitful than that of Alcinous, were vastly more expensive and more picturesque. And what makes them more interesting is the spirit of courtesy in which they were constructed. Nebuchadnezzar made them to gratify the taste of his wife, who being by birth a Mede, and accustomed to the view of mountainous regions. did not perfectly enjoy the rural prospects of the level country around her husband's capital. These gardens were four hundred feet square, and consisted of terraces raised one upon another to the height of three hundred and fifty feet. These terraces were ascended by steps ten feet wide, and supported by massy arches upon arches of solid masonry, the whole being surrounded and strengthened by a wall twenty-two feet thick. The floor of each terrace was made impervious to water, and covered with a sufficient depth of soil to support the largest trees, and the innumerable shrubs and plants with which it was embellished. And upon the upper terrace was a reservoir, which was filled with water from the river by an ingenious engine, of such dimensions as to supply the moisture required by all the terraces."

We judge from this that Nebuchadnezzar was a great improvement upon Cheops. He did more to gratify the living and quite as much to immortalize himself with posterity. Mr. Holley notices the gardens and groves of Greece, where the immortal Epicurus and Plato taught what some of the sagest of our modern sages are happy to revive, and of Rome he says : —

" The Romans were peculiarly fond of gardens. In their cities the common people used to have representations of them in their windows. And several of their noble families derived their names from their cultivation of certain kinds of garden vegetables; as the Fabii, Lentuli and Lactucini. So attached to gardens were the lowest populace of Rome, that in the inimitably artful speech of Antony over the body of Cæsar, as presented to us by Shakespeare, the last degree of indignation is excited in their minds against his murderers, by the generous disposition which they were told Cæsar had made of his gardens in his will. Antony assures them, ' Moreover he hath left you all his walks, his private arbors, and new-planted orchards on this side Tiber ; — he hath left them to you, and to your

heirs forever, common pleasures to walk abroad and
recreate yourselves.' Upon this they could no longer
be restrained, but resolved, at once, to burn the traitors'
houses."

The reader will certainly forgive me for closing
this chapter with a long extract from a discourse
well deserving to be incorporated in full in the
permanent literature of our country. There can
be no doubt it produced many gardens, in an
intellectual as well as physical sense. It ought
more and more to guide the cultured youth of our
country to an occupation grander and happier
than the pursuit of political power or inordinate
wealth.

The civilized nations of the earth are now vieing
with each other in Horticultural establishments. And
since the discoveries of Linnæus, a new and most valuable object has been extensively connected with many
of them, which has given them additional claims to
intelligent favor. I allude to the promotion of Botanic
science. Europe has numerous public and private gardens, in which the splendors of Horticulture are most
happily combined with this enchanting pursuit.

In our country there have been several attempts, by
individuals and by associations, to effect the same
agreeable combination. These attempts are exceedingly laudable, and, if duly encouraged, will insure extensive and lasting benefits. They are like to be
essentially aided by the United States government;

for, during the last year, we were told by one of its
public functionaries that the President had much at
heart the introduction into our country, from abroad, of
plants of every description not already known among
us, whether used as food or for purposes connected with
the arts, through the agency of our ministers, consuls,
and other public agents in foreign countries.

Ornamental gardening, in its broadest range, has
at one time or another been made to include almost
every class of objects, both in nature and art, from the
association of which pleasure could naturally be derived.
Milton describes the garden of Eden as containing ' in
narrow room nature's whole wealth, yea, more, a heaven
on earth.'

But the more restricted and essential idea of a garden, is that of a place where, by the aid of cultivation,
vegetable productions may be reared more excellent in
kind, and more pleasing in distribution, than the ordinary growth of nature. Beauty and use are both included, though they may both exist in almost infinite
diversity of relative proportions, according to the diver-
sities of taste, and skill, and means in cultivators.

The direct objects of gardening, in the most restricted
definition, besides earth and water, are trees and shrubs,
and fruits, and flowers, and esculent vegetables, with
the best modes of propagating, nourishing, arranging,
improving, and preserving them. To these objects the
manuring, mixing, and working of soils, the construction of fences, walks, terraces, quarters, borders, trel-
lises, arbors, and implements, are everywhere subsidiary :
while in climates subject to frosts, the wall, the hot-
bed, and the green-house, are valuable and agreeable
auxiliaries.

The successful conduct of the business of a garden requires labor, vigilance, and knowledge. Ever since the sentence of the Most High subjected man to earn his bread in the sweat of his face, labor has been the appointed means of his advancement and happiness. Without it, it is impossible for us to have healthy bodies or cheerful minds; and the worth of all the valuable possessions which we acquire is measured by the amount of it which they respectively involve. It is not wonderful, therefore, that much of it is essential to the most desirable Horticulture, though it is not merely gross corporal labor that is required.

> ' Strength may wield the ponderous spade,
> May turn the clod, and wheel the compost home;
> But elegance, chief grace the garden shows,
> And most attractive, is the fair result
> Of thought, the creature of a polished mind."

And labor is not more indispensable than vigilance—keen-sighted, unremitted vigilance. Many of the nurse-lings of the garden are so tender and so exposed to accidents for months together, that an hour's neglect may lead to cureless ruin, and disappoint hopes long and fondly cherished.

But without knowledge, labor and vigilance are vain. The accomplished gardener must know the best manner and time of performing a great multiplicity of manual operations peculiar to each season of the year, all of which are essential to his success, and the knowledge of which cannot be obtained without experience and observation. Every direct, and every subsidiary object of his pursuit, demands care, and reflection, and knowledge. He must not only know the modes and times of

propagating trees, and shrubs, and flowers, of which
there are several already understood. as applicable to
many of them ; the proper use of the pruning-knife, so
essential to some of his highest purposes ; the various
means of improving the flavor and size of fruits which
will be acknowledged to have been the most successfully introduced, when it is remembered that the largest
and most delicious apples upon our tables have been derived from the austere English crab ; the measures most
effective towards meliorating the less esteemed culinary
vegetables, which he will not consider unimportant
when he learns that some of them. now the most savory
and nutritious, were in their uncultivated state of but
little claim to notice, such as the asparagus, the celery,
the cauliflower, the potatoe ; the charming art of man-
aging flowers, by which the single and almost scentless
blossoms of nature have been swelled into much greater
compass and new varieties of beauty, and filled with intenser fragrance ; but the accomplished gardener should
understand the best method of acclimating plants not
indigenous, which may contribute prodigiously to em-
bellishment and use, and which involves the knowledge
of botanical geography. And he should have all that
science which may be conducive to the utmost possible
perfection of every subject of his care. To this end,
chemistry, natural history, and botany, are necessary.

The productions of the garden are affected either for
evil or for good, in different stages of their growth, by the
most minute and the most magnificent objects in nature,
by the bugs. by the worms, by the flies, by the birds,
by the clouds, by the air, by the sun. The knowledge of
these objects, with all their means of favor or annoy-
ance, and the superadded knowledge of all the other ob-

jects and means by which the effects of these. so far as they are good, may be promoted. and so far as they are evil, may be prevented. should be embraced within the scope of his acquirements. The science of Horticulture, therefore, does not merely admit, it demands. excites, and favors the most extensive and diversified intellectual attainments.

But it has pleasures to bestow which amply repay all its demands both upon the mind and body.

It gratifies all the senses.

The feeling is gratified by its smooth walks. its soft banks, the touch of many of its leaves. and fruits. and flowers, and by the refreshing coolness of its shades.

The smell is agreeably excited from unnumbered sources. — from the lowliest pot-herb to the stateliest tree ; from the humble violet and mignonnette to the splendid tulip and queenly rose, — a garden is the unrivalled repository of fragrance.

The gratification of the ear in a garden is adventitious. not of man's procurement. but nevertheless certain and real. The most tasteful of its animal creation, in their flight from one end of the earth to the other. discover no spot so alluring to them as a well-replenished garden. The birds are fond of its shade, its flowers, and its fruits. Amidst these they love to build their nests, rear their young, and first win them to that element which seems created to be their peculiar field of joy. And if they sometimes commit unwelcome inroads upon the delicacies which we prize, they more than compensate us by their cheerful and continual songs, and by destroying innumerable insects and more dangerous intruders in the air, in the trees, upon the plants, and on the ground.

The taste finds its choicest regalement in the garden, in its sweet roots, its crisp and tender salads, its nutritious and acceptable pulse, its pungent and salutary condiments, its fragrant and delicious fruits, with a countless list of other palatable productions, all existing in such inexhaustible variety that the art of cookery takes more than half its subjects from that overflowing storehouse.

But the eye delights in a garden, as if all its labors, its cares, and its knowledge had been dedicated to that single sense. From every quarter, and border, and arbor; from every bank, and walk, and plant, and shrub, and tree, and every combination of groups, spring forms of beauty, natural though cultivated, innocent though gay.

Horticulture gratifies the higher faculties of our nature, the intellectual taste, the reason and the heart.

CHAPTER XVIII.

ANTI-MASONRY.

Had Mr. Holley, when he retired from public service, consulted his own personal tastes, the home, the garden, and the education of his chil_dren would have absorbed the rest of his life. But two great social questions were at the door. No man more than he was qualified to answer. One of these questions concerned the social value of the institution of Free Masonry. It is recorded of this institution in the State of New York, in the History of Ontario County, page 63 : " The order in 1826 numbered in the state 360 lodges and 22,000 members. Ten years later, and the lodges were 75 and the members 4,000." A similar shrinkage, though perhaps in a lower ratio, occurred in other states, within the same period. No subject, except that of slavery, has ever produced intenser excitement in this country than broke out in regard to Free Masonry in Central New York in 1826, and prevailed for ten years. Mr. Holley, though

never himself a mason, had family connections
and political friends who were. If any good grew
out of that excitement,—and probably the opinion
that much did is now as strong inside of masonic
lodges as outside,—to no one man is it due more
than to Mr. Holley. The lesson to mankind,
which reformed, if it did not extinguish, the order,
was, in its most impressive shape, his. It was
delivered with disinterestedness, dignity, and
masterly force. Justice cannot be done to his
character and acts in this behalf without some
detail of the facts. Though he was not a mason
himself, the husband of one of his daughters was.
The order everywhere embraced men of the highest respectability, with whom he had been intimate
in public life. Therefore, when it was said in 1826
that a large number of masons had together committed a crime, the highest known to the law, and the
order justified it, he was not one of the first to
believe it. It was not till he clearly saw, to his
astonishment, that the courts of justice were obstructed and overawed, that he applied his mind
to the study of the facts and the character of the
institution. And the moment he had reached a
firm conclusion, he did not confer with flesh and
blood. Masonry became, in his mind, a thing

which had no right to exist, and he gave his reasons on every fitting occasion, at any sacrifice of his personal comfort.

Of course this was very natural. For a man to whom the family was the focus of human happiness, and justice the vital principle of human society, any institution which segregated a body of men from the rest of the world, including the wives and daughters of their own families, under oaths of secresy, backed by horrible penalties, could have no attractions. He never had any time or taste for anything of that sort. But when it became plain that such an institution could be used and had been used, not only against the family, but against free government, he became its uncompromising enemy.

In the ten years' excitement about Free Masonry its history was thoroughly scanned. Some of the ablest scholars were engaged in the search. All the records of the past were ransacked, from the remotest times down, by those who were interested to confirm its pretensions to a venerable antiquity, as well as by those who were willing to overthrow them. Not the faintest ray of any historical document or monument could be found to sustain these pretensions back of 1717. In that

year, at the Apple Tree Inn, in London, some ingenious romancers set up the institution, with its
odd rituals, secret grips, monstrous oaths, professions of philanthropy, sanctity, and hoary
antiquity. And as the glory of Solomon and his
marvellous temple was then unquestioned, everybody was ready enough to believe anything which
apparently added to it. The pretended masonic
history seemed to confirm the sacred. The sacred
history certainly does not confirm the masonic, but
in these days has too much need of confirmation
itself. The most thorough and painstaking excavations have revealed nothing of a temple existing
before that which Titus destroyed. And if it did,
and revealed the dimensions described in the
sacred writings of the Jews, it is difficult now to
believe that 22,000 oxen and 120,000 sheep were
sacrificed in it in the fourteen days of the dedica-
tion. The building was not large enough, even
if furnished with modern machinery. Solomon
seems to have had enough to do in providing en-
tertainment for a fabulous amount of female
society, without founding lodges exclusively of
males, in which to go through those not very
amusing ceremonies described by William Morgan.

Incredible as now it may seem, Free Masonry

spread rapidly in Europe. It had certain social advantages, mutual aid, a resource against peril among strangers. The lodge was a convenient *nidus*, in which to hatch plans of resistance to ecclesiastical or political persecution. In America, it enjoyed considerable popularity before the revolution, as a benevolent and patriotic institution, and it did not conflict with ecclesiastical domination, because it professed profound respect for the Bible as a divine revelation. A number of the leaders of the revolution, as Washington and Lafayette, were, or rather had been, brothers of the "mystic tie." But plainly enough, the institution could not have had any weight to throw in favor of the separation of these colonies from the mother country, if it did not weigh against it. It was only too weak, if it had wished, to prevent a separation, when justice required it. During the revolution it flourished considerably in the American army, and had movable lodges. Gen. Henry Sewall, during the anti-masonic excitement, said he was induced to join that he might fare better in case he should be made a prisoner. Its chief use seems to have been to relieve the tedium of long intervals of inaction.

At a later period, after the war of 1812, Free

Masonry began to grow rapidly, and developed political significance, especially to those who were watchful observers, in regard to minor offices. Doubtless it was this feature which led to its trouble. The secresy of the order was the more precious, and the more jealously to be guarded, the more it had political aims. That it had such aims not only turned out to be the fact, but it was indiscreet enough in the person of one of its orators, W. F. Brainard, Esq., of New London, Ct., to boast of it. An oration which he delivered, June 24, 1825, in that place, has this remarkable passage, which does not seem to have attracted any notice or comment till after the abduction and murder of Morgan in the year following.

" *What is Masonry now? It is powerful. It comprises men of rank, wealth, office and talent, in power and out of power; and that in almost every place where power is of any importance; and it comprises among other classes of the community, to the lowest, in large numbers, active men, united together, and capable of being directed by others, so as to have the force of concert throughout the civilized world! They are distributed, too, with the means of knowing one another, and the means of keeping secret, and the means of co-operating, in the desk; in the legislative hall; on the bench; in every gathering of business; in every party of pleasure; in every enterprise of government; in every domestic circle; in peace and in war; among enemies and friends; in one place as well as in another! So powerful, indeed, is it at this time, that it fears nothing from violence, either public or private; for it has every means to learn it in season, to counteract, defeat and punish it."*

When it became known the next year that a band of Masons had assumed powers belonging only to ministers of the law, had bound a man, confined him in a government fortress and put him out of sight, then it was discovered that Orator Brainard was only describing an accomplished fact. All the courts of Western New York were completely in the hands of the masonic fraternity, and bound by extra-judicial oaths *not* to do justice.

It is of no consequence to the present narrative

what the motives of William Morgan were in publishing the secrets for which he was put to death. Whether he was patriotic or not, his act resulted in a most fortunate deliverance for his country. Free Masonry deserved its punishment, if a republic deserves to exist. About all of Free Masonry that exists now is the name, which is not objectionable. There must be clubs, cliques and coteries, for people who do not fit elsewhere, or for whom the actual world is unfit. But they must not govern the whole.

Secresy is good in the right place and for honorable purposes. But it becomes a crime when it shields crime from justice. For publishing secrets, some of which were criminal, Morgan was secretly murdered — secretly in regard to the outside world, but not to the masonic world. To the free-masons, for at least fifty miles on every side, Morgan's destruction was deliberately predetermined, none dissenting, if all did not consent. There was no form of trial. It was a foregone conclusion that he must die. The only deliberation or hesitation was as to the best method of effecting the murder so as to conceal it from the public, and here in the multitude of counsellors the free-masons supposed there was safety. In the darkness of night, as is now known beyond doubt, they dropped him into Lake Ontario with a weight attached, and reported he had fled to Canada. The executioners fled, and were supported by the money of the order beyond the reach of the ministers of public justice, if the latter should ever come to suspect who they were. But it was all in vain. In fact, the concealment was overdone.

In spite of the combined efforts of hundreds of free-masons to suppress the revelation, even by setting fire to the office where the printing was going on, and abducting and murdering its author, the little pamphlet got into existence and silently spoke to the living after the lips of its author were sealed in death at the bottom of Lake Ontario. It professed to give the silly rites and execrable oaths of the first three degrees, which was the whole of the writer's masonic experience. Masons, high and low, were either ominously silent, or sneered at the thing as a sham, unworthy of the slightest attention. But wise men like Myron Holley, who had never been inside a lodge, began to ponder. One thing was certain, Morgan was not to be found. That fact became every day more important. Mr. Holley had a distinguished

son-in-law who was a free-mason.   The father-in-
law was proud of him.   His best friend in his
great canal enterprise, De Witt Clinton, had been
a free-mason.   Free-masons were all around him
in the highest ranks of life.   He was not the man
to accuse them of participation in such a crime,
but he could ask them,— why, if Morgan is anywhere in this world alive, your order being
co-extensive with the world, don't you produce
him, and quiet this terrible excitement?   If this
revelation of his is of no consequence, why should
you not show that you so regard it by bringing
him back to his family?   At any rate, if he has
not been murdered, why do you not bestir yourselves to let the public know what has really
become of him?   But they did not.

The excitement grew more and more intense.
It blazed up in every family in Western New
York.   It burned into the adjoining states.   In
spite of the united efforts of masons everywhere to
smother it under wet blankets, it continued to
spread.   Presently masons of the most respectable
character began to confess the truth of Morgan's
disclosures and abandon the order.   This was the
inevitable result of the outside investigations
which in not many months ascertained beyond a

reasonable doubt the names of more than a score
of persons actively concerned in the abduction and
incarceration of Morgan. Many of these were
persons who had been highly respected. They
were all, without a single exception, masons.

On the 9th of February, 1828, an encampment
of Knights Templars at Leroy, N. Y., after a
protracted struggle between members who approved and disapproved the Morgan outrage,
resolved by a majority to disclose all the secrets
and diabolical oaths known to them, and this
included twelve degrees of masonry beyond those
revealed by Morgan. In the July following,
these were published, with eighteen more added,
making thirty-three in all. In 1829 a very able
committee, including the names of Samuel Weeks,
Harvey Ely and Thurlow Weed, reported to a
State Convention assembled at Albany, "More
than four hundred initiates, within our own State,
including members of every degree, from the
Entered Apprentice to the Thrice Illustrious
Knights of the Holy Trinity, have publicly
renounced the institution. Thousands have silently withdrawn." It was thus demonstrated beyond
any possibility of contradiction or doubt, that the
fraternity were bound by oaths from the top to

the bottom, not only to do in any similar case what had been done to Morgan, but to screen from punishment any crime committed by a mason, not excepting, in some of the degrees, Murder and Treason. It was found that bribery and counterfeiting had been thus screened to an enormous extent. At every step upward into the high-sounding degrees the oaths grew more and more horrible, which accounted for the fact that so many of the best of men had stopped before ascending very high.

The address of this convention to the people of the State of New York was the work of Myron Holley. The following paragraphs will show its force and spirit:

Fellow Citizens, — A great crisis has occurred in our social condition. The peace of this community has been extensively disturbed, the domestic security of its citizens openly violated, their property unlawfully invaded, and the life of one of them, without doubt, feloniously destroyed. And these calamitous events have proceeded from a source which threatens our most valuable institutions, and all those possessions which make life desirable.

We will not disguise the painful conviction of our minds, and we cannot suppress it. that we are commencing a course of action, which will necessarily bring with it much disquietude and distress. The intercourse of business will be obstructed, the laudable associations of neighborhoods will be convulsed, and many of the best sympathies of our nature will be violently turned away from their customary channels. Such a course of action should not be commenced for slight or transient causes. Nothing which does not affect the essence of our freedom, and which does not manifest itself in the most decisive and solemn forms, can justify it. But when the public peace, our domestic safety, our property, our life, our reputation, our equal rights as citizens, are all assailed, by the concerted action of numerous, wealthy, intelligent and powerful bodies of men ; and the regular operation of our constituted authorities is found unable to protect us, then, it is equally becoming to our minds and hearts, to our self-respect and the most cherished interests of human liberty, that we should protect ourselves, whatever evils may ensue.

The address then goes on to state succinctly the circumstances of the abduction and the way the free-masons concealed and protected the perpetrators, — closing as follows, after recommending political action :

" To this resort we are summoned by every fear and every hope which can affect the souls of free men. Our country appeals to us to make this effort in a cause as sacred and high as any that ever was promoted by human means ; and by all the sorrows and joys, by all the proudest blessings, vaunted recollections, and exulting anticipations, of our social condition. And let us not fear the charge of too much ' excitement.' In

such a cause, excitement brings blame only to those
with whom it is weak or wavering. What individual
has ever satisfied himself in a good cause, without excitement? What nation has ever wrested its liberties
from the grasp of tyranny without excitement?
Whence originate the purest virtues, and the most ex-
alted achievements, of created intelligences but from
powerful excitement? The strongest love of justice,
the quickest indignation at wrong, and the most impas-
sioned admiration of beneficence are the appropriate
signatures of a superior nature; but these are only
other names for high excitement. And such excitement the cause we are engaged in both requires and
sanctifies."

The Anti-Masonic movement culminated in a
National Convention, held in Philadelphia, on
the 11th of September, 1830, on the recommendation of this State Convention, held in Albany. Eleven States were represented by 112
self-elected delegates, eleven of whom were
seceding masons, some of high degree. Among
these delegates were such men as Pliny Merrick
and Amasa Walker, of Massachusetts; Nathaniel
Terry, Zalmon Storrs and John M. Holley, of
Connecticut; Henry Dana Ward, Francis
Granger, William H. Seward and Myron Holley,
of New York; Thaddeus Stevens, Joseph Ritner,
and Harmar Denny, of Pennsylvania; William

Slade, of Vermont; Frederick Wadsworth, of Ohio; and Ellison Conger, of N. J. That convention put forth an "ADDRESS TO THE PEOPLE OF THE UNITED STATES," from the pen of Myron Holley, and signed by the 112 delegates. It was like the appearance of a disciplined and invulnerable police force in the face of an unarmed mob. It won a victory without striking a blow. Masonry saw by that address, that Anti-Masonry had made up its mind to carry the war into politics, and that its only chance of saving even its name was by backing out of politics. And it did back out. Never since that has any political party dared to build a hope on the masonic character of a candidate. Lodges simply courted oblivion. Any unprejudiced person has only to peruse that overwhelming address to see that its grand idea triumphed in its utterance, though for some years an anti-masonic organization was kept up to show that anti-masons were in earnest.

In 1828, though the anti-masons had no prospect of a majority in the state for the choice of Governor, as neither party would put up a candidate opposed to masonry, they voted to a considerable extent for a candidate of their own. The vote stood for Governor:

Democratic, .   Martin Van Buren,   136,794
Whig, .   .   .   Smith Thompson,   106,444
Anti-Masonic,   Solomon Southwick,   33,345

In 1830, both the leading parties professedly
ignored masonry as an issue, but the Whig party
had the wisdom to select for its candidate a declared anti-mason, while his democratic rival was
supposed to be neutral.   This in effect made the
Whig and Anti-Masonic parties identical, though
nominally the anti-masons had a candidate in the
field.   The vote stood :

Democratic, .   .   Enos T. Throop, 128,842
Whig & Anti-M.,   Francis Granger, 120,861
Anti-Masonic.   .   Ezekiel Williams, 2,332

The reduction of the aggregate vote nearly ten
per cent. from the previous election must be accounted for by the large number of democrats
who had renounced masonry, but were not ready
to join their old opponents, the whigs, or condemn
their past by joining the anti-masons.   Doubtless
more than 20,000 voters felt the stunning blow of
the Philadelphia Convention and were not in a
mental condition to vote at all.   By 1832 the
local excitement had somewhat subsided and
national politics resumed sway.   William L.

Marcy as democratic candidate for Governor received 166,410 votes, and Francis Granger, absorbing all the anti-masonic votes, received 156,- 572. In 1834, the year of the anti-abolition mobs of New York, a new question began to loom up, which so far as it then affected politics at all, tended to strengthen the democratic — or rather undemocratic — party. That year William L. Marcy had 181,905 votes for Governor, and William H. Seward, a Whig, and also decided anti-mason, had 168,969. In 1836, the Whigs committed the mistake of dropping Seward and taking up Jesse Buel, an inoffensive sort of man who did not satisfy the strong anti-masons, so that Gov. Marcy walked over the course. The vote for 1836 stood:

Democratic, . Wm. L. Marcy, . 166,122
Whig, . . Jesse Buel, . . 136,648
Anti-Masonic, Isaac S. Smith, . 3,496

In 1838 the Whig politicians of New York were astute enough to see that Seward's opposition to masonic government and leaning towards abolitionism, were not obstacles in the way of his being Governor of New York, and he was elected by a vote of 192,828, against 182,461 for Marcy. This was substantially the final victory of the anti-masonic principle. After that another question took the field. The growth of the popular movement against secret political organizations and extra-judicial oaths, is pretty well indicated by the following growth of gubernatorial votes : —

1828,	.	.	.	.	33,345
1830,	.	.	.	.	123,193
1832,	.	.	.	.	156,572
1834,	.	.	.	.	168,969
1836,	.	.	.	.	140,144
1838,	.	.	.	.	192,882

Throughout the whole of this anti-masonic war, while alive to all the interests of peace and social progress, Mr. Holley was in the thickest of the fight. It has been already said that he was the author of its most effective manifesto. It has been well said, in praise of Daniel Webster, that he won his cases by the clearness of his statement. Mr. Holley's statements of fact were in the highest degree clear, Websterian, and judicial ; and when he had convinced the understanding he warmed the heart. While he denounced the institution, he was tender towards its victims. Of its members he said : " A large proportion cherish no part of the spirit of the institution. Invited to join, by its lofty pretensions, in early life they entered its threshold. And though disgusted at every step, for the purpose of understanding an institution which they had once consented to enter, they suffered themselves to be raised to the second or third degree. Nothing could induce them to go further. Such were most of the masons whose illustrious names have been so often abusively and boastfully arrayed to shield the institution from the consuming reprobation now everywhere provoked against it, in unprejudiced minds, by its full and accurate exposure. These men in the bottom of their souls have all renounced it."

Most striking confirmations of the truth of this were brought out during the anti-masonic excitement, including such men as Chief-Justice Marshall.* The national address of 1830, in a

* The following is an extract of the touching letter of Chief Justice Marshall to Edward Everett, dated Richmond, July 22, 1833. He had not attended a lodge for thirty or forty years :—

"I thought it, however, a harmless play-thing, which would live its hour and pass away, until the murder or abstraction of Morgan was brought before the public, — that atrocious crime, and I had almost said, the still more atrocious suppression of the testimony concerning it, demonstrated the abuse, of which the oaths prescribed by the order were susceptible, and convinced me that the institution ought to be abandoned as one capable of producing much evil, and incapable of producing any good, which might not be effected by safe and open means."

masterly way, goes over all the means by which the republic might expect to relieve itself of this tyrannous "Old Man of the Sea," which had fastened himself upon its shoulders, and comes to the conclusion that they reside in the elective power reserved to the people themselves. "In the first address of Mr. Jefferson, as President of the United States," says Mr. Holley, he denominates 'the right of election by the people a mild and safe correction of abuses, which are lopped by the sword of revolution where peaceable remedies are unprovided.' This is the only adequate corrective of freemasonry, — that prolific source of the worst abuses. And to this we must resort."

His final appeal to the hearts of the people of the United States is as follows : —

" FELLOW-CITIZENS, — Are we called to be anti-masons by the best feelings of our natures? Are our objects the highest that can affect the civil character? Are our means the most approved and indispensable? Unite with us, — not for our sakes, but your own. Aid us in working out the redemption of our country from free-masonry. We are misrepresented and calumniated, as the chief public means of defeating the cause we have espoused. Examine by whom and inquire into their motives. Be not deceived. If individuals among us are in fault through ignorance, or passion, or interest, or profligacy, refuse them your confidence. But do not, therefore, betray your rights, and those of your country; nor let those beguile you into their support who prefer secrecy to publicity, and free-masonry to republicanism. We are for practical, peaceable, and most necessary reform, — not for destruction, but for the establishment of right. Freedom, in every beneficial sense, is the soul of anti-masonry.

Further revelations of the ceremonies and principles of free-masonry are not required, for these are perfectly exposed; and the exposition is so confirmed as to be incapable of material modification. It will go down to posterity among the undoubted records of imposture and guilt. But we cannot suppress our anxiety to commend our cause to the decided confidence and active support of all nominal members of the fraternity. Among such there are many who have long possessed, and who still possess, our high esteem, and to whom we are attached by bonds of the most inseparable and holy brotherhood, those of a common nature, common wants, and a common destiny. We earnestly invite them to come out, with us, in defence of our common interests. Our course has been adopted after diligent inquiry into facts, and an honest comparison of free-masonry with the first principles of civil order; and we have no misgivings. We respectfully suggest to them similar comparison and inquiry. In proportion as men do this we find our numbers increasing; and knowing the inquisitive character of the people of the United States, it is scarcely more in our power than it is in our wish to exclude the anticipation of success. We know free-masonry cannot meet with their deliberate approval. When it was least suspected of evil, and highest in its harlequin attractions; when that holiness to the Lord,

which is inscribed upon its gaudy garniture, and that
charity with which its dark chambers are labelled, had
not been publicly detected as wholly counterfeit, — we
know it was not a subject of their complacent regard.
Shall the crimes with which now it is ineffaceably
blasted, and the pertinacity with which it justifies them
pass without their condemnation and rebuke? Shall
that abuse of their confidence, which first brought their
names in connection with the mountebank retainers of
the order, be an argument for sustaining the mounte-
banks, when their party colored garments are seen
dripping with the blood of the innocent, and we perceive their power to strike away all the pledges of our
common safety?

We know that the private opinions of such members
will concur with ours. We beseech them to concur
with us in giving to those opinions a public and decided
expression; for that will make them effectual to the
only end we have at heart, the overthrow of free-masonry. We want not, and we expect not, the aid of
the sinister, or dissolute, the slaves of office, of prejudice, of vice, or of faction; but we anxiously covet the
association of all who are willing, on all occasions, and
at all times, through evil report and through good report, to contend for the great interests of truth, and justice, and freedom, and that security intended to be
conferred upon these interests by our laws and constitutions. With such we are proud to labor, and, if need
be, willing to suffer, for we shall not labor and suffer in
vain. But we perceive on all sides the presages of our
success in the unspeakable importance of our cause; in
the intelligence and self-respect of our fellow-citizens;
in the peaceable and just means with which alone we

mean to promote it ; in the favoring sympathies of the enlightened and wise of every name and clime ; and in the undergoing, insuppressive, and inspiring hope with which we may seek for it the protection of that Great Being in whose hands are all the allotments of nations, and whose law is that of perfect liberty."

Myron Holley had been induced to take this decided and uncompromising position of making anti-masonry a permanent political issue by two things, his love of the family and his love of free government. The latter object of love was for the sake of the former. Yet a man whose strongest affection is for his family, has sometimes to sacrifice his own domestic interests, for the interests of that government which is the best protector of all domestic interests. The scant and tardy justice accorded to Mr. Holley's claim after long and expensive attendance on the legislature did not leave him the means of supporting a large family and at the same time doing what the anti-masonic exigency required the ablest man to do. His little property was all in real estate, in Lyons and Rochester. As early as 1829 he was straitened for money. His oldest daughter, Caroline, was married to Graham H. Chapin, a lawyer originally from Salisbury, Ct., and settled near him in Lyons. His next daughter, Clarissa, for whom his pet name was Tatty, had just been married to Dr. A. L. Beaumont, and was settled in Pennsylvania. Neither of these gentlemen seem to have favored the anti-masonic side of the great and bitter controversy. Dr. Beaumont, who was in easy circumstances, offered in 1829 to loan his father-in-law $1,000, which he seems to have much needed. It is highly characteristic of Mr. Holley that while thanking his son-in-law for this offer, he says, "I answer your letter with a pleasure, which I should express with greater energy and more in detail, were it not that in consequence of your intention to oblige me with the loan of $1,000, such expression would wear a little too much the appearance of being purchased by the loan. Money is good, for the important uses to which it may be applied, in all the debt and credit business of life; and honesty requires that money obligations should always be justly remembered and faithfully discharged." He then proceeds to detail to his son-in-law things not to be purchased, proposes to secure the loan by a mortgage on his Rochester land, and says, "On the subject of those political distinctions, which have been alluded to in our correspondence, though my convictions are perfectly decided, and my conduct will correspond with them, yet they contemplate nothing of persecution. They appear to me to rest upon the imperious necessity of defending great fundamental principles upon the preservation of which the prosperity of all depends. And I earnestly hope and confidently believe, that all political array, in their behalf, will soon be rendered unnecessary, by their universal adoption and practical acknowledgment. I pray for this daily, for I have no political ambition, and have objects other than political, to which I should be glad to devote myself exclusively." By that time the masonic fraternity were raising throughout the country the cry of "persecution," and "political ambition" against all, whether seceding masons or outsiders, who were striving to rescue the country from their almost established domination. And they found powerful support in this, outside the lodges. Their tactics failed, as they well deserved to. It is probably true that Mr. Holley's sons-in-law lived to be proud of the course from which they would have dissuaded him. His daughters now alive must surely be proud of it.

After this letter of Dr. Beaumont came the great address to the people of the United States, already quoted from.

One effect of this address and the published
proceedings of the exceedingly able Philadelphia
Convention was to produce a sort of alliance, or
co-operation, of the masonic and ecclesiastical
influences in central New York. Religious re-
vivals, among the various sects, had been common in that region from the first settlement.
Protracted meetings to promote them had become
an established fashion among the Baptists, Con-
gregationalists and Presbyterians, as well as the
Methodists. The churches and the lodges, much
as they seemed to differ, had one thing in common — the male element grasped all the power.
The lodge would not trust a woman with a secret,
the church would not allow her to open her lips
as a religious teacher. It is hard to tell which
held her, practically, in the greatest contempt.
A large number of the leading preachers, of various sects, were free-masons, and by no means
all of them withdrew on the exposure of the
shameful and criminal secrets. On the contrary,
without admitting there was anything wrong in
the mysterious order, they applied themselves
more sedulously than ever to the cultivation of
fanatical religion and the upbuilding of the
churches. To get up a counter popular excite-

ment was the best, if not the only, means of escaping from that which threatened to sweep the very name of freemasonry from the face of the earth. That diversion was in some degree successful.

Mr. Holley wrote his first letter to his fourth daughter, Sally, or Sallie, as she herself spells her name, while on a visit to his birthplace, in the winter of 1830. She was then at home in Lyons, and young enough to have him say in a postscript at the end of a long letter, "If there are any words in this letter which you do not exactly understand, get a dictionary and look them out, and so learn and remember the definitions of them."

She is the Sallie Holley, who since the anti-slavery war, has been so well known as one of the teachers of the school at Lottsburgh, Va. In Jan., 1831, she was attending the boarding school of a Miss Thurston in Lyons. Her father took the liveliest interest in her education, both intellectual and moral, as if conscious of the peculiar importance of her future — as if he foresaw the model school at Lottsburgh.

One day there occurred in Miss Thurston's school a scene which aroused the deepest indig-

nation of Mr. Holley's soul. It was not an uncommon occurrence at that day, and is doubtless
in some places repeated in our day, without any
reprobation of parents, the newspaper press, or
the secular authorities. The revivalists invaded
the schoolroom — but Mr. Holley himself shall
state the facts. They are here copied from his
eight-page foolscap letter, closely written, to Miss
C. Thurston, dated Lyons, Jan. 31, 1831, and
containing nearly as long and as able a sermon as
ever was preached on religious education.

After politely disclaiming any intention of tres-
passing on "the delicacy due to her sex," Mr.
Holley thus states his grievance : —

"My daughter informs me that in place of the usual
exercises, at your school on Saturday last, the whole
time, till noon, was consumed in prayer to God, and in
solemn conversation with the scholars, in respect to
their hopes of eternal salvation, — that soon after the
school hour arrived, the Hon. David Eddy, of a remote
town in this county, and Mr. Newell Taft, of this village, came into the schoolroom and partook with yourself and one of your larger scholars in leading these
exercises, — that in addition to their prayers with the
interesting family of your pupils, one or both of these
gentlemen put such questions and made such quotations
as the following to them, one by one : 'Do you think
you have got religion?' 'Do you hope to be saved?'

'Will you renounce all the vanities of life, the idle talk, the amusements and pleasures, of this world, and love Christ?' 'The bible says, " He that believeth shall be saved, but he that believeth not shall be damned."' — that the effect of these exercises upon your pupils was, to produce much fear and many tears, — that all the children wept a great deal — that one little girl, when she was questioned, cried out, ' O, take me home. I want to go home,' — that when you were asked by one of your pupils if she should not recite her lesson in philosophy, you put the question to her, whether she felt more concerned about her philosophy, than she did about the salvation of her soul? — that neither she, nor any other of your pupils, during the whole forenoon, attended at all to their usual studies and recitations — and that, before the school was dismissed, you invited them all to attend a prayer-meeting the same afternoon.

" This account is only a specimen, not a complete statement."

Mr. Holley, it is to be understood, while rejecting certain theological dogmas, was a decided theist and Christian, in a moral sense. He did not object to prayer — wrote prayers for his children, and prayed himself — but did not believe that souls could be saved by fear, or gloom or asceticism. He objected to this course of conduct in Miss Thurston's school under three heads :

"1st. Because it was an abuse of prayer.

"2d.　Because it was an abuse of religion.

"3d.　Because it was an immoral infringement of my rights."

Page after page he gives sound reasons for these positions — reasons that could be supported by plenty of scripture texts — but which could stand firm without them. What is more to the purpose of this narrative, is his disposal of the interference of Eddy and Taft, and it pungently illustrates exactly what the various religious bodies of to-day are doing with nearly all of the secular schools, in their pretence of saving souls :

"But the most offensive part of the transactions of Saturday, to which I object, is the interference of Mr. Eddy and Mr. Taft. These persons interrupted the proceedings of your school, in a manner grossly inconsistent with my rights. You undertook to teach my child certain branches of knowledge, in consideration of which I undertook to pay you a certain sum of money. While you were engaged fulfilling your undertaking, these persons came in and altogether arrested your customary instruction. They have injured me in proportion to the value of that knowledge, which might have been acquired during the interruption, and was prevented from being acquired by it : and in proportion to the perversion of the mind and feelings of my child, arising from the injurious fears and pernicious senti-

ments. which they inculcated. If there is one right
connected with the paternal relation. more dear than
any, or than all others. it is that of protecting the mind
of a child from error and pollution. So dear. in this
case. is that right of mine. which has been invaded.
If these men came to your school and arrested the
order of its proceedings. and substituted a course of
their own, against your will. you can obtain a just
redress by resorting to the laws: and thus protect
yourself from similar intrusions. in future. If they
came, and conducted, according to your invitation and
request. much of the blame. it cannot be disguised. at-
taches to you. They had no right to visit your school.
except by your invitation. They are not competent to
teach children the branches of education. in which you
can well instruct them. and they are men of *bad moral
character*. If you invited them there. I have no doubt,
it was with good intentions, though I think it was very
indiscreet and neither has produced. nor will produce
anything but mischief. They would probably pretend
that they came there with good purposes. But I have
no confidence in the honesty of their pretensions.
Though they both pretend to be christians. they have
taken upon themselves obligations. the most anti-
christian. unprincipled and infamous. *Publicly* professing subjection to that authority which says, ‘ Thou
shalt not take the name of the Lord thy God in vain.’
they have *secretly*, in a state of indecent nudity. with a
rope round their necks and a bandage over their eyes,
kneeling before a mock altar. laid their hands upon the
open bible. with a square and compass upon it. to impart additional meaning to the ceremony, called upon

God to witness, that they always would ' hail. ever conceal. and never reveal any part of the secrets of freemasonry, which they had received, were about to receive, or might thereafter be intrusted with,' and to the full performance of this promise they pledged their lives, most unlawfully and immorally. to be taken, in case of failure in the performance. I know you have too much good sense and real piety, madam. not to be shocked at the profanity and degradation of the name of God and the bible involved in such a transaction. You can also justly appreciate the crime. worse than self-murder, committed by a moral agent, who voluntarily foregoes the use of his understanding, in relation to the bearing of a proposition. and adopts it, when such a proposition may require of him perjury. murder, treason, and any other crime, and especially if he pledges his life. without any mental reservation. equivocation or evasion of mind, to the adopted proposition, and calls God to witness his pledge. These are but a small part, and not the most profane and degrading, of the masonic obligations, which have been taken by the men in question.

" It is well known that these oaths and others of an equally infamous character, have actually led freemasons, of as good repute before, as either Mr. Eddy or Mr. Taft, feloniously to steal a free citizen, and murder him ; and then to array themselves against the laws of the land. and the safety of the state. so as effectually to prevent, for the most part, their judicial and just punishment. Some of these manstealers, if not the murderers, are well known to Mr. Eddy and Mr. Taft, whose moral characters are nevertheless so

low, that they have not yet publicly and openly renounced a masonic connection with them. Can men be
sincere Christians, and come out and renounce the
world, and teach little children to renounce the innocent amusements, and the rational pleasures of life, who
yet refuse to renounce a selfish and corrupt association,
which they know retains in its embrace notorious per-
jurers and convicted kidnappers? Such men are not
worthy of respect, while they are so stupid and so
wicked as to live in sins of so deep a dye, as are im-
plicated in the oaths and conduct above alluded to,
though we may compassionate their blindness, and la-
ment their iniquity, we must guard ourselves against
the contamination of their society. While they remain
in such a state, Christian charity can only weep over
the increasing depths of guilt into which they plunge
themselves by professing a tenderness for their own
souls, or the souls of others, exhort them to a thorough
application of the most searching self-examination, with
a view to the most mighty efforts of which they may be
capable to raise themselves from the horrible pit and
miry clay into which they are fallen, and commend
them in our prayers to the mercy of God.

"Having thus expressed myself with decision and
plainness, upon what I consider the injury I have received, and the impropriety which occurred in your
school on Saturday, permit me to conclude by saying
that I can easily forget all the concern you have had in
them; and if you intend to conduct your school hereafter, with the same attention to the several branches
of human knowledge, by which it has heretofore been
characterized, and without drawing into it religious

fear, or gloom, or grief, I shall cheerfully continue to
send my daughter to you. Wishing you every blessing
in this life and that which is to come, I am in all charity and with much esteem,

"Your very obedient,

"MYRON HOLLEY."

It is not to be wondered at that after this experience of the affinity between the masonic and
the ecclesiastical fraternity, there succeeded four
years of editorial labor, in which he directed his
energies, in a large measure, but not exclusively,
against the masonic institution and its iniquitous
oaths as the most vulnerable point of the allied
forces of social evil. His first editorial engagement was in conducting the "LYONS COUNTRY-
MAN," commencing on the 3d of May, 1831. The
files of that good-looking weekly periodical testify
to the fact that for about three years its sub-
scribers enjoyed better instruction than ordinarily
comes from either press or pulpit. No public or
domestic interest was neglected. The dignity
and courtesy with which he treated his adversaries were as conspicuous as his overwhelming
force of argument.

In his salutatory he formally stated one of his
objects to be the complete overthrow of free-

masonry, and said : "While we muster in that battle all the forces we can command, we shall by no means forget the great interests in behalf of which we wage it."

In this opening of his editorial career, in 1831, he laid down principles broad enough to justify all that he did as a moral and political agitator in the years of his life after free-masonry had ceased to excite the apprehensions of patriots. He says, and he grandly lived up to his promises : "We will not, knowingly, cherish any illiberal sentiment, or take a single step, under the influence of a persecuting spirit. There is not a human being on earth to whom we bear ill-will. There are no means of real good that we shall designingly oppose. We intend on all occasions which bring them into question, to advocate the interests of truth, of justice, of freedom, of knowledge, and of benevolence ; because we are thoroughly persuaded that these are our own personal interests, and the interests of all others, and that they are the indispensable means of all genuine social and individual advancement."

"We set up no claim to extraordinary exemption from errors of opinion, or mistakes of fact, or prejudices of mind. But we will strive earnestly to divest ourselves of these, and we promise, in no case, to pursue a purpose after we shall learn that it has no better foundation than these to rest upon. Feeling ourselves connected with all human beings by strong and durable sympathies, and rejoicing in the connection with all our soul, we mean to contend faithfully, in our little sphere, for human improvement. We are thoroughly convinced that the race to which we belong can never be improved by inequality of conventional privileges, by distinction of ranks, by hereditary transmission of authority, or by any factitious and lasting separation of individuals from the common lot. Every institution, therefore, which embodies such inequality, distinction, transmission, or separation, we most decidedly reprobate, and will labor to overthrow. In these labors may we not expect the concurrence of all our free fellow-citizens?"

A man fighting free-masonry on these principles must have been an immediate abolitionist, whether he was conscious of it or not. The question had only need to come up to have him side with the friends of the largest liberty. He stood by labor and the laborer, whether employed in agriculture or the useful arts. He stood by literature and science; by education, high and low, "solid, extensive, and universal." "Feeling ourselves," he writes, "impelled by patriotism, by philanthropy, by a proud remembrance of the immortal asserters of our freedom, and by our farthest-reaching hopes, to the grateful labor we shall, with zeal and constancy, bestow our best efforts in behalf of such an education."

This newspaper was not a paying concern, and as the two leading political parties were interested to crush out the rising third party, and the massonic fraternity, so deeply rooted, was seconding their efforts by the cry of "persecution," and by the parade of being exceedingly good and zealous Christians, it was by no means wonderful that Mr. Holley's editorial labors exhausted his pecuniary resources. In 1833 his anti-masonic friends, of his own Assembly district, nominated him for their candidate to the Assembly. The politicians, and especially those of the dominant "democratic" party, were intensely frightened. To let a man of his power of pen, and still more of voice, with his grand integrity, into the Assembly, might revolutionize the Empire State. If he were let alone there was almost a certainty of his election. Hence a grand battery of the basest calumny ever known in our political history was trained and opened upon him, — and of course, near enough to the election day to prevent his reply from taking much effect. The party organs raised the old cry of "defaulter," which the legislative journals and statute-book had silenced five years before, and laid the calumny in large print and with every semblance of proof before every voter of the district. All that Mr. Holley could do was to prepare a reply in the form of a broadsheet to be posted on election day. The antidote would probably have conquered the poison if it had been administered in season. But at the top of society corruption had been going on — such as high politicians know too well how to practice — long before the stink-pots of calumny were thrown. To this it was due that some of Mr. Holley's trusted friends, and even family connections, sided with his enemies on this trying occasion. But the grand pioneer of labor, civil and religious liberty, justice and humanity, did not wilt. His "poster" for election day deserves to go down to posterity to the latest generation, and I believe it will, for the encouragement of all champions of the right and honest voters against political chicanery.

One printed original, at least, of this interesting document was preserved by Henry O'Reilly, Esq., of Rochester, a pioneer in the great telegraph industry, with a view of placing it in the archives of the New York Historical Society. While it was in his hands the following exact copy was made for this memoir : —

DO ME JUSTICE ! !

I ask no man to support my nomination against his conviction of duty. The sense of duty is the most precious bestowment of the Creator upon our rational nature. Let it never be violated. But I ask to be protected from persecution — to be treated by my honest fellow-citizens of all parties according to the great rule of social justice. And I ask no more. The last " Western Argus," in a postscript, accuses me of being a defaulter, and of defrauding the state out of about $30,000; and heaps upon me a multitude of defamatory epithets, which, if they are truly applied, ought to deprive me of all favor from the community. Are these accusations and epithets *truly* applied?

In 1828 my accounts with the state were

finally adjusted by the following act, entitled
"An act for settling the claims of Myron
Holley, late Canal Commissioner, passed
21st March, 1828 :

"The people of the State of New York,
represented in Senate and Assembly, do
enact as follows : that the Commissioners
of the Canal fund be directed to release to
Myron Holley, his heirs and assigns, all
the interest derived to the State from the
deed bearing date the 8th Decr., 1825, and
executed by Myron Holley, Wm. II. Adams,
John M. Holley, Mindwell P. Granger,
Francis Granger, and John A. Granger ;
and to assign to the said Myron Holley all
the securities taken, and to pay to him all
the monies received on the sale of such
parts of the estate conveyed by said deed
to the said commissioners, as shall have been
sold : Provided the same shall be received
by the said Myron Holley in full *satisfaction
and discharge of all his claims* and demands
against the State."

Previous to the passage of this Act the
commissioners of the canal fund had re-

quired of me the surrender to the state of
all my property, real and personal, including
in their rigor even the wearing apparel of
my wife and children. I had complied with
this requisition to the minutest particular.
and the persons named in the act, being, as
bail or otherwise. interested in the real property, had joined me in conveying it. After
the conveyance the commissioners of the
canal fund had sold some of the property and
received payments and securities thereon,
and the legislature itself had restored to me
all my personal property. My bail were well
known to be abundantly responsible for any
deficiency in my means of accounting to the
state, and the property conveyed was of
considerable value. The state had given me
the appointment of canal commissioner. It
had the highest authority and the amplest
means to investigate and decide upon my
conduct under that appointment ; and with
full means in its possession, to enforce all
the claims of justice against me, it did investigate and decide upon it ; and by the
law above recited, it solemnly declared that

I was not a defaulter in a single cent, and ordered, as you will see, the complete and immediate restoration of my property. In my claims upon the state, an humble individual, opposed, slandered, and persecuted by some leading politicians in every legislature for four years, I stood, without wealth, without the sympathetic favor of influential political associates, without any means of success, but such as clear justice and the public character of the state afforded me, *and my rights prevailed.* Was this a crime? Did this success show that I was a *defaulter?* Did I *defraud* the State?

In the Senate my bill passed by a majority of 20 vs. 4, including in the affirmative the names of Benton, Dagan, Enos, Oliver, Stebbins, Todd, Throop, and several others belonging to the political majority of that body ; in the Assembly it passed by a majority of 69 vs. 31, including in the affirmative the names of Armstrong, Brinkerhoff, Butler, Emmet, Hoffman, Livingston, Monnell, Paige, Tallmadge, Westcott, and many others belonging to the political majority of

that body, and now most high in favor with
my political adversaries. If I defrauded the
state it must have been with the concurrence of these men! The charge is false.
Reflect upon it a moment and you will see it
is. It is uttered in the madness of mere
party denunciation. And by whom is it uttered? By Chapin and Chapman, each of
whom has, before his criminal support of
free-masonry had been required, solemnly,
under his hand, asserted his belief in *my
integrity*, in reference to my whole conduct
as canal commissioner, and, by petitioning the
legislature in favor of an act like that above
recited, become a party to the fraud!! Deliberate inconsistencies always betray guilt.

'The extracts in the "Argus" are garbled,
and all, when corrected, admit of easy ex-
planation; but it would be too long to
explain them all now. In the last report
made by the legislature, respecting my
claims, the very able chairman of the committee from whom it came, Mr. Paige, of
Schenectady, then and now a decided friend
of Gen. Jackson and Mr. Van Buren, says :

" The claim of Mr. Holley has already undergone the examination of committees of several legislatures. Those committees have *uniformly* decided in favor of its validity and *justice*." " The committee feel themselves *constrained* to conclude that the claim of Mr. Holley is founded in justice, and is either a legal or an equitable demand against the state."

" Although the committee have *unanimously* come to the above conclusions, yet some of its members conceive that the bill referred to them ought to contain a provision requiring that the release of the property therein referred to, to Mr. Holley, should be accepted by him in full satisfaction of all claims upon the state, so as fully. upon its face, to express that it provides for the payment of a *demand due* him by the state." The bill, upon this last suggestion, was amended by the addition of the proviso which it contains. This report is found in Assembly Journal of 1828, page 744, &c.

Now, I ask all men, who are not the slaves of party, and who do not mean to *persecute*, whether in executing duties so arduous and responsible, — when labors, and hazards, and perplexities were so continually pressing upon me for more than seven years, and when, with untiring vigilance and great abilities against me, and nothing but the sense of justice on my side, with the acknowledged importance of my services, the passage of such a law as the one above, in favor of my claims, by the highest tribunal in the state, was effected, — I ought not to have for my family peace and exemption from interested and malignant aspersions? To the free voters of the land it belongs to suppress persecution in the last resort, and they alone can effectually point the dagger which the interested and base have drawn upon me. Before such voters drive it home to the mark at which it is aimed, they will consider,—whether they can justly impeach my character for truth and honesty in my dealings with any man? whether they can charge me, on any occasion, with a want of public spirit? whether my drawing up two-thirds of all the official documents proceed-

ing from the canal commissioners for above
seven years, while I was a member of that
body, was an evidence of zeal for their interests? whether my letter to the committee of the Assembly, in 1820, signed by
three commissioners only, and opposed by
the other two, but which caused the construction of the canal west of the Seneca
River, simultaneously with the eastern section, was useful towards the speedy completion of a work which has raised the value
of all their lands and multiplied their means
of an honorable livelihood? — whether, finally, the resolute assertion of the rights of
the people and the supremacy of the law,
to which I have devoted myself since the
murder of Morgan, has proceeded from disinterested rectitude of purpose, and been in
conformity with the true principles of equal
rights? And upon such consideration I
calmly repose the issue of the nomination
with which I have been honored.

MYRON HOLLEY.

Nov. 2, 1833.

The documents Mr. Holley here refers to, in

self-defence, incontestibly prove not only that he was never a "defaulter," but that the State of New York, when he retired from the office of Canal Commissioner, in plain equity, owed him a large sum. It still owes it, with interest, to his heirs. This rests on the testimony of the most able and intelligent of his political opponents.

As to the veritable fate of William Morgan, which proved so much dynamite to Free Masonry, I interviewed the venerable Thurlow Weed, at his quiet home in New York, and obtained the following information :

Thurlow Weed was sued for libel, damages $10,000, for charging —————— with paying money to Whitney and others, abductors of Morgan, in order to enable them to evade justice. He expected to prove the truth of his statement by Whitney himself, who had returned from his flight, and was ready to testify for the benefit of Weed. But the prosecution claimed that the defence could not produce testimony to the fact of the payment of money to the witness without first proving that the libellee *knew* that the witness was guilty and was fleeing from justice, and with the intention of aiding his escape, and on this plea Weed's witnesses were all ruled out and the verdict was against him to the extent of $400! Afterwards Mr. Weed invited to lunch with him this same Whitney and a friend of his who was also a friend of Weed. In the course of the conversation Whitney's friend urged Whitney to make a clean breast of all he knew about Morgan's abduction. To this Whitney assented, saying that he had long thought of it, and could have no peace without it. He could not hear a blind rattle at night without dread of the sheriff. He then proceeded to say that he, with two other men, took Morgan from Fort Niagara, bound around the body with a rope, to the two ends of which weights were attached, and having conveyed him down the river in a boat till they reached the deep water of the lake, threw him overboard! "Now Weed can hang you," said his friend, to Whitney. "But he won't," said Whitney.

Mr. Weed did not meet Whitney again till he attended the Republican Convention in Chicago which nominated Lincoln. Just on the eve of the convention the two met, and Whitney expressed a wish to have Weed take down his confession in writing, to be published after his death, saying he had not long to live. But Mr. Weed, being exceedingly busy, put him off till after the adjournment. But he was so much disappointed that the convention preferred Lincoln to Seward, that he resolved not to wait for the adjournment, and set out immediately to take the earliest train homeward. On his way to the cars Whitney met him again and urged his purpose of confession, but Mr. Weed excused himself on the ground that he should lose his train. After his return Mr. Weed addressed a letter to Whitney, at Chicago, on the subject, in favor of complying with his wishes. No answer came, but the letter was returned through the dead letter office, for Whitney himself was dead.

See *Gould* vs. *Weed*, 12 Wendell's N. Y. Reports, to fill the blank on the previous page.

CHAPTER XIX.

RESIDENCE IN HARTFORD.

Though Myron Holley had won by far the most honorable place in both the canal history and the anti-masonic history of New York, he was the victim of this cruel calumny, launched against him by the faction which was then governing the state in the interest of the slave-power, aided by that which was ambitious to take its place. But he by no means lost caste with the best and wisest men anywhere. The anti-masons of Connecticut, his native state, were about to establish a weekly paper as the organ of their cause, called the "Free Elector," and they engaged him to edit it — at a moderate salary, no doubt, though what it was does not appear — for the term of one year at least. Averse as he was to leaving home, his debts obliged him to accept the offer, and for the next year, 1834, he resided in Hartford.

His long letters to the members of his large family let us into the heart and character of the man. Those of that year would fill a volume as large as this. Some extracts must suffice.

HARTFORD, 26th January, 1834.

MY DEAR SALLY. — Since I left home my most prevailing affections and anxious thoughts have been with you, and all the other precious tenants of my heart's love at Lyons. You have had my daily prayers, my best wishes, my most interesting recollections, and my most cherished hopes. There is nothing, in the past, upon which I dwell with more satisfaction, than those occasions, in the evening and on the Sabbath, when I have sat listening to you when engaged in reading from the holy repository of that wisdom which cometh from above. . . . . . Never admit the thought, my dear daughter, into your heart, that speculation, or mere mental conviction and emotion, under any name, however plausible and honored, will be sufficient. *Practical duty* is the only legitimate end of all speculation, conviction and feeling, and without this, grace, faith, and every other name to live are empty sounds ; *with this*, and *tending to this*, they are the very gates of heaven, the bright livery of the spirits of the just made perfect.

Before I came here you told me I should see Mrs. Sigourney. You were a true prophet. A few evenings ago Mrs. Willard, of Troy, was in this city, as I learnt by receiving an invitation to take tea in her company. The invitation was brought by a bookseller here, a Mr. Huntington, who is highly respectable, and treated me with great politeness. Mrs. Willard was at his house. At seven o'clock in the evening, after a busy day with me, I went to comply with my invitation, and soon

found myself in very intelligent and agreeable company. The circle was small but social, characterized full as much by cordiality as by ceremony, though nothing of either was wanting which good breeding enjoins. Besides Mrs. Willard and Mrs. Sigourney and Mrs. Huntington. there were the sister of the latter. Mrs. Phillips, and two other ladies whose names I did not learn, and there were also, besides Mr. Huntington, his brother, Doctor Lee, Mr. Sigourney, and a young gentleman. .
. . . . The subjects of conversation were chiefly the exertions making by the ladies to sustain a school for females in Greece. For this object Mrs. Willard said more than two thousand dollars had been raised, the school is established, and in it young women are learning to become teachers, at the cost of the contributors to the school fund, who, after they are sufficiently educated, if they can get employment as teachers at a certain rate of wages in Greece, are to pay back annually to the school fund a certain sum. Mrs. Willard's book of travels is selling off, and the avails of it, beyond remuneration for the expense of publication, will go to enlarge this fund. Other subjects of conversation were, somnambulism, Swedenborgianism, phrenology, with a small spice of politics, and such other topics as were less weighty and not improper. All the ladies at the little soiree were very neat in their dress, and showed great deference to each other. without any interrupting eagerness to put in a word here and there to mend each other's conversation. or exhibit their own superior accuracy of recollection, or facility of invention. In all these respects their example is worthy of imitation. Love me, remember me, and write to me. Good-by, my dear.   MYRON HOLLEY.

HARTFORD, 6th Feb., 1834.

MY DEAR ROBERT, — In a letter which I received a few days ago from your mother, she informed me that you had started for Albany, and I address you this line for the purpose of ascertaining whether you are in that city or not. I feel towards you an irrepressible and immortal sympathy, which will be greatly lacerated if I do not occasionally hear from you, and hear that you are well. Your faculties and your accomplishments for business are such as make me happy to think upon, and it would give me the truest gratification to aid you, in every way in my power, to get into business, reputable and profitable. Is there anything I can do for you in Albany? I know many gentlemen there, and am respected by a considerable number.* If my writing to them in your behalf would be of use to you, let me know it, and letters shall be immediately forwarded. My situation here is very comfortable, and I am getting into respect rapidly, because I keep myself engaged in my proper employment, and run into no idle, expensive, or profligate associations. My life, as you know, has not been unassailed by malice and persecution. The consciousness of my integrity, and the general praiseworthiness of my pursuits, and the hopes I cherish, have raised me above all the mischiefs of those evils.

* Thurlow Weed, in his reminiscences of stage-travelling, before the completion of the Erie Canal, says: " It was an unusual circumstance to find a stage-coach with fair weather and good roads, between Rochester and Albany, that was not enlivened by conversation, for there were almost always two or three intellectual passengers. Myron Holley, for example, with a gifted and highly-cultivated mind, had committed to memory, and would recite by the hour, gems from the British poets."

If life ends with the dissolution of the body, the course of innocence, integrity, and kindness to others, is the only way of enjoying it. But, my son, I have no doubt that our spirits are immortal, and that immortality may be infinitely blessed by the sturdy practical exhibition of these qualities, and immortality would be wretched without it. Pray let me hear from you soon, and often, and from your heart.

Most affectionately yours,

MYRON HOLLEY.

Mr. Holley, from first to last, believed, or rather undoubtingly took for granted the personal government of the universe by a supreme intellect, the existence of the human intellect after death, progressively and perpetually, and in the canonized Bible as a revelation of God's nature and will, without ever appearing to explain to himself or others how these beliefs were consistent with adverse phenomena or facts testified to by our senses, or how the Bible is any more, or better a revelation than all other literature. Practically, however, he seems to have derived the divinest wisdom from all sorts of literature, and to have regarded nature itself as a revelation. His detestation of the masonic institution did not in the slightest degree alienate his affections from the families of his daughters, the male heads of

two of which had taken sides in its defence against
him. To an impartial observer it would seem that
the divinity was *in* him, rather than personally
outside of him, and that while the abstract principles of love and justice so ruled his own heart
and life, there was no need of his belief in the
over-ruling *personality* assumed by the popular
creeds, and that it was of no consequence whether
personalities exist outside of matter or not, he so
deeply reverenced the personality and personalities
inside of it. His conception of God seems practically not to have differed from that of an abstract
verity. It was a comfort to him to personify it.
He never lifted a finger nor uttered a word to
compel any other person to do the same.

He had twelve children, all but two of whom
were born in Canandaigua. They had different
qualities and dispositions, but he treated them all
with equal affection. His discipline was nothing
but persuasion and kindness. In the following
letter to his eldest daughter, Mrs. Chapin, he
touchingly communicates the wisdom of a kind
father, derived from large experience :

HARTFORD, 23rd August, 1834.

MY DEAR DAUGHTER, — Not long ago I received a
very interesting letter from you, and more recently

Elizabeth has informed me that your health is not good ;
that you are feeble so as to be able to do little more
then walk about the house. I hope you are perfectly
restored before this, and that you will not fail to take
all needful care of yourself. Your situation is one of
great importance, involving necessarily much solicitude
and many duties. I pray that you may have health to
meet them and discharge them, in full accordance with
your own pure wishes. Habitual prudence, cheerful-
ness and hope, are very requisite to you ; and I expect
you to cherish them continually. With them, there is
no situation in life, in which a woman can be placed,
more truly dignified, useful, or interesting, than yours.
God surrounds us with objects of affection and care, to
call forth our highest powers of mind and heart. And
when they are called forth worthily, as they always are
in the judicious bringing up and education of a little
flock of the immortal birds of Paradise, they will ensure
the most substantial and permanent enjoyment that
human beings have any right to aspire to. The tender
relations of parent and child are prominently and often
referred to in the scriptures to illustrate and impress
upon us the ever-wakeful and intense benevolence of
our Maker towards all the beings he has made. And
human life affords no means so effectual as these relations are, to draw out our spirits from the cold degradation of mere selfishness, to the delightful exercises of
that disinterested love which is destined to supply our
motives to virtuous action more and more forever. Let
not the cares, then, of your numerous family, oppress
your spirits on the one hand, nor stimulate you to such
exertions of labor and fatigue on the other, as may impair your constitution. Calmness, self-government,

and consistency, always obeying the law of love in taking charge of children, will be the best means of rendering them obedient and docile. And when they have their perfect work, they secure us such rewards as can no where else be reaped — the rewards of a conscientious and kind performance of the most essential duties, and those of seeing the objects of our efforts and affections continually enlarging their qualifications for usefulness, respectability, and enjoyment. In the allotments of life this is generally true, though not always. There are exceptions. The most virtuous parents may sometimes suffer the unhappiness of seeing their children do ill. I pray that this suffering may never fall to you, and think your hope of escaping it is as well founded as that of any mother of so large a family. But I have no doubt that suffering in life is designed, by our Infinite Governor, as much for our good as enjoyment is. By sufferings we become more tender, more patient, more resigned, more sensible of the presence of our Heavenly Father, than we should otherwise be; and these qualities are absolutely essential to our highest exaltation. To be sure, to produce these effects, we must suppose the suffering to be disciplinary and limited. And so in my view will all suffering prove to be. Without suffering we should manifestly be less capable of enjoyment. With it, believing undoubtingly in the existence and government of God, and that he is good to all, we are affectingly taught our dependence, our need of help from Him who is Almighty, and the indispensable duty of trusting in Him at all times.

In the vicinity of this city, one mile south of it, on a beautiful and healthy elevation of ground, is a Retreat for the insane. I went to see it yesterday for the first time since my residence here, and I felt greatly interested. There are now 120 inmates of the buildings, which are very large, and surrounded with many very charming objects. Without being abrupt at all in ascent, the site of the Retreat is sufficiently elevated to be easy to be kept clean, and to afford a wide and variegated, and ornamental prospect. All report agrees in representing the management of this establishment as being eminently kind and effective. I was strongly impressed with what I heard and saw, though there were so many persons there as visitors that I concluded to postpone to another time enquiries which I had designed to make. I went through the lower hall of the building, however, and walked across its ample grounds. Within half a mile of the building one constantly hears songs, shouts, screams, and clamor from the inmates. There are uttered such tones as healthy organs are never tuned to, indicative of distress, rage, and every passion. I heard female voices, harsh, rapid, shrill, and sorrowful, all mixed up in a manner to me very novel and afflicting. Going from the edifice down one of its last walks, about 100 rods from shelter, in the corner of a field, we found the saddest spectacle of quiet melancholy that ever met my eye. A man looking to be about my age, tall, thin, and silent, was slowly walking backwards and forwards on a path not more than 30 feet long, where in weather not particularly intemperate he is to be found, at all hours of the day (except those in which he is called to sleep and eat), saying nothing and scarcely regarding anything. He answers shortly and mournfully if spoken to, and seems occupied exclusively by some sad spirit. I intend to see him again, if I can, and by expressions of that sympathy and good-will for him which I feel, learn from himself his history. His path is as hard as any part of the highway, and as much worn. I imagine his grief is of domestic or religious origin. This life has many forms of intense distress which you and I have never witnessed. I pray that neither we, nor any of ours, may ever feel them.

With love to all yours.

Most affectionately,

MYRON HOLLEY.

While residing in Hartford Mr. Holley appeared before a committee of the legislature in favor of a law against extra-judicial oaths. He drew up the committee's report, and the bill it recommended. Perhaps a grander piece of wisdom was never committed to a legislative pigeon-hole. The bill is good law, whether it was enacted by the next Assembly or not. It is one of those laws, however, which must enforce itself. Perhaps the only way in which the government can do anything effective towards its enforcement is to set the example of dispensing with oaths altogether in its own practice, as some of the best lawyers now hold that they are utterly useless there, if not pernicious. Only the free-masons know whether *they* have dispensed with them in their practice.

REPORT AND BILL.

The Joint Committee, to whom was referred the Petition of Gaius Lyman and others, praying for the passage of a law to prohibit the administration of extra-judicial oaths, respectfully report:

That they have diligently examined the allegations contained in the said petition, and have enquired of witnesses under oath, and consulted documents of indisputable authority concerning the truth thereof, and concerning various other facts connected therewith, and they are of opinion that they are true, and that the best interests of the state require the interposition of the legislature in the premises.

The facts relied on in the petition, and the proofs obtained, are all connected with the institution of free-masonry, and show that institution to be distinguished by the following features, viz.:

It is a voluntary institution, embracing *men* only, between non-age and dotage, neither idiots nor madmen.

Its professed object is the promotion of charity and science.

Its most indispensable requisition is that of inviolable secrecy in respect to its essential peculiarities.

It secures this secrecy by oaths, with most of which is connected the penalty of death in case of their violation.

Its secrets consist of its ceremonies of initiation; its oaths, the crimes committed by its members against the public, including the highest known to the law; and its pass-words, grips, signs and cyphers for private communication.

Its oaths are imposed under false pretences and taken without being at all previously considered and understood by the persons taking them, and they contain injunctions utterly irreconcileable with moral rectitude in those who obey them, with impartial justice in the most important business of life, and with the safety of the state.

Its ceremonies are grossly indecent and shockingly profane.

In reference to the first of these characteristics : by excluding from its embrace, in the outset, the most helpless sex, feeble infancy and old age, with all such as are born slaves, or suffer under the most afflicting disabilities of life, we perceived the sphere of its charity is very much circumscribed. Its arrangements, on this head, are rather made with a business-like and prudential regard to possible necessities among its members, and those immediately depending on them, than with any more generous views. But such provision, if adhered to with fidelity and involving no injustice to others, is in a certain degree commendable. If, however, the funds raised by the contributions of all persons initiated into the society under the expectation of their being devoted to charity and science are chiefly applied to the purchase of useless and vain decorations, buildings to accommodate its meetings and to rent, and refreshments often needless and pernicious, there seems to be connected with this feature of the institution more of fraud than of charity ; and that such are the chief applications of the funds was satisfactorily proved. Passing from this most prominent of the professed objects of the society, the committee are fully convinced that its profession of promoting science is intended as an allurement to the increase of its members, and wholly illusory. The witnesses examined knew of no useful discoveries ever made by freemasonry, of any publication of useful books, or any establishment or endowment of any seat of learning.

The next in order of its characteristics, as we have stated them, is its secrecy. Is there any standing pursuit in which a good man can engage that requires secrecy? In the administration of criminal justice, secrecy is required for a time, that is, till the accused is secured for legal trial; and the selfishness of nations, in their wars and negotiations, sometimes enjoin temporary secrecy. But secrecy always implies injustice, shame, or crime somewhere. Can freemasonry require secrecy for any injustice, shame, or crime, *except its own?* If it requires it for this, is it not the duty of the legislature to frown upon it?

The secrecy of freemasonry is secured by oaths; without these the society would not continue long to exist. The penalty of these oaths is always unlawful. It amounts to death in most of the degrees. No man has a right to kill himself, or voluntarily to put his life in hazard, without the authority of government, to which he owes allegiance, or a necessity occasioned by a violent invasion of the great rights he derives from his Maker. But the oaths are promissory, and the promises are many of them unlawful and criminal. We beg leave here to state some of them.

In the first oath the officer of the lodge, who administers it, makes the candidate swear that he will always hail, ever conceal, and never reveal any part of the secrets of freemasonry which he may afterwards be instructed in — the officer always knowing that among such secrets, if the candidate advances to the third degree, are included crimes against the state.

In the second oath, the candidate swears that he will obey all regular signs or summons handed him by a brother of that degree, or sent him from a lodge, without any exception but that of its being to be obeyed within a certain distance from him, and excluding all objection arising from the illegality or criminality of the summons.

In the third oath the candidate swears that, on receiving the sign of distress from a brother of that degree, he will fly to his relief if there is a greater probability of saving the life of the distressed than of losing his own ; that he will not speak evil of a brother of that degree, neither behind his back nor before his face ; that he will apprise him of all approaching danger, if he can ; that he will yield the same passive obedience as in the foregoing oath : that he will keep the secrets of a brother of that degree, when communicated to him as such and he knowing them to be such, as securely as the criminal himself would keep them, *murder and treason excepted*, and they left to his discretion.

In the oath of the seventh degree the candidate swears to aid a companion of that degree, and, if in his power, to extricate him from any difficulty, *whether he be right or wrong;* to conceal his crimes as in the preceding degrees : only murder and treason, in this degree, are explicitly not excepted, as most usually administered.

It is important to observe that these oaths are taken to be obeyed absolutely and on all occasions, without any exception in favor of the laws of the land or any other civil. moral or religious obligation.

The nature of the promises, penalties and ceremonies contained in the oaths of freemasonry being criminal and indecent. affords strong ground for the secrecy of the order. Such promises, with such penalties and accompanied by such ceremonies. no man would have the effrontery to impose in the face of the world. and no man would take upon himself. understandingly, because they are decidedly at war with every republican sentiment, with every moral feeling, and with explicit Christian precept.

These oaths are not binding. — they are promissory. A promissory oath is the calling upon God to take notice of what is promised. and invoking his vengeance by the promiser upon himself if it is not performed. Promises are not binding where false or erroneous representations and inducements are held out to those who take them. The representation made to the candidate before admission. that the oath will affect neither his religion nor his politics. is of this character. and so are the pretensions of the society to the promotion of science.

To take an oath is a solemn and deliberate act of the mind. Understanding is essential to its obligation, on which account oaths impose no obligation upon, and are not administered to. idiots. lunatics, madmen. or young children. they not having sufficient knowledge of the nature of the things promised. nor of the penalties of non-performance ; and both of these sorts of knowledge are requisite. There can be no moral obligation, in any case. without knowledge ; and in respect to the nature of the promises and penalties in the oaths of freemasonry, all the persons before alluded to as being free from the obligation of oaths for the want of understanding, have as much knowledge as the wisest of the brethren had before the oaths were taken.

The right to administer oaths is a prerogative of sovereign power and cannot be enjoyed concurrently by the government and its subjects. It would be both wrong and ridiculous for any individual, not authorized by law, to pretend to a natural right of administering oaths in such form, with such penalties, and for such purposes as he might choose to dictate; and such pretension would not be made valid by his finding any man, or number of men, who would consent to take them. Even if the form, penalties and purposes were all good, this would be true. The right of administering oaths does not exist anterior to the establishment of government nor independently of it. It springs from the necessities of government after its establishment. It is a right of the most sacred character, serving the most solemn purposes of civil organization. It cannot exist in individuals or associations, except when conferred upon them by government.

There is no rightful government in our country but that of religion and the laws adopted under our civil institutions. Christianity commands, " Swear not at all." Civil government has not conferred upon freemasonry the right to administer any oath. Would it not be a violation of every man's conscience and a scandalous breach of his allegiance to our government for him to administer an oath under pretence of authority from any foreign government? It is equally so under pretence of authority from freemasonry. None of the oaths of that institution are authorized by our

laws; they are therefore unlawful and not oblig-
atory.

The performance of some of the promises in the
masonic oaths is in all cases unlawful. and of many
others of them, in some cases. it is so.   A promise to
conceal crimes. to give notice of approaching danger
from legal prosecution for crime. to assist any out of
difficulty. right or wrong. is always unlawful, the
promiser being under a prior obligation to the contrary.   From such prior obligation what shall discharge
him?   His promise?   His own act and deed?   But an
obligation from which a man can discharge himself, by
his own act. is no obligation at all.

An oath can never bind a man to do what is morally
wrong.   If it is a bond of duty. let us consider what
is the authority of duty.   It is the command of God,
or general utility, opposition to which is the very definition of wrong.   It is both preposterous and impious to
call upon God to take notice of what is in opposition
to his command.   To make a promise under such circumstances is deeply sinful; to break such a promise
always a duty.

Our laws regard the due administration of oaths as
of great importance in ascertaining the truth in the
most important concerns of individual right and the
public safety.   And it is wholly inconsistent with their
due administration to have them administered at all
without authority.   To assume the power to administer them without is a flagrant criminal and dangerous
usurpation of sovereign power.   Unauthorized swearing is profanity, subject to punishment by our laws;
and the offence of such profanity is amazingly enhanced by circumstances of premeditation, indecency

and mockery, and, most of all, by the deliberate usurpation of authority to commit it. The Father of his Country, in his farewell address, emphatically asks, " Where is the security for property, for reputation, for life, if this sense of religious obligation desert the oaths, which are the instruments of investigation in courts of justice ? "

In the administration of the masonic oaths we have said the ceremonies are grossly indecent and shockingly profane. To show this we need only refer to those of the first degree, which, however, are not so deeply revolting as those of some of the higher degrees.

Such false professions, such criminal and dangerous oaths, such indecent and profane ceremonies we are convinced should be strictly prohibited by law ; and in order to effect such prohibition we have proposed a bill, which we report herewith, and recommend to be passed into a law. All which is respectfully submitted.

Signed, per order: GEORGE SPOFFORD,
                      Chairman.

An Act in addition to an Act concerning Crimes and Punishments.

Be it enacted by the Senate and House of Representatives in General Assembly convened : That every person who shall hereafter knowingly and wilfully administer to any other person, any oath not by law authorized or required, and shall be thereof duly convicted, shall for every such offense forfeit and pay the sum of one hundred dollars.

And every person who shall hereafter knowingly, wilfully, and willingly receive any such oath, and shall be thereof duly convicted, shall for every such offense suffer a like penalty.

The impression he made on his native State, and which its semi-capital made on him, may best be discovered from a long letter addressed to his daughter, Mrs. George Kingman:

HARTFORD, 19th Oct., 1834.

MY DEAR ELIZABETH, — Your last excellent letter was duly received, and gave me great pleasure, though I have not been very prompt in answering it. All the expressions of affection which it contains my heart has responded to every day since I received it; and will respond to when its pulsations are lost in the ethereality of our spiritual nature. The only comforts I have enjoyed, in this place, have arisen from my consciousness of being honestly employed, my hopes of meeting the members of my family soon in health and undiminished affection for me, and the excellent letters with which so many of them have favored me. But my exile seems long. How many long evenings I have passed in lonely but tender recollections of my dear children, their connexions, their new relations, their increasing social interests, their past history, with all the endearing incidents which have made up my domestic experience! My person is in Hartford: my senses are conversant with its scenery; but my mind, my thoughts, my hopes, and my love are far to the west, occupied with far dearer images associated with all my true enjoyments upon earth, and which to me must essentially contribute to the bliss of heaven. Do not from these

remarks imagine that I am destitute of the respect
of those with whom I live. Seeking to do no mischief. and prosecuting my employment in a spirit of
good will toward others, though I have not much
society. reasonable evidences of estimation wait upon
me wherever I go. But the regards of strangers,
especially such as pertain to the calculations of a
sordid utility. and are offered to the mind more than
to the heart, and imply the expectation of remuneration in some shape or other, have very little in them
to satisfy the cravings of a free and social nature.
They constitute commodities condemned. by all the
higher powers. as contraband. in the intercourse of
love. Hartford is prosperous in its business, has far
more wealth than any other place in Connecticut. and is
enlarging its business and population. It is two hundred years old. Several generations are deposited in
its burying grounds. among whom individuals were found
that were of energetic character and commanding virtues. Its early settlement was opened and made safe
and successful, by public spirit, enterprise and hardi-
hood. that deserved the name of a fearless and generous philanthropy. Its infancy. like that of most other new
settlements, was noted for the neighborly sympathies
which it manifested ; and the hazards by which it was long
surrounded called forth and cultivated much vigilance
and shrewdness and self-reliance. These qualities still
distinguish it. in the channels of business. They are
not the only qualities needed to make society desirable.
Where they prevail to the exclusion of quick moral
sense, and all true relish for that spiritual communion
which builds up the inner man. and fits him for those
enjoyments which lie beyond the power of time and

sense, they are only coarse means to coarser ends.   I
fear Mammon has more devoted worshippers here than
any other God.   Johnson says, in one of his satires :

> This mournful truth is everywhere confest,
> Slow rises worth, by poverty deprest ;
> But here more slow, where all are slaves to gold,
> Where looks are merchandise, and smiles are sold.

And it seems to me to apply more to this place, than
any other to which my acquaintance has extended.
But censure is not an agreeable employment, and I will
break off from this strain.   I was led to it by a sensa-
tion, perhaps too keen, of my personal want of sympa-
thizing companionship.

We had an anti-masonic state convention here last
Wednesday and Thursday. in which, being one of its
members, I took part, which gained me credit.   My
manner of conducting the *Free Elector* too was cordially approved by that body.   These circumstances
are gratifying to me, and on that account will please
you.   The anti-masons wish very much that I should
engage with them for another year, and are trying to
gain patronage for the paper in such a degree as shall
induce me to remain.   But I can be no longer separated from my family.   If nothing better can be done
for them, I must come home and get disencumbered of
my debts by surrendering all my property, and so be
at liberty to start anew, and devote myself to their
society, to their support, protection, comfort, and the
education of the little ones.   I hope a better lot awaits
us, but will not be discouraged if my fortune takes this
color.   My health is good, my character I trust is not
deteriorated, my sense of duty to my family is strength-

ened, and I will work for them with the constancy and
ardor of the truest affection. I cannot live thus away
from them. My days and nights are troubled with
apprehensions of their suffering for necessary food
and fire, and clothing. I shall soon write to your
mother, and I hope to be able to send her some
money. Tell George I thank him for what he has done
for them, and hope he will keep them along and not let
them suffer. I shall be able to pay all yet. If my interest at Rochester is advertised for sale on the mortgage, and George should find it out, I wish he would
send me a paper containing the advertisement. Perhaps I could make some arrangement here to my benefit
with it.

Remember me most affectionately to your mother,
Grace, Bolly,* Sally, and all my other friends.

As ever yours,

MYRON HOLLEY.

---

* This was his pet name for his youngest son, Bolivar. On
all the generous minds of that age the conduct of the great
South American patriot and liberator produced a profound
impression. To the Senate of Colombia (afterwards divided
into the republics of New Grenada, Venezuela and Ecuador),
Simon Bolivar said: " I beg as fervently of my country as I
would for the lives of my children, that you will never consent
that clime, or color, or creed, should make any distinction in
your republic."

Again, to the Legislature of Bolivia and Peru he said :—
" Legislators! Slavery is the infringement of all laws. A law
having a tendency to preserve slavery would be the grossest
sacrilege. Man to be possessed by his fellow man! Man to
be made property of! The image of the Deity to be put
under the yoke! Let these usurpers show us their title deeds!"

So when his editorial engagement was at an end, in spite of the earnest entreaties of his Connecticut friends, he hastened home to his cosy stone cottage in Lyons, not to live long among his quince and mulberry trees, but to do what he could to relieve the little property he had left from the incumbrances which burdened it. After much struggle he effected the sale of his house and five acres in Lyons, and bought a farm of 120 on the Genesee below Rochester — and no farmer ever enjoyed life more than he did on that beautiful spot. The place was broad, fertile, genial and unpretentious, like himself. A grand, pensile willow tree standing near the commodious house he built, will assure the stranger that he has found the sacred home where he lived at the sublimest period of his life.

CHAPTER XXI.

LIBERTY PARTY.

In spite of the Declaration of Independence, which in words abolished slavery as emphatically as it separated the colonies from the mother country, and in spite of the constitution of 1787, which created the United States as a nation without re-establishing slavery, that abominable and inhuman institution existed in nearly all the states in the early years of the present century; and while Myron Holley was so bravely battling with the more local masonic usurpation, the extension of slavery was the governing interest of the nation. The South claimed that human chattelism was entrenched in the constitution, and the people of the North, almost without exception, admitted that claim. Constitutionally and legally, it was not a question of race or color at all. The assumption was, *partus sequitur ventrem.* Once a slave forever a slave, whatever the race or complexion of the mother. Physical human slavery

no longer exists in any of the United States. It
abolished itself by its own inherent unwisdom.
It was not by any political foresight or integrity
of the North that it met its fate. The slave power
might have continued to govern the nation had it
not insisted on suppressing the freedom of speech
and the press by brute force, and on using the
national power to restore fugitive slaves. The
great civil war was by no means a crusade against
slavery, though it well enough might have been,
and probably would have been, if Captain John
Brown, instead of James Buchanan, had been
President of the United States.

Morally speaking, the crime of slavery resided
no less in the north than the south. New England ships imported the slaves from Africa and
sold them chiefly in the southern colonies, because there their labor was more profitable than
on the rugged hills of New Hampshire and Massachusetts. But even after the Declaration of
Independence, slaves were held in the northern
states. They were held in New York so late that
perhaps Myron Holley may have owned one for
domestic service in Canandaigua. Some others,
in his time, certainly did. But the institution
gradually faded out at the north, till "Mason and

Dixon's line" divided the slave states from the free, and in 1820 that line was extended, virtually, to the Pacific, by a "solemn" compromise.

Little did the great slaveholders of that day dream what was to happen in the next two or three decades. The Yankee Whitney, in giving them the cotton-gin, had opened to them a vision of wealth beyond all El Dorados. Cotton was now King, and the whole commerce of the north bowed the knee in allegiance to his majesty. The white race of the south, enriched by the labor of the slaves, had nothing to do but to govern the nation. The negroes raised the cotton, the sailors carried it to market, and Calhoun thought Charleston would soon be more powerful than London and Rome combined. Did not the soil of the south have more sunshine than that of the north, and the monopoly of a plant with which the subject looms of England and New England could clothe and bed the world?

But while the ingenious southern statesmen were dreaming these dreams, Myron Holley was patiently and enthusiastically digging that ditch through the marshes and swamps of New York, which in 1825 was to let the enterprising, well schooled white free laborers into the vast forests

of Ohio, Indiana and Michigan, and into the
boundless prairies of Illinois and Wisconsin.
These became rich states, while, as to the mass of
the white population, all the south became poor.
More and more the great trading metropolis of the
east, New York, derived its wealth rather from
this new west than from the south. By ten years
after the Missouri compromise, so cunningly contrived by Henry Clay, the north and new west
were ripe for a moral movement to emancipate
public sentiment from its servility to the slaveholders. This was an all-important step in the
solution of the great problem. The ignorant
masses of the great cities and large towns could
not be relied upon to aid it. It was too easy to
make them believe it was an attack on their means
of living rather than a vindication of their rights.
Even their patriotism, no less than their prejudices, was appealed to against it. Neither were
the powerful Christian sects, or churches, to be
relied on. To them it was a theological civil war.
And, as organizations, they stood by an institution which at the south was as much in the church
as in the world. As obstructions to the moral
movement, the churches were far more effective
than the mobs. The pulpit everywhere — with a

very few exceptions — either justified slavery from the scriptures, or denounced abolitionism as a pestilent sin.

The germ of the moral movement against slavery was in the heart and head of William Lloyd Garrison, a young printer, born in Newburyport, Mass., in 1805. His heart and head, from early manhood, were full of the Golden Rule and the Declaration of Independence. He had never been schooled into Jesuitism. Till it shone out in him, there had been no solid basis for any moral movement against the bad system, for even such a devoted abolitionist as Benjamin Lundy proposed only gradual emancipation, thus giving up both the Golden Rule and the Declaration. Garrison, when he joined Lundy, in Baltimore, in editing the "Genius of Universal Emancipation," in 1828, at the age of 23, advocated, with a most refreshing and contagious vigor, the duty of immediate abolition, personal and national. He denounced the pretension of property in human beings as absolutely false, and every act of ownership as a crime, law or no law. Here was a solid logical foundation, on which a man could stand without stultifying himself. When you asked a man or woman how would you like to be a chattel, sold on the auction block, even for a single day, there could be but one answer. For gradual emancipation, especially if accompanied with colonization or deportation of the emancipated, the slave power cared little, if anything. But Garrison's new doctrine was, in their view, treason to the state and blasphemy to the church. Of course it was not long before he was in a Baltimore prison, and it was on complaint of a Newburyport slave trader, whose name is elsewhere handed down to posterity. Arthur Tappan, a very benevolent Christian silk merchant of New York, effected his release. Garrison soon after established his famous LIBERATOR in Boston, which, in spite of all sorts of persecution, mobocratic and theocratic, continued to be issued weekly till the slaves were proclaimed free, at the close of the rebellion.

There never was a more foolish act of persecution — unless we except two or three recent instances against the free use of the United States mails — than throwing young Garrison into a Baltimore prison. It was terribly ominous of what happened to the Confederacy of Jefferson Davis about 37 years afterwards. If Garrison had been wrong, his doctrine would have died of itself. Right as it was, possibly it never would have triumphed if he and his followers had not been persecuted. He owed his success, seemingly, rather more to the folly of his persecutors than to his own wisdom and perseverance.

While Mr. Garrison deserves more glory than he has received, or perhaps ever will receive, for being the uncompromising leader of the moral movement against chattel slavery, he was subject to some, perhaps inevitable, but unfortunate, limitations. He accepted the prevalent theory that slavery was entrenched behind guarantees in the Federal constitution. So that he fought not only against the slave power, but against the constitution itself, as a "Covenant with death, and an agreement with hell," fondly quoting Jeremiah, whereas with a reasonable interpretation making the instrument consistent with itself, there was not a clause or word in it which could operate either as a guarantee or justification of chattelism or property in a human being.* On account of

---

* The fault of the Constitution was not that it authorized or guaranteed slavery, but that it did not, in express terms, forbid it. By fair implication it did. But ignoring the existence of the foul injustice, the framers of the instrument left it to be abolished by the states, giving Congress and the federal courts no power to act upon it, except in the District of Columbia, the territories and the commerce between the states. This was the "compromise." Doctor Franklin at

this opinion, apparently, if not on account of the
doctrine of non-resistance derived from the Sermon
on the Mount, in the New Testament, he confined
himself entirely to the moral movement, and never
encouraged any direct or distinct political action.
Such action, however, grew inevitably out of his
moral teaching, in spite of his personal aversion
to it.

Slavery begins in war, and there is no peace
till emancipation comes. Hence civil war existed
in the colonies and in the United States till 1865.
It was at first confined to the masters and slaves
as the belligerents. After the formation of the
American Anti-Slavery Society in 1833, it broke
out decidedly in the July mobs in New York, in

the time wrote to a bosom friend, who expostulated with him
about it : —

"It is a little sop to Cerberus—the best thing that can be
done at present—it cannot last long; there is too much virtue
in the country. As fast as men become *honest* they will drop
slavery. Every *honest* man knows the laborer is worthy
of his hire; and would just as soon keep your purse, that he
had found, because fortune put it in his possession, as he
would compel a poor man or woman to bear the heat and burden of the day for him without reward. There is not one
shade's difference between the two; and further,—

> What he to Afric's child would do,
>   He'd do to thee and thine.
> So guard your spoons and daughters too,
>   Whene'er he comes to dine."

1834. Slavery fired upon the peaceful settlers of Kansas before it did upon Fort Sumter.

The one man who did more than any other to start the political movement which culminated in 1860 in the victory of a party opposed to any further geographical extension of slavery was Myron Holley. At the latter date, with California and New Mexico added to the Union, it was plain enough to the slaveholders that if slavery could not be extended to them, the system, and the power founded upon it, was doomed. So they put themselves in the attitude of carrying out their chronic threat of dissolving the Union, and committed the serious military blunder of attacking Sumter, instead of occupying Washington. If the southern leaders had had the boldness of a good cause, or even the usual wisdom of a bad one, they would have stayed under the old flag at Washington, barred out Lincoln, and inaugurated Breckenridge. Their folly was fortunate for the slaves and for us all. Still, it was the grand political movement which grew out of the little Liberty Party of 1840 that drove the slaveholders into this folly. The party that voted for Fremont in 1856 and for Lincoln in 1860, was as clearly the natural result of that which voted for Birney in

1840 and 1844, as an oak is of a well-planted acorn.* It was the last great labor of Mr. Holley's

* The growth of the Liberty Party, through the names of Free Soil and Republican, up to victory, is evidenced by the following series of figures, giving the votes cast against the pro-slavery candidates, compared with the whole popular vote, in six presidential elections : —

	Liberty.		Free Soil.		Republican.	
Year, ...	1840.	1844.	1848.	1851.	1856.	1860.
Candidates,. . .	Birney.	Birney.	VanBuren.	Hale.	Frem'nt.	Lincoln.
Votes, ...	7,069	62,263	291,342	155,825	1,341,264	1,857,610
Presidents elected {	Harrison & Tyler.	Polk.	Taylor & Fillm're.	Pierce.	B'chan'n.	Linc'ln.
Whole vote, . .	2,395,900	2,678,121	2,872,056	3,143,679	4,053,967	4,645,390

Though Lincoln did not have a majority of the popular vote, he had a large majority of the electors, and really represented a vast majority of the people, counting as people all the women and enslaved men—not allowed to vote—and also a majority of the virtue, intelligence and worth.

The Liberty vote in 1840 seems ridiculously small compared with the whole vote, and it was fairly so compared with the voting abolitionists, then embodied in Anti-Slavery Societies, who could have numbered not less than 70,000. It was generally reported by the newspapers — if at all—as "scattering." The following are the official returns, as collected by Mr. Greeley, though he does not give any for Indiana, where some votes were certainly cast for Birney.

VOTES FOR BIRNEY AND EARLE IN 1840.

Maine, ...	194	New York,. . . .	2,808
New Hampshire,. .	126	New Jersey, . . .	69
Massachusetts, . .	1,621	Pennsylvania,. . .	343
Vermont, ...	319	Ohio,.	903
Rhode Island, . . .	42	Michigan, . . .	321
Connecticut, . . .	174	Illinois, ...	149
New England, . .	2,476	Other states, . .	4,593
			2,476
		Total, .	7,069

life to plant that acorn. It grew in the soil his earlier labors watered, and which his recent labors had been ploughing and harrowing. His life had been making both the physical and moral preparation for the growth of such a party. He was just the broad, sensible, far-seeing man to be the father of it. And it will go down to the remotest future that he was; — that he, almost alone, of all the prominent abolitionists of his day, insisted on planting the acorn when it was planted; and but for him it certainly would not have been planted then, if ever.

It was not till the winter of 1837, when Mr. Holley had become comfortably established in his new home of Rose Ridge, on the Genesee, two or three miles below Rochester, that he began to take a practical interest in the slavery question. His son-in-law, Hon. Graham H. Chapin, was then in Congress, and under date of Feb. 23 he writes to his daughter Caroline, who was with her husband in Washington: "The things most deeply interesting to me in the proceedings of Congress,

---

The "Political Text Book" of Greeley and Cleveland, and Johnston's "American Politics," state the total as 7,609, but this is by an error of transposing figures. The Liberty men, however, were right in saying that they had in 1840 "seven thousand men who had not bowed the knee to Baal."

during the present session, relate to the question of slavery. And these things I am persuaded will become more and more interesting at every future session of the national legislature, till slavery is abolished. By the same mail which carries this I send to Mr. Chapin a copy of an abolition address which I delivered here at Rochester a short time ago. If you or Mr. Chapin read it, you will perceive that it is written without passion, and that it was prepared without reference to many documents. At Washington I presume a diligent inquirer might find many evidences of the state of public opinion in all the states on this subject, at and subsequent to the Declaration of Independence. A collection of such documents, copious and authentic, would be very valuable. As Mr. Adams, the late President, has read and preserved everything almost connected with every question agitated much in the course of our national progress, I have thought that he may have made a speech which is published with reference to such documents. If he has, it would oblige me very much to receive a copy of it."

But for the "abolition address" here referred to, Mr. Holley would probably soon have been in Congress himself. He was by far the ablest representative that could then be sent from his district. His long anti-masonic service was in his favor, rather than otherwise. The whig party controlled at that time a decided majority in the district, and offered the nomination to Mr. Holley, on the condition that he would not agitate the slavery question. He rejected it, rather than be gagged on that question, for to act against slavery was all that could tempt him to leave his family and his delightful home. Congress, in those days, lost many valuable members by such action of the dominant political parties. William Leggett, of New York, was a signal instance, in the democratic party. As editor of the *N. Y. Evening Post*, he had shamed the city authorities into suppressing the anti-abolition mobs of 1834, and his party dared not trust him in Congress without a padlock on his lips, on that subject.

But the abolitionists who were then organizing with zeal in all parts of the free states, were wise enough to avail themselves of such a champion as Mr. Holley, and in Dec. 1838, he writes to his daughter Mrs. Kingman, at the close of a long and interesting letter in which he pictures the happiness of family ties, " I intend in a day or two to go out in this county and give lectures upon anti-slavery, and after trying it a week, if I can stand it pretty well, to continue it for three months. I am offered $130 for such services three months." The testimony of those who heard them is, that no lectures made a deeper or more lasting impression than his.

On the 7th of February, 1839, there occurred in the Senate of the United States the most astounding declaration of sentiments on the slavery question which ever proceeded from the lips of any man called a statesman in the nineteenth or perhaps any previous century. It may fairly be considered as the declaration of that war which ended at Appomattox. The dominant citizens of the District of Columbia, of course slaveholders, had got up a petition to Congress praying it to stop the agitation of the slavery question by refusing to receive any petitions for its abolition, there or elsewhere, and it was of course signed by hundreds of non-slaveholders, who, whatever might be their opinions, did not dare to refuse. This was placed for presentation in the hands of Henry Clay, whose voice in its favor would obviously be more effective than that of John C. Calhoun. Mr. Clay in presenting it, outdid all that Calhoun had ever done, and at once received the hearty congratulations of that champion of human bondage. The great orator of Grecian Liberty, the legislator who had won the hearts of the northern Crœsuses by his "American," or tariff protection "system," here made the mistake of his life and threw away his chance of being either the next president, or the next but one. His expressed terror lest the morality of the Declaration of Independence should get into the ballot-box, induced at least a few of the "ultra-abolitionists" to resolve that it should go there without loss of time, — and stay there till it should effect its object.

Mr. Clay was, in any good cause, probably the most forcefully eloquent man who ever spoke in the Senate of the United States, or in the popular house. On this occasion he exhausted his electrical energy, and there never was a more diabolical justification of a diabolical institution, as will be seen by consulting the *Appendix of the Congressional Globe*, Vol. 7, page 355, where it stands carefully revised by himself. Here are some of his exact words with his own italics :

" Mr. President, it is at this alarming stage of the proceedings of the ultra-abolitionists that I would seriously invite every considerate man in the country

solemnly to pause, and deliberately to reflect, not merely
on our existing posture, but upon that dreadful precipice
down which they would hurry us. It is because these
ultra-abolitionists have ceased to employ the instruments
of reason and persuasion, have made their cause political, and have appealed to the ballot-box, that I am
induced upon this occasion to address you. . . . .

"I know that there is a visionary dogma which holds
that negro slaves cannot be the subject of property. I
shall not dwell long with this speculative abstraction.
That *is* property which the law declares *to be* property.
Two hundred years of legislation have sanctioned and
sanctified negro slaves as property. Under all the
forms of government which have existed upon this
continent during that long space of time — under the
British government — under the Colonial government
— under all the State constitutions and governments —
and under the Federal government itself — they have
been deliberately and solemnly recognized as the legi-
mate subjects of property. To the wild speculations
of theorists and innovators stands opposed the *fact*,
that in an uninterrupted period of two hundred years
duration, under every form of human legislation, and
by all the departments of human government, African
negro slaves have been held and respected, have descended and been transferred, as lawful and indisputable property."

He then goes on to cite as a British concession
of the right of property the paying of £20,000,-
000 to free the slaves in the West Indies, and proceeds, with stupendous audacity, to say : —

" If, therefore, these ultra-abolitionists are sincerely determined to pursue their scheme of immediate abolition, they should at once set about raising a fund of twelve hundred millions of dollars to indemnify the owners of slave property. And the taxes to raise that enormous amount can only be justly assessed upon themselves, or upon the free states, if they can persuade them to assent to such an assessment ; for it would be a mockery of all justice, and an outrage against all equity, to lay any portion of the tax upon the slave states to pay for their own unquestioned property."

In thus converting the slave power into a money power the astute politician forgot how the people had lately overthrown a money power of only some sixty millions, and still dreaded its recovering ascendancy. If there was concentrated at the south another 20 times as great, what could they expect but eternal subjection to it? Two days later an honest democrat, Thomas Morris, of Ohio, who had seldom opened his lips in the Senate during the five previous years, presented the petitions of thousands of abolitionists in Ohio, praying for abolition in the District of Columbia, with an exceedingly modest but manly speech, which deserves to be in all our school books. One of its points was that Mr. Clay's money power of twelve hundred millions had only to join the great

Biddle Bank monopoly to extinguish our liberties and rule the world.

Undoubtedly this atrocious and thoroughly brutal speech of Henry Clay excited a profound emotion in the breast of Myron Holley. For him it struck at the foundation not only of his politics but his religion. I have already said he was a deeply religious man. But his religion, though he took for granted that it grew out of the Bible, where the slaveholders also found their sanction, was really better expressed by the Declaration of Independence. He was that sort of Christian that for some years he had found a more congenial atmosphere outside of churches than in them, and was very commonly spoken of as an infidel. Being invited to deliver an oration in Perry, N.Y., on the Fourth of July, 1839, he took occasion to give his views of the slavery question at considerable length. A few extracts from this production will serve to show the logic which underpinned the Liberty Party.

FRIENDS AND FELLOW CITIZENS.— To honor our parents is a natural duty, of which the obligation is equally plain and imperative. It is the first commandment with promise; and no man is so dull as not to perceive its beneficial tendency. Those who bring us into being, who nourish, protect, instruct, encourage

and guide us, are entitled to our gratitude, reverence
and obedience. Their affectionate solicitude and continual labor for our well-being and advancement, can
be repaid only by our performance of all our filial
obligations.

Enlarging the application of this natural duty beyond
the confines of the domestic hearth, we are assembled
this day to offer a reasonable homage to our civil fathers.
Never has human life presented a day so worthy to be
consecrated to such homage as that which we are
engaged in celebrating ; and never were a people bound
to their civil fathers, by obligations so numerous, precious and persuasive, as those under which it is our
privilege to live. With what words — with what
emotions — with what principles — does it become all
the children of this great republic, to mark the anniversary of their national freedom, and to honor its
illustrious founders ! Every honest heart will respond
— with none but the words of truth and soberness —
with none but emotions of the most expansive patriotism — with none but the principles of equal and
universal liberty can they be duly marked and honored.

The day we celebrate was not one of inconsiderate
exultation or unmanly depression — of unchastened
revelry, or gloomy mortification — of frivolous distinctions, or unproductive ceremony. It was a day when
good men spoke freely, and sincerely and ardently —
when they thought anxiously and intensely, but clearly
and candidly — when they acted bravely, consistently
and perseveringly. The great subjects which filled
their minds were the rights, duties, improvement and
happiness of social life. These subjects they examined
and discussed, with an earnestness, comprehension and

sagacity new in the history of nations, because they regarded them with the deep interest of the most extensive and permanent self-application : and the results at which they arrived, they resolved to maintain, with the legitimate force of truth, with a fortitude which no trial could discourage, and with a philanthropy the most unlimited and beneficent. Their labors, their sufferings, their achievements, their disinterestedness, have excited the sympathies and admiration of mankind. Their words have already come to be considered as the living, imperishable and inspiring accents of freedom. Their thoughts are set in the polished framework of our constitutions, where they glow and shine, with unclouded and genial lustre, for our warmth and guidance ; and where, I devoutly trust, they will continue to glow and shine, with lustre undiminished, till, like the lights in the firmament of heaven, they warm and guide the world.

He then proceeds to describe the character of the men who peopled our continent from the old world. They were chiefly law-abiding, but more disposed to value themselves as creations of the Supreme Being than as subjects of the state. They were men who could not be driven from their sense of duty by any amount of persecuting force. How those men faced, defied and overthrew British usurpation, he depicts in vivid colors.

They were republicans. They loved liberty, as indispensable to all pure enjoyment and elevated hope.

They looked upon it as of God's appointment, without which there could be neither right, nor duty, nor improvement, nor happiness — and these were the ends of their creation — the great objects of their care for themselves and for their children. They had been born and bred to freedom. They had long inquired, and conversed, and learnt, and labored, and loved, and hated, and lived without unreasonable restraint. And they could bear everything better than *to think* under the supervision of human authority ; to *talk* in a bondsman's key ; to *profess* opinions they did not entertain ; to *countenance* sentiments they despised ; to *feel* the new-forged collars of servitude burning and blistering their bodies, and their inevitable effects corrupting the immortal wealth and obscuring the inextinguishable light of their souls.

They fought ; they conquered. Their outward preparation was small, and their muster mean to the eye. But they had the highest and holiest preparation of the heart and understanding. Their battle was gallant and long sustained against the most formidable odds. Their cause was the mighty cause of the human race, and the Great Being who keeps that cause as the apple of his eye, crowned it with success. The names of our fathers will be forever sweet in the mouths of men. Their praise is already in all the earth. And every nation shall yet repeat, throughout all its multitudes, and in the fullest joy of self-appropriation, the glad song of their victory.

Showing how the republican government commenced its career on principles that did not admit the existence of slavery, and how it practically

excluded it from the common territory of the
states, and how the universal expectation was that
it would cease in twenty years, he proceeds to say :

Since our nation was thus solemnly pledged against
it, slavery has increased in the United States more than
in any country in the world. It has multiplied five-
fold. More slaves are now annually smuggled into this
country than ever were imported in any single year of
our colonial existence, and there are, probably, more
open slave-traders in the southern states than there are
on the whole Guinea coast of Africa. The nations of
the earth, in the aggregate, have scarcely more capital
embarked, in this detestable traffic, on the high seas,
at this moment, than the great Atlantic cities of this
Union have, and derive less pecuniary profit from it.
Virginia sells annually, of her own native children, into
the most cruel bondage, to the estimated amount of ten
millions of dollars. The merchants in New York alone
have legal claims upon the persons of men, women and
children, endowed with the same natural rights as they
enjoy, to secure debts, as upon articles of property, to
another amount estimated at ten millions. Our national
authorities have given to the trade in slaves imported
from Africa, the name of piracy, and have then winked
at its perpetration by pardoning convicts under the act,
and by permitting the sale of imported slaves in our
country! They have admitted new states into the
Union, in which all that industry which constitutes the
great basis of national wealth was to be discouraged,
by the infamy and restraints of slavery ; and yet, in
consequence of this infamy, the authors of it are to

enjoy political power to dispose of national wealth, and determine who shall fill the most important of our public offices, much greater than that of an equal number of honest freemen. They have purchased immense Territories, at the common cost of the nation, in which they have extended the institution of slavery and the same unjust political power. And they, by sheer usurpation, have introduced laws creating slavery in the District of Columbia, and have long witnessed there the sale of free citizens to pay jail fees, by their own officers, without any expression of disapprobation, thus destroying all justice and humanity in the spot consecrated by the name of Washington — where the national honor especially dwells, and where they are constitutionally endowed with the right to legislate, in all cases whatsoever.

At this moment the two great political parties of our country, sharing the favorable wishes, exertions, and purses of a majority of the people fancying themselves free, are emulously exerting themselves to cast the highest honor of the nation upon men, one of whom has prostrated his dignity and insulted the nation by committing himself to oppose the abolition of slavery in the district (where it exists only in defiance of the Constitution which he has sworn to support), until such abolition is consented to by the slave States! and the other of whom has publicly affirmed that human beings may become property, chattels, articles of traffic, whenever barbarous and sordid legislation shall so enact; and he a man, too, who, as a representative of this nation, a few years ago, signed his name to a treaty in which the traffic in slaves is said to be irreconcilable with humanity and justice, and publicly bound his country to use its best endeavors to effect its entire abolition! Many men of intelligence, abilities, high station, and influence, at the South, have come out before the public and represented slavery as a blessing, and these men and their abettors have violated the highest rights of their free countrymen, and all the obligations of the constitution, to prevent its discussion, and to hinder the spread of free principles. They are sustained by the apathy or open support of a large majority of politicians, professing Christians, and printing-presses, in all the free States. Nowhere in the land consecrated by the ashes of Washington and Jefferson, is any man, professing openly their most important sentiments, safe from the cowhide or tar-barrel, the bowie knife or the rifle-ball. In the person of Amos Dresser, freedom and Christianity were publicly scourged in Tennessee! In the person of Aaron W. Kitchell, they were rode on a rail, and tarred and feathered in Georgia! In the person of Peter John Lee, they were kidnapped and sold into slavery in New York! In the person of J. B. Mahan, they were ruthlessly delivered up in Ohio, and sent for long incarceration in Kentucky! In the person of E. P. Lovejoy, they were murdered in Illinois! "O! what a fall was there, my countrymen! Then you and I, and all of us, fell down, whilst bloody treason flourished over us!" And yet government—the government set up by our fathers—framed upon the model of Christianity, under the wing of which they trusted their children, and children's children, would forever sit in security, was, in the entire letter, yet existing. Its spirit and provisions were standing out on the unmutilated face of the national charter, in obvious and direct condemnation of these enormities.   This spirit and these provisions can take effect only through human agency, and the administrators of the government can alone employ such agency.   But they said nothing, did nothing.   Worse than this, they encouraged these atrocities, and committed others of equal enormity.   Deputy post-masters rifled the mails with which they were officially entrusted. The post-master general, sworn to guard that great depar ment of public power from all illegal encroachment, when openly apprised of these proceedings, refused not only to discharge the delinquents, but even to censure them!   And the President of the United States lent all his influence to countenance these alarming assaults upon the common rights of the people, and officially recommended measures to extend them!

How can the principles of our government be reinstated and perpetuated?   I answer, by resorting to the same powers through which they were originally established.   These powers, we have seen, were the inculcation of moral and religious truth, by precept and example, and the application of it to all the purposes of government.   The practical application of truth to government is political action.

It has become fashionable with many of late to degrade the word political into a signification narrow, sordid, grovelling, selfish, and personal.   This is because those who have chiefly controlled it have betrayed it to services characterized by these epithets.   It should have, and may have, a much higher meaning; and must be wholly reclaimed from its base significance, or the memory of our fathers and the hopes of their children will perish.

It was eloquence of this sort that kindled a fire in Central New York which the political leaders could not entirely ignore, which caused the Whigs, at their convention in Harrisburg, Dec. 4, 1839, to set aside their favorite Henry Clay, and nominate Wm. Henry Harrison on no platform at all. He was a northern man, with no principles about slavery which had ever been very distinctly declared; but the slaveholders, with good reason, trusted him, having a vice-president of their own behind him. He was elected, and both Webster and Granger had to sell themselves to the slave-power for places in his Cabinet.

But before Harrison was nominated, Myron Holley's eloquence, wisdom and perseverance, in spite of the wrong-headedness, timidity and stupidity of the mass of the abolitionists, had put in nomination a hero and patriot worthy of the name, a man against whom, four years later, the Whigs ventured to pit Henry Clay, and by that act won an ignominious defeat.

It must be understood that the great body of the abolitionists, previous to Mr. Clay's declaration of sentiments in 1839, were solid against any distinct political action or party organization. The American Anti-Slavery Society had repeatedly put itself on record against it. The most that was recommended was to vote for the candidate who was most favorable to the abolition of slavery in the District and Territories, of whichever party he might be. It could only have been at this very harmless use of the ballot-box that the great Whig orator took alarm. The times were terribly hard, and many of the abolition organs stopped for want of patronage. In the face of Mr. Clay's speech, which, if anything could, would have aroused all the voting abolitionists to act together as a unit, even so late as October, 1839, a great State Anti-Slavery Convention at Cleveland, Ohio, went largely against separate nominations. But at that convention appeared Myron Holley, who brought forward a proposition to make an immediate nomination of President and Vice-President. It was opposed by President Mahan, of Oberlin, Blodget, Wade, and others. "This," says the *Emancipator*, "called up Mr. Holley, who made a most gallant defence of his resolution. When he spoke of the dignity of the elective franchise, and the solemn responsibility of every elector to use it firmly and save the Republic, he was surprisingly eloquent." He failed to find any support. With exceptions that could be counted on

the fingers, the 400 delegates present at that convention entirely failed to appreciate the hope-
lessly pro-slavery attitude of the two parties, or
that true power of the ballot-box, which Clay had
so overwhelmingly demonstrated. Nothing can
better illustrate this than Henry B. Stanton's
reply to a letter which had been written him just
before the convention, urging him to use all his
influence to have the nomination made then and
there, and let it be followed up by other conven-
tions as they should take place.*

* This letter was strictly confidential, and rather hasty.
Of course, it was not laid before the Convention. But being
stolen from Mr. Stanton's hat while dining at a hotel, it was
soon after published in the *Liberator*, as an effective mis-
sile against the " new organization."
   That organization doubtless had in it men actuated by unworthy motives and prejudices. It certainly had in it some
men of genuine anti-slavery zeal, and some martyrs. What
attracted to it some highly practical men was, that, at the
start, it favored, or professed to favor, distinct political
action, while the " old organization" bitterly opposed it.
The old organization, however, must have the credit of man-
fully asserting the *rights of woman*, which the new one soon
turned out to oppose, and thus put itself miserably in the
wrong. Gladly would the Slave Power have seen this feud,
on "the woman question," absorb all the energies of both
sides, for it well knew that the male religion of Christendom,
from its inventor, Paul, downwards, was the Power which
held woman in mental bondage [see the great historian,
Michelet's *Le pretre, la femme et la famille*], and that negro-
slavery would be safe for a century or two, if that was to be
settled *first*. Such men as Henry B. Stanton, Samuel E.

CLEVELAND, Monday, Oct. 28, '39.

DEAR WRIGHT, — I believe your brother, whom I saw at our meeting, is to give you a notice of it for the *Abolitionist*, therefore I will simply answer your good letter, for which I thank you.

Myron Holley brought forward the subject of nominating Anti-Slavery candidates for Pres. and V. P. The discussion lasted ½ an afternoon, the whole of an evening, and ½ a forenoon. The proposition was finally laid on the table. My main reason for voting for this disposition of it was this : — To have nominated candidates would have been a surprise on the great mass of our friends.

Nothing of the kind was indicated in the call. It was a local meeting, called for special objects at the west. It was local in its representation, being confined chiefly to Ohio. The measure was as extraordi-

Sewall and William Jackson had not a word to say against granting to woman every right, political, social, financial or religious, claimed by man. Nor had JOHN G. WHITTIER, whose "PASTORAL LETTER," crying "shame on ye, parish popes," will ring down the coming ages till there shall not be a male politician or judge mean enough to refuse to his mother or his wife any right or privilege which he claims for himself. But they thought it wise to postpone this question till the slaveholders were brought to their senses.

Mr. Oliver Johnson, the venerable and amiable historian of the *Life and Times of Wm. Lloyd Garrison*, in a private letter to the writer, demurs to, or rather denies, the statement that the "*streak letter*," so called, was stolen. He must settle that question with Mr. Stanton. Mr. Garrison must have known that the publication of that letter put its author in a cruelly false position with some of his best friends, because in his haste he used the phrase, "this confounded woman question," without explaining it.

nary as would have been a dissolution of the Society, and therefore our auxiliary societies would have been aggrieved by it. greatly. A nomination made before we see whether the parties will put up anybody for whom we can go, would, by the mass of our friends, have been deemed premature — and had we made a nomination, and the Whigs had put up Scott and John Davis, and *we had called a Convention in New York State to nominate an A. S. electoral ticket, that Convention would have declared it inexpedient to do so, and thus nullified the whole thing.* It would have been thought a trick; getting away out here and doing what we knew we could not do at the centre.

No; so extraordinary a move as the nomination of national candidates, in my opinion, should not be made by the Am. Society without due notice to that effect. Give due notice, and then all are bound to take notice, and be present, or forever after hold their peace.

This is my plan. Wait till both parties have nominated [the Democratic did not do it till May 5, 1840], and then if Clay and Van Buren are the men, call a great Convention to consider the wisdom of nominating. This will go strong. Anything short of this would split the Society and prove a failure.

Our meeting was a grand one. 400 Delegates. No miserable woman question, non-resistance, nor 15-minute rule to perplex, confuse and gag us.

Haste, thine, H. B. S.

As we have seen, Clay was not the man, but the North Bend hero, who had declared that the discussion of slavery was unconstitutional and that "the schemes of the Abolitionists were fraught with horrors upon which an incarnate devil only could look with approbation."

The *Liberator* rejoiced over the defeat of Mr. Holley at Cleveland, as having saved the Anti-Slavery cause from being dashed on the breakers. But Mr. Holley was not discouraged. He had already procured the passage of a resolution in favor of a distinct nomination, in the Monroe County Anti-Slavery Convention a few days previous, and on the 13th of November a much larger Convention assembled at Warsaw, N. Y. There he laid out his full strength, and carried the meeting as by storm. There was made the first Presidential nomination for the celebrated "Log Cabin and Hard Cider Campaign" of 1840. The following letter conveyed the intelligence to the leading candidate, and must have taken him somewhat by surprise: —

ROCHESTER, 18th Nov., 1839.

Hon. JAMES G. BIRNEY:

DEAR SIR. — As a committee of an abolition convention held the 13th and 14th days of this month, at Warsaw, in Genesee County, we beg leave to address you. The convention after having adopted, with great harmony, a resolution expressive of their opinion, that every motive of duty and expediency, which ought to control the action of a Christian freeman, required the abolitionists of the United States to organize an independent political party, for securing their great object, proceeded to nominate suitable persons to be supported for election to the offices of president and vice-president of the United States, at the next presidential canvass. And subsequently, on the report of a committee, the convention concurred, unanimously, in the nomination of James G. Birney, of New York, for the first office above referred to, and Francis J. Lemoyne, of Pennsylvania, for the second.

A summary account of the proceedings of the convention at Warsaw having been already forwarded to you, and relying fully upon your just appreciation of the object and motives of the convention, and the vast importance of the distinct political action of the abolitionists, we earnestly hope you will favor us with your consent to the use of your name, in conformity with the wish of the convention. To obtain such consent is the object of this communication. Devoted as we are, and as we know the convention to be, to the most active support of the nominations above referred to, and firmly persuaded that the great anti-slavery enterprise can never succeed, without the organization of an independent abolition party; and that such organization can never commence at a time so auspicious as the present, nor under names more acceptable to the community, we repeat the hope, that you will concur with the views of the convention, and favor us, at your convenience, with the expression of your concurrence.

In behalf of the convention, we are, sir, with great respect, your ob't serv'ts.

MYRON HOLLEY,

JOSHUA H. DARLING,

JOSIAH ANDREWS,

Committee of Corres.

Both candidates declined to accept this nomination. Dr. Francis Julius Lemoyne, a working abolitionist of Washington Co., Pennsylvania, out of sheer modesty, and because it would interfere with his profession; and Mr. Birney, because he preferred not to accept it till it could come from a nationally called convention. But it at once struck hundreds of abolitionists, in all parts of the country, that the nomination of James G. Birney was one exceedingly fit to be made. He had stood so high in Alabama, before he became an abolitionist and emancipated his slaves, that the highest judicial office in the state was within his reach; in case of election he would have stood in all points of dignity and statesmanship above the average of presidents; he had faced detraction and mob violence with the grandest heroism and moral success; in every point of view he was a man so immeasurably superior to either Harrison or Tyler, that as soon as these men were put on the Whig ticket, every intelligent abolitionist, who could vote at all, saw an excellent opportunity of using his suffrage against such candidates with self-respect and a good conscience. Accordingly, soon after the Whig nomination, a call was extensively signed by leading abolitionists for a National Convention to meet at Albany, April 1, 1840, to take into consideration the formation of a Liberty Party.

The movement was ridiculed by abolitionists opposed to political action, as the April Fool convention. Nevertheless, it assembled to the number of at least 76 members — generally self-elected — from six states. The opponents of political action took care to be well represented, especially from Albany and Troy. The Convention promptly assembled in the City Hall, the use of which had been courteously granted by the City Council, and 121 members were enrolled. It was quite obvious that many of them, though professing abolitionism, had enrolled themselves on purpose to vote against distinct nominations. The Convention was organized by the election of the following officers :

PRESIDENT:

Alvan Stewart, N. Y.

VICE-PRESIDENTS:

Benjamin Shaw, Vt.
John A. Paine, N. J.
Ichabod Codding, Me.
Charles T. Torrey, Mass.

SECRETARIES:

L. P. Noble, N. Y.
Joshua Leavitt, N. J.

COMMITTEE ON BUSINESS AND RESOLUTIONS.

Myron Holley, N. Y.
Joshua Leavitt, N. J.
Ichabod Codding, Me.
Elizur Wright, Jr., Mass.
Edwin W. Clarke, N. Y.

COMMITTEE OF CORRESPONDENCE.

Alvan Stewart, N. Y.
Gerrit Smith, N. Y.
Wm. Goodell, N. Y.

Letters approving the proposed object of the Convention were read from J. P. Miller, of Vt., J. G. Whittier, of Mass., Gerrit Smith, H. N. Robinson and Hiram Corliss, of N. Y., from B. F. Hoffman, Levi Sutliff and O. Clark, of Ohio, and from Thomas Earle, of Penn. These gentlemen regretted their inability to attend the Convention, and their words of cheer proved their regret so genuine, that it was fully equalled by that of their friends who were present.

On the first day, and the morning of the second, while the Convention was waiting for the Report of the Business Committee, speeches were in order, and a good many of them were designed to drench the object of the Convention with cold water in advance. One, particularly, by Rev. S. S. Beman, D. D., of Troy, which immediately preceded the report, displayed a great power and

aptitude for ridicule. The reverend Dr. treated
the principles of the abolitionists with the highest
respect, but depicted the means they proposed to
employ in so inadequate and grotesque a light,
and with such a lambent lightning of wit, that if
the question of nominating had been voted on
immediately after he sat down, the Convention
would have been a failure and a joke worthy of
the date.

Mr. Holley reported the Resolutions, of which
he was the author, about eleven o'clock, A.M., and
occupied nearly two hours in a speech advocating
the first, which was taken separately, as a test,
and was to be voted on by *yeas* and *nays*. Comparatively few members of the Convention knew
of him, and what they did know was, perhaps,
colored by prejudice. But his presence was simply grand. His voice was smooth, distinct, mu-
sical, intensely human. The contrast of his
weighty, earnest sentences, with the badinage of
Dr. Beman, must have been painful even to that
master of raillery. He had not spoken five
minutes before many eyes began to moisten, and
he commanded the rapt attention of every auditor
till he took his seat. The remark was common
afterwards : " That was the most eloquent speech I

ever heard." "Eloquent," said one member, "is no name for it. It was divine." At all events, it went to many hearts. If the *yeas* and *nays* had been taken immediately, there would probably have been few of the latter. But the Convention took a recess for dinner, and in the afternoon the opponents rallied a little. Dr. Beman had already exhausted his forensic ammunition, and confined himself to private influence. Rev. David Root, Moses Breck, and Calvin Pepper, Jr., a young lawyer of Albany, successively took the floor, and did their best to turn the tide, and establish an ebb. But they were met by such men as Beriah Green, Joshua Leavitt, L. P. Noble and others, and at last Alvan Stewart left the chair, and in a few words, which would have put back-bone into mollusks, closed the debate. The close belonged to Mr. Holley, but he said, "Let us not waste time," and the *yeas* and *nays* were then called. Forty-four of the 121 enrolled members declined to vote, and let their names drop out of history. Those who did vote, put themselves on record, as follows :

Yeas.

MAINE, . . .	Ichabod Codding, . .	Hallowell.
VERMONT, . .	Benjamin Shaw, . . .	Weston.
	Charles Sexton, . .	Burlington.

MASSACHUSETTS,	Charles Smith, . . .	Middlefield.
	John E. Cathcart, . .	Williamsburgh.
	Charles T. Torrey, . .	Worcester.
	Joseph Hulburt, . . .	Curtisville.
	Josiah Hayden, . . .	Haydenville.
	Thomas W. Ward, . .	Shrewsbury.
	Elizur Wright, Jr., . .	Boston.
CONNECTICUT, .	M. G. Pierce, ...	Middletown.
NEW YORK, . .	L. P. Noble, ...	New York.*
	E. W. Goodwin, . . .	Albany.
	Benjamin Paul.	
	Joseph Strain.	
	E. P. Freeman.	
	Samuel Martin.	
	James Porter.	
	Christopher Hepinstall.	
	Daniel E. Bassett, . .	Poughkeepsie.
	Samuel Thompson, . .	"
	John Wilkinson Sleight,	Dover.
	William Barnes, . . .	Johnstown.
	S. S. Wheeler, . . .	Athens.
	D. R. Norris, ...	Warsaw.
	E. M. K. Glen, . . .	Minnville.
	Myron Holley, ...	Rochester.
	Isaac Pierce, ...	New York.
	William Goodell, . . .	Utica.
	Alvan Stewart, . . .	"
	Edmund C. Pritchett, .	"
	Beriah Green, ...	Whitesboro.
	E. W. Stewart, . . .	Camden.
	J. N. T. Tucker, . . .	Apulia.
	E. Willard Frisbie, . .	Phelps.
	James Brown, ...	Oswego.
	E. W. Clarke, ...	"

* This residence may be erroneous. I think Mr. Noble hailed from northern New York at that time. The residence of the six following Mr. Goodwin, is not indicated in the report, but probably it was Albany.

New York,	D. Cushman,	Exeter.
	Geo. W. Peavy,	Troy.
	G. W. Roberts,	"
	Wm. S. Gates,	Scoharie.
New Jersey,	Joshua Leavitt,	Bloomfield.
	John A. Paine,	Newark.

—43

Nays.

Massachusetts,	Moses Breck,	Northampton.
	David Root,	"
	Levi Stockbridge,	North Hadley.
New York,	Calvin Pepper, Jr.,	Albany.
	T. Fassett.*	
	Israel Smith.	
	R. Winslow.	
	W. B. Sims.	
	John Alden.	
	A. G. Alden.	
	S. J. Penniman.	
	H. Blackmore.	
	A. Stowell.	
	S. A. Parmelee.	
	William Crapo.	
	W. Tillinghast,	
	Geo. Cuyler,	Albany.
	Thomas Little,	New York.
	E. A. Lambert,	"
	A. Wheeler,	"
	Samuel Lightbody,	Utica.
	John Rhodes,	Troy.
	R. Wales,	"
	P. A. Moon,	"
	W. H. Seymour,	"
	H. G. Hayner,	"

* The names without indication of residence were probably all from Albany or Troy. From the latter certainly came two leading party politicians, one a whig and the other a democrat, both *nays!*

New York, . . Sam. N. Lawrence, . . Troy.
               William Stimpson, . .   "
               Charles Sheldon, . .   "
               N. C. P. Ives, . .   . West Troy.
               Gurdon Grant, ...   "
               George Brainerd.
               Uriah Moore.

—33

Among the *yeas* were men who had plenty of office within their reach, if they would suppress their humanity, men who could face present contempt and ridicule out of respect to themselves, — and among the *nays* were some who could not. This crisis passed successfully, the names of JAMES GILLESPIE BIRNEY, and THOMAS EARLE were inserted in the second Resolution, which Mr. Holley had reported in blank, by a unanimous and *viva voce* AYE, and the whole series was passed as reported with some trifling verbal amendments. There never was a fairer or more patent victory of good temper and pure reason over the stupid *vis inertiæ* of stereotyped conservatism. It seemed as if the broad humanity and sound common sense of the Fathers of the Republic had come down there.

Liberty Party Resolutions always occupied space enough to be exhaustive and leave no escape for a "doughface." This admirable series is too

long to be copied here. It ought to have dis-
armed all opposition among the abolitionists, for
it is conceived in the most catholic spirit, and
expresses nothing but cordial approbation of the
moral action of those who confined themselves to
that. But I cannot abstain from copying the
preamble to the nominating Resolution, which is
as follows :

Whereas, large bodies of freemen, in the United
States, have adopted the pledge embodied in the constitution of the American Anti-Slavery Society, " to do
all that is lawfully in our power, to bring about the ex-
tinction of slavery ; "

And *whereas*, a National Convention of Abolitionists
holden in this city on the 1st of August, 1839, solemnly
and deliberately resolved that they would neither vote
for, nor support the election of any man for President
or Vice President of the United States, who is not in
favor of the immediate abolition of slavery ; And
whereas, in the judgment of this Convention, it becomes
the anti-slavery electors of our country to unite their
votes upon well qualified candidates for these high
offices at the ensuing election, and, in our estimation,
no such candidates are yet nominated and none are
likely to be, without our interference ; Therefore, Resolved, That we owe it to the sacred cause of HUMAN
RIGHTS, and our desire to advance it by all peaceful and
constitutional means, to make such nomination, &c.

This movement of Myron Holley, — for the
Liberty Party was practically his achievement, —

cannot be historically appreciated without a view of the cotemporary public opinion and feeling, which can only be learned by the way in which the public press, both anti-slavery and pro-slavery, religious and political, received it. A few examples out of hundreds that could be cited, must suffice.

It is with pain I cite the expressions of the *Liberator*, for Mr. Garrison was the author of that most weighty and imperative sentence which Mr. Holley quotes in the first clause of the preamble to his first resolution. That he could so descend and go back on those who would follow the straight path he had himself so nobly and clearly marked out, is a sad proof of the weakness and imperfection of human nature.

[" Liberator," Editorial, April 3, 1840.]

" INFIDELITY. — After a careful examination of all the reasons which have been urged in favor of another political party, we are satisfied that they spring from a lack of faith in God, and those simple instrumentalities which it is His good pleasure to adopt for the suppression of evil and the salvation of the world."   .

[" Liberator," Editorial, April 10, 1840.]

ALBANY CONVENTION. — By yesterday's " Abolitionist" we are furnished with an account of the proceedings of the SOI-DISANT National (!) Convention, which was

held on the first day of April at Albany, and a more
ridiculous farce than appears to have been enacted on
the occasion, in the nomination of presidential candidates, we have never had occasion to place on record.
As we prophesied, in point of numbers, it was really
contemptible. Of 121 persons who enrolled their names
on the occasion, 48 belonged to Albany, and 104 to
the State of New York. There was 1 from Maine, 0
from N. H., 2 from Vt., 11 from Massachusetts, 0 from
Rhode Island! 1 from Connecticut, 2 from N. J.! 0 from
Pa.! 0 from Ohio, Indiana, Illinois, Michigan!!!!   A
National Convention forsooth! Why it was not as
large as a common village meeting. Will it be credited
by the abolitionists of the United States the handful of
abolitionists thus brought together had the folly, the
presumption. the almost unequalled infatuation, to put
candidates in nomination in their behalf for the Presidency and Vice-Presidency of the U. S.! — namely,
James G. Birney, of Kentucky, and Thos. Earle, of
Pa. This nomination was sustained — Yeas, 44!!
Nays, 32!! Majority, 11! But we are compelled to
omit all comment on this political farce in our present
number. We can only say, that the reasons which
induced Mr. Birney to decline a similar nomination
made a short time since still exist in full force. We
have too high an opinion of the good sense and sound
discretion of himself and Mr. Earle to believe that they
will consent to stand — nominated as they have been,
in fact, by a majority of only *eleven persons.*

Mr. Garrison here appears to have mistaken
the vote on the *question* of nominating for the vote
on the candidates. Though the Convention was

divided on the propriety of nominating, it was quite unanimous in the choice of candidates.

The Boston "Daily Advertiser" of April 8, 1840, with its proverbial promptitude, gave the news of the nomination of Birney and Earle on the first of April, with these significant remarks, showing how anxious the great parties of that day were to keep clear of all taint of abolitionism.

"We are happy to learn that the abolitionists have resolved to support their own candidates for the presidency. They are surely not wanted as adjuncts of the Whig party. . . . It will now be distinctly understood that the abolitionists are not Whigs. They have political objects of their own to promote, entirely at variance with those of the Whig party." *

* The Boston Whigs in 1840 were glad enough to see abolitionists opposed to separate political action, for if they did not get for Harrison and Tyler all the white abolition votes they got nearly all the colored ones. But their ingratitude for this political aid soon showed itself in a remarkable manner. On the death of Pres. Harrison the Mayor invited "all citizens" to join in a public funeral procession in his honor. The colored citizens who had been allowed to vote for him, at once met, appointing a marshal, and offered to join the procession in a body. The Mayor, Mr. Chapman, and the Chief Marshal, Josiah Quincy, Jr., under the apprehension that such a proceeding would excite a mob, endeavored in vain to dissuade them. At last Mr. Quincy sent to their Marshal, Mr. Alexander, the following curious note :—

"CITY HALL, Tuesday, April 20, 1841.

"If the colored citizens intend to appear as an organized body, they will take position in rear of ward No. 12.

"JOSIAH QUINCY, JR.,
"Chief Marshal."

But the most amusing expression of opinion was that of the great Whig organ at Washington, the " National Intelligencer," which attempted to make the country believe that the Liberty Party was plotted by Van Buren to debilitate the Whigs at the North.

[" National Intelligencer," Editorial, April 7, 1810.]

" A man might as well whistle in a whirlwind, and expect to be heard, as expect the people in the north now to contend for abolition in the South, when there is nowhere such a need of abolition as in the North itself, prostrated as is its trade, and chained as are all its energies by the power of the federal office holders. This last device of Mr. Van Buren to regain New York, and to recover Massachusetts, will turn out to be as contemptible as it is ridiculous. Indeed the abolitionists themselves laugh at it." *

It is needless to say that the colored citizens, who chiefly belonged to the Beacon Hill Ward, No. 6, declined this Negro Pew arrangement, and those who ventured to take their proper places in the procession, as *unorganized*, were, as the Mayor and Marshal predicted, ignominiously mobbed off. At the next Presidential election they took care to vote the Liberty Ticket.

* This arrogance of the old parties prompted the following lines, which appeared in Wm. Goodell's " *Friend of Man*," showing that the little sprout was not to be discouraged by huge trunks that were rotten at the core.

LIBERTY PARTY.

Will ye despise the acorn,
  Just thrusting out its shoot,
Ye giants of the forest,
  That strike the deepest root?

This was the *Intelligencer's* way of calming and quieting the whigs of the south, who had been so much alarmed by the speech of Henry Clay the year before that they were almost ready, in their fright, to join the "Democratic" or Administration party, as the surest defence of slavery. Its logic, however, was too "childlike and bland" to have any considerable effect. With the aid of those abolitionists who were more *ultra* than *practical*, the Whig party stood firm both at the

> Will ye despise the streamlet
> Upon the mountain side,
> Ye broad and mighty rivers
> On-sweeping to the tide?
>
> Wilt thou despise the crescent,
> That trembles, newly born,
> Thou bright and peerless planet,
> The queen of eve and morn?
>
> Time now his scythe is whetting,
> Ye giant oaks for you;
> Ye floods, the sea is thirsting
> To drink you like the dew.
>
> That crescent, pale and trembling,
> Her lamp shall nightly trim,
> Till thou, imperious planet,
> Shalt in her light grow dim.
>
> And so shall wax the party,
> Now feeble in its birth,
> Till liberty shall cover
> This tyrant-ridden earth.

north and the south, till the next presidential campaign, when Mr. Van Buren's plot, if such it was, not only defeated his great rival, Henry Clay, but sent Mr. Van Buren himself home to Kinderhook, there to meditate himself into some degree of fitness to be the FREE SOIL candidate of 1848. It had been the cherished plan of the great whig slaveholders of the south to cement the slave power and the national bank power, and by controlling both to control the nation. But

> That party, as we term it,—
>   The party of the WHOLE—
> Has for its firm foundation
>   The substance of the soul.
>
> It groweth out of reason,
>   The strongest soil below;
> The smaller is its budding,
>   The more its room to grow.
>
> Then rally to its banners,
>   Supported by the true,
> The weakest are the waning,
>   The many or the few.
>
> Of what is small but living,
>   God makes himself the nurse,
> While "Onward" cry the voices
>   Of all his universe.
>
> Our plant is of the cedar,
>   That knoweth not decay;
> Its growth shall bless the mountains
>   Till mountains pass away.

General Jackson had exploded a torpedo under the National Bank, and the chief object of the Whig campaign of 1840 was to repair that mischief, and the north was really made to believe that the destruction of the Biddle Bank monopoly, and not the depravity of its ally, the slave system, was the cause of the miserably hard times which then prevailed. The slave-ridden south was always the hot-bed of bankruptcy, and the north at last learned that when better times came, they came from western rather than southern trade, as abolitionists always taught. Only those who paid fair wages were good customers.

The grand argument, inside the anti-slavery ranks as well as outside — and especially in the churches — against party political action was, that it "let down the moral sublimity of the cause." How much more it did so than voting for the least pro-slavery of two thoroughly pro-slavery candidates, was never shown. Wm. Goodell, editor of the *Friend of Man*, was one of the earliest abolitionists, and one of the most sincerely religious persons, remaining so till his death, and always an admiring friend of Mr. Garrison. His testimony as to the origin of the Liberty party is, of course, valuable. He said in the Fifth Annual

Report of the N. Y. State Anti-Slavery Society, of which he was secretary, Sept., 1840 :

"Among those who were the most early and decided in recommending the policy of independent nominations, were the editors of three anti-slavery papers, whose arguments and views exerted a well-deserved influence on the anti-slavery community. Myron Holley, of the *Rochester Freeman*, (which our western friends would have done well to have sustained), Joshua Leavitt, of the *Emancipator*, New York, and Elizur Wright, Jr.,* then of the *Massachusetts Abolitionist*, Boston,— these were among the prominent writers by whom the new policy was vindicated and recommended. Our own paper, the *Friend of Man*, has been open to the discussion from the first, admitting freely and impartially the principal writers on both sides, but taking no decisive editorial stand in favor of the measure until some time last spring."

But no man did more than the modest and laborious William Goodell to sustain the "moral sublimity" of the Anti-Slavery cause. Reviewing an Address of the Managers of the Massachusetts Anti-Slavery Society, in which the Liberty Party was criticized in a tone pretty nearly bordering on cant, he wrote :

" The managers say, by nominating abolition candidates we shall let down the " moral sublimity " of our

* The " Jr." was dropped at the death of his father in 1845, and he himself had been dropped from the *Abolitionist* prior to April 1, 1840.

enterprise. We ought to " shun the very appearance
of evil " — alluding to the sacred text, 1 Thes. v. 22,
"Abstain from all *appearance of evil*." Here we protest
against the interpretation. The Apostle's own Greek
phrase, we think, means only, Abstain from every sort
of evil. But if it must be translated *appearance*, it is
that which appears evil to oneself. and not to the world.
The common interpretation does not hold true in
morals. It is by no means our duty to abstain from
everything which appears to be evil to others, while it
seems right to ourselves. The fashion of the world in
wrong in this respect. We care too much about our
appearance; what others say of us and our motives ;
and at the same time we are too ready (is it prompted
by our self-knowledge?) to condemn the motives of
others. If a third party really is the best way, as it is
confessedly a rightful one, to knock off our brother's
chains, and we take it, shoulder to shoulder, the pro-
slavery public may *say* of us what they will, they will
certainly think none the less highly of our " moral
sublimity." Indeed, what is that moral sublimity good
for, if it cannot sacrifice its reputation for sanctity, and
incur the odium of the tyrannical and the inhuman, in
order to seize the best means of accomplishing its
object? But we suspect there is a little self-righteous-
ness to be sacrificed. Have we not set a rather high
value on our own *purity?* Is it, after all, anything
very much out of the reach of common saintship to
wish to see our own countrymen more free and our
country relieved from disgrace? We incline to think
not, but that an immense majority in the free states
may be brought to the same " moral sublimity " by the
right *lead*."

CHAPTER XXII.

ON THE STUMP.

A certain species of political oratory, better known in this country than any other, takes its name from the fact that in our western states the stump of a large tree frequently became the pulpit or rostrum from which a candidate for office or a political adept addressed his fellow citizens. From the time, in 1838, when Mr. Holley declined to accept office from the Whigs, on the condition of being gagged on the subject of slavery, he was much on the stump, besides editing the *Rochester Freeman*, a weekly sheet specially devoted to the abolition cause. From the first he held that anti-slavery sentiment must make itself a political channel, or fail of any effect. And wherever any anti-slavery sentiment existed, his addresses produced conviction. It was this conviction, widely extended by him, that effected the nomination, on the first of April, 1840. In him there was no faltering or despondency about the result. He labored in a hope, not born of feverish enthusiasm, but cool judgment. He had a distinct vision of the means as well as the end. Writing from Rochester to his daughter, Mrs. Beaumont, who was then living in Lyons, in March, 1839, he says : — "Anti-slavery sentiments seem slowly to be gaining ground in all the north, and they are undoubtedly producing effects favorable to abolition in all the union. I have no doubt that slavery will be abolished in North America within twenty years. If the slave states are wise or prudent they will, before that lapse of time, abolish peaceably, and if they will not, the first war that shall occur between our country and any considerable foreign power will compel a bloody abolition. I pray this may be prevented." He goes right on to speak to his "dear Tatty," as he called her, of his own labors. "I have often thought with some mortification of my lecture delivered when I was last at Lyons. The pleasant society which I enjoyed all the day with my children and grand-children absorbed me so much during the day that in truth I was very ill-prepared to give a lecture. But I thought the few abolitionists at Lyons wanted sympathy and encouragement, and that by coming out as I did, I should somewhat strengthen their faith and fortitude.

Odium, misrepresentation and persecution have ever awaited those who set themselves earnestly to cast off great abuses. So many men of wealth, intelligence and influence have their feelings, habits and prospects thoroughly mingled up with great social abuses, that whoever exposes, resists and seeks to overthrow the abuses, must expect trouble. And if they have not a faith and firmness leading even to martyrdom, if need be, the reform will not be carried."

Notwithstanding this modest self-depreciation, no doubt the "few abolitionists of Lyons" were encouraged when they saw the gentleman who had given them their canal, and whom *they* well knew to be the wisest man in the state, standing by them. Here was a man who could show them how to *do* as well as to think and feel.

Never did he lecture without inspiring action, which always implies hope. After the nomination, he gave himself to the work of the stump with the full spirit of martyrdom, seemingly well aware that he was crowding ten or twenty years of life into one, and that the Liberty vote to be gained was worth the cost.

The little despised Liberty Party was very far from commanding the sinews of · political war

which a party wielding the anti-slavery sentiment
of the country should have had. It resolved to
establish a daily paper in Albany as its organ, and
after much delay it was done in a small way, the
martyr Charles T. Torrey becoming its first editor.
The best it could do was to promise $40 a month
to keep Mr. Holley in the lecture field. And on
that slender stipend he labored with the vigor of
a Hercules through all the months succeeding the
nomination till the election. In writing to his
son William who had fallen sick in Buffalo, in
September, he reveals the effect of these labors
upon his health, as well as the manner of them.
"We want very much to be with you in your distress, and regret that our situation and means,
at present, forbid it. We should like to hear
further particulars. and if you are not getting
better or are growing worse, your mother will
come out if possible. I am now engaged in serving the anti-slavery cause, and get forty dollars a
month, which is better than nothing. I find,
however, that speaking so much as I have occasion
to do, or something else, has given me a pain in
my breast and reduced me below good working
condition. Yet I must persevere. I start away
from home (Rochester) again to day. . . .

A few days ago I was within eleven miles of Buffalo passing from Aurora to Fredonia, and I wished amazingly to come there, not knowing however that any of you were sick, but I had not an hour to spare, and tore myself on westerly."

From this "pain in the breast" he did not recover. His speaking or "something else" had exhausted his vitality and sleep did not restore it. That "something else" was partly the excessive fatigue of constant travelling, for at that day the railroad system, with its multitudinous branches, hardly existed. In the Empire State there were not then 500 miles of railroad where now there are more than 5,000; for the Central was not opened from Schenectady to Buffalo till 1841, and the Erie reached only from Piermont to Goshen. As to the fatigue of travel, it is easier to stump all the northern states now than the single state of New York then. But it was mostly the deep thought and sense of responsibility which exhausted him. It is only sleep which restores the thinking power of the brain, and the sleeping-car had not yet been invented. The best and soundest thinking is done directly after sound natural sleep in pure air. If the air of the sleeping-car could be kept fresh and free from dust, perhaps, by virtue of the vibration, it would be the best sleeping place in the world. Mr. Holley was naturally a good sleeper. He never disturbed that important faculty by stimulants or narcotics, — those pests which are filling the world with insanity, — for he never took anything stronger than a single cup of coffee in the morning. To this undoubtedly his farsightedness, equanimity and steady persistence may be largely attributed.

Mr. Holley's lectures, it must be remembered, were never superficial. He had a great fund of humor, and power to amuse any audience, but he confined it to the parlor, or the company in a stage coach, or packet boat. Before an audience in a hall, few or many, whatever his subject, he went to the bottom of it as thoroughly as if he were addressing the Senate of the United States. And if there was in that audience any thinking power, he set it in action. His appeal was never to prejudice — no vituperation — no personality — no sarcasm — but a mountainous accumulation of unquestionable facts laid directly at the door of practical common sense. The early years of the anti-slavery cause were full of oratory, — the bare names of the orators would fill a page, — in which

irony, denunciation, invective, ridicule, wit, blistering satire and indignant rebuke conspired to produce philippics as much grander than that of Demosthenes as the object was more deserving of them.
Witness the speeches of that giant of the New York
bar, ALVAN STEWART, who, presiding at an anti-
slavery meeting in Utica in 1835, tossed the leader
of a mob of respectable citizens, who invaded the
church and penetrated to the pulpit where he sat,
to break up the meeting, down on to the crowd of
his followers below, and then coolly put the resolutions of the meeting to the vote which formed the
New York State Anti-Slavery Society. Witness
the speech of the young WENDELL PHILLIPS
when he burst out on that "recreant" New Eng-
lander, Hon. James T. Austin, Attorney General
of the Commonwealth, who dared in Fanueil Hall
to class the fiends who murdered Lovejoy with
the men who threw the tea overboard in Boston
Harbor. Here was a king of Macedon, face to
face, surrounded by his grim myrmidons, defam-
ing the fathers of our republic. The young
Demosthenes rose, pointed to their pictures on
the walls, and said, "I thought while he was
speaking those pictured lips would have broken
into voice, to rebuke the recreant American — the

slanderer of the dead." "Take back that word,"
howled the liveried slaves of slavery. No. He
went on, and the plaudits shook the old Cradle of
Liberty as it was never shaken before. The
words of the orator were true in the grandest
sense, — the earth did open and swallow Austin.
All this, every breath of it, and more of the same
sort, was necessary to rouse the people from their
fatal lethargy. But there was another sort, perhaps fully as effective, and it was even earlier.
As far back as 1832 there was a young "divinity
student" who hated slavery in every shape,
whether it was the lash or the bottle that produced
it. He had the natural gift of eloquence to such
a degree that when he talked against alcohol, deal-
ers went home, rolled the whiskey barrels out of
the back door and knocked in the heads. When
he talked about negro slavery in an Alabama
parlor, James G. Birney became an abolitionist
and liberated his slaves. He it was that revolu-
tionized Lane Seminary against the opposing
power of its president, the great father of the
Beechers, and sent nearly all its students to
Oberlin, which became a celebrated station on
the underground railroad. He it was who, in a
course of lectures in Steubenville, Ohio, put so

much abolitionism into a young democratic law student, who attended to refute him, that he held his peace on the subject till he became Lincoln's Secretary of War in 1861. Perhaps if Judge J. Black had attended that course, it would have saved him from making a deplorable donkey of himself. And shall I forget "Carolina's high-souled daughter," who afterwards became the excellent wife of the orator just mentioned? She, soon after the first mobs and before the murder of Lovejoy, kindled coals in the Legislature of Massachusetts, in spite of the freezing mixtures of election sermons and the awful frowns of the clergy. The names of these will be remembered without marble.* Mr. Holley's stump oratory was of the same sort. It seems to me impossible to believe that if one hundred leading men of the South, including John C. Calhoun and Jefferson Davis, could have listened to him for two hours, there would ever have been a Mexican War or a Southern Confederacy.

---

* After voice and health failed this eloquent pair, they settled at Fort Lee, on the Hudson, for a while, and there compiled from a vast stack of southern newspapers that terrific pamphlet, " SLAVERY AS IT IS; OR, THE TESTIMONY OF 1,000 WITNESSES," which was the precursor, and afterwards the justification, of Mrs. Stowe's " UNCLE TOM'S CABIN."

CHAPTER XXII.

HIS HOMES.

THE homes of great and good citizens, whether the first or the last, are the most sacred places on earth. They are apt not to be so durable as those of tyrants and oppressors. The world did not begin much to admire the genius of Homer till it had forgotten in what city he was born. Yet his name and his fame may outlast the pyramids. The homes and habits of Cadmus are not known. Would we not give as much to know them as to see the Colosseum or the Vatican? It is rather painful and depressing to behold a grand house, built by a small, ignoble, or detestable man, whose name would otherwise have been forgotten; or a magnificent cathedral, which was built and presided over by some cold-hearted inquisitor, whose gaudy garments smelt of the smoke of burnt heretics; but who does not feel his heart warmed and enlarged by looking on the home-picture on which the eyes of a Howard or a Shakespeare rested with delight?

Much do I wish that I could show my kind readers, in the present beautiful style of the graphic art, the house where Myron Holley was born, the four which he himself successively built for his family, and the last one where his dust now reposes, built for him by the kind hand of mother Nature in one of her sweetest groves, and beautified by the gratitude of the little band of Liberty Party Abolitionists three or four years after his death. I can but point out the spots.

It was as early as 1821 that Mr. Holley removed his wife and ten children from their pleasant home in Canandaigua to Lyons, where he had provided a spacious double house, two stories high, on the main street, with doubtless all the then modern improvements. It is to be remembered that his good father was a man of considerable wealth, and that his Canandaigua property was desirable. He could well afford to live in a good house.

Lyons is hardly less beautiful than Canandaigua. It has exceedingly fertile hills, of easy ascent, but with wide and charming views of valley scenery. It is at the head of navigation on the river Clyde,

an affluent of the Seneca, formed by the junction of
Mud Creek from the west, and Flint Creek, bearing the waters of Canandaigua Lake, from the
southwest. Either of these would be considered
respectable rivers in England or Scotland — they
only lack a Burns to be so here.

After his reverse in the canal business had
obliged him to make the most of his resources, he
built a cozy stone cottage on Phelps Street, in a
less aristocratic portion of the town, called Joppa,
situated in a five-acre fruit-garden, where he
cultivated quince and mulberry trees, and where
his family lived while he was editing in Lyons and
in Hartford.

I am told it was of this home that a Canandaigua poet, rejoicing in the name of Zebulun
Barton Stout, wrote some verses, published in the
local papers, and addressed to "Mrs. Holley,
Miss Lawrence and Miss Holley." The sense
and spirit are rather more conspicuous than the
polish or finish, but those who complain of this
rustic bard, should show they know how to give
his worthy subject a worthier treatment. American poets have never yet done justice to American
trees.

On the green margin of the peaceful stream,
   Which winds its way through Lyons' charming vale;
Stand three tall Elms — and nobler trees, I deem
   Ne'er waved their heads to heaven's salubrious gale;

Their spreading branches with thick foliage crowned,
   Partly obstruct a view, admired by all;
And thoughtlessly was a decision found,
   The ancient sturdy Elms should straightway fall.

But ere the impious axeman gave the blow,
   A voice unearthly murmured in the breeze;
The spirit of the woods, in accents low,
   Thus sighed a prayer, amid the trembling trees:

Hold, woodman! know these venerable elms,
   The wintry storms of ages have withstood;
False is the taste, and cruel, which condemns
   The stately Elm, the pride of every wood.

E'er in this vale the white man durst appear,
   These verdant branches spread their summer shade
O'er many an Indian hunter loitering here,
   O'er many a beauteous, tawny, forest maid.

The Elms, a monument, then, woodman spare,
   Of the lost race, to tell that they have been;
Their solemn dirge shall mournful winds declare,
   Dews wept from leaves, the tribute grief begin.

And when the morning sunshine shall exhale
   These Nature's tears, for Nature's children shed,
As through their boughs light winds prevail,
   They'll cheer the living while they mourn the dead.

In future, oft shall village youths repair,
   And lovelier damsels grace the jocund train;
Then, woodman, grant this happier race to share
   These blessed shades.   Oh, let the Elms remain!

Lost were these strains upon the woodman's ear,
   Had not two blooming maidens joined their voice,
In intercession sweet, with hearts sincere,
   And begged the trees might live. They live. Rejoice.

Thus wayward man can slight a voice from heaven,
   Yet woman's pleadings joyfully obey;
Woman, to thee the magic charm is given,
   At once to serve, yet bear enchanting sway.

This village has a dwelling named CONTENT, —
   In front, a dark green maple woodland grows,
Beneath whose shade, in graceful curvings bent,
   Erie's canal in silent grandeur flows.

'Tis sweet to mark at evening's pensive hour,
   Amid the grove, the decklights glide along;
Or listen,—lulled with music's soothing power,—
   To the shrill bugle, or the boatman's song.

Health to this mansion, long may joy and love,
   And blue-eyed hope, its smiling bowers adorn;
Each sun returning o'er the dark green grove,
   Forever waken still a happier morn.

Around this home of "Content" Mr. Holley's married daughters were then settled, and he himself in a long letter to Mrs. Clarissa Beaumont, dated Hartford, Sep. 21, 1834, tells how and why he loved it. Notice how he recognized in Nature a commandment more effective than any contained in any book. After expressing the longing he felt, after nine months of absence, to meet again the objects of his "most engrained affections," he says: "The divine wisdom has seen it best to

ordain that the stream of love should flow strongest
down the current of life; and so has made it
natural that parents should love their children
more than children should love their parents. If
I remember right, parents are not commanded,
anywhere in the Scriptures, to love their children.
This most necessary and most efficacious of means
of compelling human beings to do everything in
their power to increase and secure the well-being
of their race, is better accomplished by ligaments
round the heart and incapable of being severed
from it, than it could possibly be by any words—
even the commands of the Most High. They are
monsters who do not feel, or who refuse to acknow-
ledge, the force of all these ligaments. Every day
of my life the scenery most before me is that of Lyons. And the society I most enjoy is that which
gives this scenery its chief interest. Our new situation, at the Quince Orchard, with its snug comforts
and unfinished but promising accompaniments, —
the place you occupy, with its tasteful, convenient,
and multiplied means of enjoyment,—Caroline's
domicil with all its agreeable associations, and
Elizabeth's nice establishment by the river, are
almost constantly before me, in all their peculiar
features and distinguishing attractions; and my

heart is filled, sometimes with a melancholy, but more often with a cheerful interest in the living, and moving, and immortal, and responsible, and loving beings, who fill the high places of all this scenery, and, in my view, concentrate upon it the highest social delights of this life, and twine themselves inseparably with all my most solemn and most precious anticipations of the future."

Yet, though he had achieved for Lyons the "silent grandeur" of the canal which "flows" so lovingly by it, had made Wayne a county * and

---

* In those early days, whenever a new county was to be set off from one already established, there was generally a stubborn resistance from those whose power was to be diminished. I quote the following letter for two reasons; first, to show what Lyons owed to Mr. Holley, and second, how DeWitt Clinton's plan of having the Erie Canal duly celebrated, in a book of the greatest possible scientific, economical, pictorial and historical interest, written by Mr. Holley himself, fell through, because in the midst of his preparation for it, he, Clinton, was stupidly removed from the Canal Board.

ALBANY, 15 April, 1823.

DEAR SIR, — I was disappointed in not seeing you before your departure from this place.

I have received a letter from the bookseller in New York, [A. V. Goodrich & Co.] declining the overture I made on account of circumstances unconnected with any objections to the merits of the plan, but I really would advise you to proceed and execute the work, and there can be no doubt of a liberal remuneration from more affluent quarters.

Mr. Bouck thinks that the Canal Board ought to meet at Buffalo the latter end of May. Will you let me know your

Lyons the capital of it, he was not to stay in Lyons.

Soon after his return from Hartford, seeing that five acres of quinces, with some Chinese and Italian mulberry trees, would not sustain a large family, he repaired to Rochester, then the centre of the great milling interest and growing to be a great city. From some hotel there we have a family letter to his daughter, Mrs. George Kingman, then residing in Lyons:

ROCHESTER, 4 March, 1835.

MY DEAR ELIZABETH. — Your present of apples and cakes came very safe by George, and were received with great delight as evidence of your affectionate regard for me. Besides affording me a little supper last evening, they enabled me to be properly courteous to Judge E. B. Strong and Dr. Smith, who called at my room half an hour, having left the ball-room occupied here last evening for that purpose.

George informs me that you take a lively interest in

opinion in order that I may select the most acceptable period? This, however, is upon a supposition that the present Canal Board will continue. I learn that there is an excitement against you on account of the new county, which I very much regret. As to myself, I think it almost certain that an attempt will be made to remove, and I shall certainly feel no mortification at its success.

I am sincerely,
Your friend,
DeWITT CLINTON.

M. HOLLEY, ESQ.

Sally, and wish her to be sent to Caroline's in Connecticut for a year. This might be very useful to her, and possibly may take place. At any rate, I feel very sensibly obliged by the sisterly feeling in you which it indicates; and am very much gratified by the interest manifested by George in such an arrangement. I shall think of it, and if I do not come home (probably I shall) before the canal opens, shall write further on this subject. In the meantime, I cannot say that the probability is in favor of her going. I love Sally with an affection which nothing shall or can ever obliterate, and hope to aid her advancement in life more hereafter than I have been able to for some years past. I have a project of business here which looks plausible for a permanent establishment. If it can be compassed on reasonable terms, it promises me comfort, and my family more assistance from me than I shall be ever able to render them in any other way as to subsistence and profit. George can tell you what it is, but I wish it not to be spoken of out of the circle of my children.

With perfect affection, my dear Elizabeth,

Your abiding friend,

MYRON HOLLEY.

Kiss Clare and little George for me, and give my love to Sam.

It does not seem that this "project of business" succeeded, for Mr. Holley bought a piece of land — of great natural beauty and fertility — on the river, a little below Rochester, where he built a plain commodious house, and moved his family into it before Christmas, though it was not quite finished. From that place, as " ROSE RIDGE," he dates his beautiful letters for the next three years. The spot is well worth going to see, as the Genesee, after playing Niagara at Rochester, flows peacefully through a deep gorge beneath it. Nature indulges in a beautiful shrubbery of *arbor vitæ* on its banks, Here with his library, his principal room on the ground floor, he was in his element. He knew how to get as much out of his acres as any man could, and a great deal more out of his books. I must here give the reader the residue of a letter to his daughter Caroline at Washington, from which I have quoted in a previous chapter :

ROSE RIDGE, 23d February, 1837.

MY DEAR CAROLINE. — Your mother and I were very much pleased to read a very interesting letter which you addressed to her yesterday ; and as the time draws near when you will leave the seat of government, I lose no time in expressing my thanks for that and all the other evidences of your affection with which you have favored us this winter. I received the play of Bulwer and all the other articles and documents referred to by you, and have read most of them with much interest, and feel, indeed, much obliged both to you and Mr. Chapin for them.

Bulwer's play, I think, adds nothing to his reputation as an author. It seems to me feeble, and to embrace a poor subject. The intrigues, sensuality and vices of kings cannot be treated of, with much interest, in any publication without marking them with that stern reprobation, which titled and fashionable and enthroned infamy peculiarly deserves. The graces and the flatteries, and the fame of the Court of Louis the 14th of France, do only make the more disgusting the pride, selfishness and brutality of that hypocritical and unprincipled scoundrel's character. But I will say nothing more of him.

Your anxiety to get home again is natural and commendable. I think you have done well in availing yourself of the fine opportunity offered you by your husband's election to Congress, and consent that you should accompany him there, to become acquainted with the distinguished circles of Washington. And I think you have done better to make up your mind, notwithstanding the pretension, the elegance, the intelligence and the renown of those circles, to cherish an honest and deep-felt preference for the more true-hearted, artless and virtuous society with which your own village will supply you. I entertain but little confidence in the qualities requisite to distinction in what are called high societies in any country. In such societies in our country, I fear, there is increasing degradation. The most distinguished virtues, and the great improvements of our race, have always originated with the poor; and I think we must always chiefly look to them for future improvements. This is the lesson of history, and easily to be accounted for. The Christian commandment of love to God and man enters more deeply into the spirits of the reflecting poor than any others, and when this affection combines in all its strength and purity, as it sometimes does in their souls, with the highest intellectual power, and a resolution never daunted in the pursuit of good, they become the lights and guides of the world. In such persons the want of education is nothing. Every thing in nature stimulates them to inquiry and to thought, and to observation. Their best faculties become strong by exertion. And they have no prejudices, which always disable the high born and the high bred, or if they have, their prejudices are in favor of the great majority of their fellow beings, and not in favor of any little class. And all social improvements, that are true and permanent, benefit, not the few at the expense of the many, but the many together with the few.

Your mother's hand is better, though not yet so well as to enable her to write. She regrets this chiefly because it prevents her from writing to you.

If you see Mr. and Mrs. T. Childs before you start for home, give my respects to them, but do not fail to do it to my brother-in-law, Mr. Whittlesey.

We have heard no bad news from Lyons, though it is now two or three weeks since we have heard anything at all from there. Bolly is with Mrs. Kingman and goes to school. Sally is with Mrs. Beaumont and I hope considers herself at school also. Grace is all the child we have at home. She likes to hear your letters, and wants very much to have Cornelia Chapin spend the summer here. Perhaps, after you get home, and find all things there as you can wish, you will be able to come out to see us with her and some other of your family. It will give us great happiness. Give my affectionate regards to Mr. Chapin and believe me as usual yours. Ma and Grace send love.

MYRON HOLLEY.

Mr. Holley's life had not been exempt from the sorrows of the common lot. At Lyons he had lost his daughter Cornelia, a lovely child, the next younger than Sally. He felt the loss most keenly, but the neighbors who came to condole with him at his house, where a Methodist minister preached a funeral sermon, were surprised that he wore light clothes, never before having seen a man who did not dress in black and wear crape on such an occasion. At Rose Ridge, in 1838, he heard that three of his daughters, Mrs. Chapin, Mrs. Beaumont and Mrs. Kingman, had simultaneously entered on a six months probation to join the Methodist church. He sat down and addressed to the three jointly a very long and serious letter, in which he does not object to the act nor cast any reproach on the church, but very distinctly states his notion of religion. By his definition, Religion is "a practical obedience to all the obligations of our nature and just relations"— substantially identical with that of Voltaire, Paine and other distinguished deists, whom the Methodists as well as most other Christian sects are never tired of denouncing as "infidels." He expresses no anxiety about or prejudice against *belief* if only *duty* was right. While he was writing this letter, one came to him from Lockport, stating that his son Robert had just died there. He incorporates this letter, and then proceeds to speak of his son in the tenderest terms, implying that though his habits had not all been such as he could wish, he believed him not to be beyond hope. Neither the Scriptures nor his own understanding taught him that "probation was confined to this life." The whole of his most affectionate epistle taught trust in Nature as well as Christ. If the Methodist Church would apply to Miss Sallie Holley, who has preserved this letter in full, they would find it quite as edifying as any of Paul's. I wish I had room for it here.

I must give one which he addressed to his young son Bolivar, who was then a lad at school in Lyons:

ROSE RIDGE, 26th March, 1837.

MY DEAR BOLIVAR,—Grace and I have just finished a very pleasant walk down along the banks of the Genesee, during which we often thought of you. The clear sky, the bright sun, the merry birds, all attended us, and seemed to say, "Where is Bolly, whom you both love so much, and who used to walk with you here?" The best answer I could make was, our dear Bolly is at Lyons, engaged in learning many things very necessary to enable him to pass a useful and happy life; and we hope he is diligent and ambitious to make good progress. But while he is striving with all his powers, to increase his knowledge, Grace and myself, and his mother, all hope he will neither forget us, nor lose one jot of his love for us. "*That* he will not," all nature seemed to say, "and when he comes home, improved in mind and manners, and grown nearer to the stature of a man, you and he will walk here again with increasing satisfaction. Perhaps, in the course of the summer, which I am now laboring to bring forth, he, with some of his, and your, best friends at Lyons, will join you in one or two very pleasant whortleberry parties." With this and many other social enjoyments which we hope to experience with him, we make ourselves contented in his absence, praying to our heavenly Father, that he may have the grace to be always good, which we are sure will make him always happy. Mother and Grace send their best love to you and Elizabeth and Caroline and Tatty and all their children and friends.

Affectionately your father.

The great cause of human liberty did not allow Mr. Holley to spend that summer on his farm of Rose Ridge. He hired a house in Rochester, nearer his work. His labor was on the press and on the stump. He felt that to be the crisis of a new birth. Not a moment was to be lost. We have seen how effectively he labored.

Thus to pull up stakes was costly, difficult and slow. Debts must necessarily be incurred. The times were excessively hard. The industrious north had trusted the slack-twisted financial honor of the south, and it failed. The backers of the *Rochester Freeman* had not the backbone to sustain it. Late in the fall of 1840, after Mr. Holley had finished his great work of planting a new party on the immortal Declaration of '76, he completed the sale of his beautiful farm, received money enough to pay all his debts — which he did with a relish only known to honesty — and had left $400 in hand. Just before the canal froze up he visited his daughter, Mrs. Kingman, then settled in Buffalo, much enjoying with his family a trip which his earlier labors had made possible.

He returned to his hired house at Rochester to die. I find no letter from him later than one addressed to J. W. Alden and Samuel E. Sewall, in reply to an invitation to attend the Massachusetts State Liberty Party Convention to be held on the 24th of February, 1841, in the Marlboro Chapel in Boston. It was dated Feb. 1, 1841, — only a month and four days previous to his death, and closed thus :— "I pray God to endow you with divine wisdom and render your convention a

mighty instrument of disabusing our cause of the
visionary notions which have so much impeded it,
and placing it firmly in the strong arms of Christian
principles and practical good sense.

With much respect,

Your obedient servant,

Myron Holley."

The Last Home.

Its site is among the beautiful, tree-crowned
river hills, on the Genesee, above Rochester — in
a cemetery well named Mount Hope. A plain
and modest monument marks the spot, whose history does honor to another great man, who loved
him like a brother, and whose own memory will
grow greener and greener with his.

At a convention of the Liberty Party of the State of
New York, held at Canastota, Sep. 20, 1843, Gerrit
Smith offered the following Resolutions. They were,
after a few remarks by him. passed unanimously — the
members of the convention standing whilst the votes
were taken. The blanks in the 2d and 3d resolutions
were filled with the name of Gerrit Smith.

1st. Whereas of all the public and private honors,
which cluster so thickly and brightly around the name
of Myron Holley, there is none so prominent and
enduring, as his devoted friendship for the slave ; and
whereas amongst the evidence of that friendship, none
is so worthy of record, as his agency in founding the

Liberty Party : Resolved, therefore, that for this party
to incur the expense, and have the credit of erecting the
monument on his grave would be strikingly appropriate ;
and that now, when this party is travelling so rapidly
towards its bloodless and blessed victory over American
slavery, is a peculiarly fit time to erect it.

2d.   Resolved, that —— ——, be authorized to erect
the monument at the expense of about two hundred
dollars ; and that the only testimony to Mr. Holley's
worth which shall be inscribed on it be as follows :

THE LIBERTY PARTY

OF THE

UNITED STATES OF AMERICA

HAVE ERECTED THIS MONUMENT

TO THE MEMORY OF

MYRON HOLLEY,

THE FRIEND OF THE SLAVE,

AND THE MOST EFFECTIVE, AS WELL AS ONE OF THE

VERY EARLIEST OF THE FOUNDERS OF

THAT PARTY.

3d.   Resolved, that each member of the Liberty
Party have the privilege of contributing one cent, no
more, towards the expense of erecting the monument ;
and that the said —— —— be authorized to appoint a
person in each of the free states and free territories,
whose duty it shall be to gather the contributions of his
respective state or territory, and send the same to him,
the said —— ——.

4th.   Resolved, that the first day of October, 1844,
shall be the period when these contributions shall cease
to be made ; and should their aggregate exceed the cost

of the monument, the excess shall be given to Mr. Holley's family.*

This was the day of small things and great hopes. The next Presidential election showed less than 70,000 Liberty Party voters. If there had been enough at one cent apiece to have given to Mr. Holley's family any excess over the cost of the monument, perhaps the victory over American slavery would have been "bloodless," as was then hoped. But some thousands gave their cent. Mr. Smith procured the monument, which was of Stockbridge marble, made by Mr. Dixon, of Albany, under the superintendence of Orville L. Holley.

* At the date of this Canastota Convention the activity of the Liberty Party leaders was such as thoroughly to frighten the Whig politicians. They had no other cause of fear. Their idol, Clay, had won the south by the atrocious speech already cited. All they had to do, was to hold their ascendancy at the north, by keeping their voters from going over to the Liberty Party. Neither high rhetoric nor fair argument was sufficient for that. At the last fortnight of the canvass in 1844, the Michigan Whig State Committee concocted against Mr. Birney the basest and most inexcusable forgery, of a letter alleged to have been written by him to a Mr. Garland of Saginaw, selling himself to the democrats for a seat in the legislature. It was worse than a lie. Supported by bets in the highest quarters, it doubtless cost the Liberty Party thousands of votes, but it did not save Henry Clay.

On one side it bears the inscription :

MYRON HOLLEY
BORN IN SALISBURY, CONNECTICUT,
APRIL 29, 1779.
DIED IN ROCHESTER,
MARCH 4, 1841.
HE TRUSTED IN GOD, AND LOVED HIS NEIGHBOR.

A fine medallion likeness by Carew, of Boston, in Italian marble, is inserted in the same side of the shaft.

On the opposite side were inscribed the words above cited in the second resolution.

The monument was dedicated June 13, 1844, under a blue sky, in the presence of six thousand persons.

A characteristic eulogy was delivered by Gerrit Smith, and the following hymn, composed for the occasion, by John Pierpont, was sung to the tune of *"God Save the King."*

> Here, where young Summer weaves
> A screen of tender leaves
>   Over thy grave,
> And the wood-robin's wing
> Around is fluttering
> Thy requiem we sing,
>   Friend of the slave.
>
> Here, in this leafy aisle,
> A monumental pile
>   To thee we rear;

HIS HOMES.

That strangers as they're led
These shady paths to tread
May linger by thy bed
    And drop a tear.

Why, brother, should we mourn?
Long hast thou bravely borne
    A false world's frown : —
Yet He for whose dear sake,
Thou did'st that burden take
Well knoweth how to make
    Thy cross thy crown.

How glowed thy lips — thy pen
When for thy fellow men,
    For e'en the thrall,
Thy spirit dared to be
With God's own freedom free,
And publish his decree
    FREEDOM FOR ALL!

Tears — manly tears — will yet
These cold, mute marbles wet,
    Servant of God;
And clouds in mourning drest,
Low greeting from the west,
And stars that watch thy rest,
    Bedew thy sod.

CHAPTER XXIII.

HIS CHARACTER.

The family is the ultimate test of character. It is the furnace where gold is distinguished from every other metal. The man or woman who can pass that ordeal, and, like an autumn sunset, shine brighter to the last, has a better title to heroism than any other mortal. Well ordered, loving families are the only stuff that a real republic can be made of. If the average family is a sham, so will the republic be. If the general fact is that the family is harmonious, husband and wife worshipping each other and living for each other — children, if any, worshipping mother and father — no matter what the creed or the wealth may be, the country will be happy under almost any government, if not under none. It cannot help being a republic.

It was the glory of Myron Holley's life, that all his unparalleled devotion to the public service, his facing persecution for rectitude, his far-seeing and self-sacrificing patriotism were founded on his love for his family. It was on that theatre that his magnificent and beneficent powers of body and mind had full play. With delight he tossed his babies, and his children's, in the air, and when their minds began to open, poured his light into them, as the sun does into the opening buds of spring. Let us hope the time will come when the republic will put its supreme trust only in such persons.

The idlest of all dreams is, that there can be patriotism and cohesion in a republic, when there is not love, harmony, order, justice in the family. If chains of arbitrary will and hoops of theological creed are what hold the family together, no government other than arbitrary, plutocratic and theocratic, as well as military, can hold society together.

That our rather over-lauded democratic republican government has not gone into utter disintegration long before now, is doubtless owing to the fact, that scattered over our vast country, of all creeds and none, are, in large proportion, happy, self-supporting, fondly loving, proudly laboring, and comparatively free-thinking families. These families are self-centred units; and to them the *e pluribus unum* flag is more significant than any

theological emblem.   It teaches them to ostracize
no man or woman.   Under it, they are learning
that deep wisdom which the great English bard,
nearly three centuries ago, put into the mouth of
a heroic woman who essayed the healing art :

> " Our remedies oft in ourselves do lie,
>   Which we ascribe to Heaven.   The fated sky
>   Gives us free scope; only, doth backward pull
>   Our slow designs, when we ourselves are dull."

It is now more than *forty* years since Myron
Holley was laid beneath the sod, wept by high and
low, rich and poor, white and black — the sky
weeping too.   Others may have forgotten, but
his sons and daughters worship him more and
more.   The few that knew him personally at all,
do so too ; and their only regret is that they did
not know him more intimately.

Under the date of March 19, 1878, Henry
O'Rielly, one of the most enthusiastic and honest of
the men who spread the telegraph wires over the
continent, wrote me about Mr. Holley : —

" A long life has not enabled me to see a man
more worthy of honor and love.   I use the last
word warily — for his was a truly *lovable* character.   When I came to know him (for he was my
neighbor for several of his later years), I 're-

pented in sack-cloth and ashes' (metaphorically speaking) for what I saw was the injustice done towards him by many of the partizans with whom I was associated, persons in whose prejudices I, *for awhile*, participated — *but only for awhile;* for unfounded prejudice gave way speedily, as I became acquainted with the excellence of his whole character. Few *could* know him so well as I knew him — for I knew him in *adversity* for several years." In this letter Mr. O'Rielly also says : " I first cleared up and laid out the 'Triangle Tract' in Mt. Hope, on which our lot is next to Mr. Holley's monument — where a tablet records the simple fact that ' Capt. Henry Brooks O'Rielly of the Army of the Potomac fell in May, 1862 ' — defending in the field what Mr. Holley courageously advocated in a life of severe trial, in the latter part of which life none knew him better than I did."

Mr. O'Rielly, who took a leading part in the enlargement of the Erie Canal, was able to, and kindly did, furnish incontestible documents, proving what has been stated in the foregoing pages, to wit, that, to the practical sagacity, zeal and self-denying devotion of Myron Holley, New York and the world owe it, that the original canal did not stop at Oswego, and probably that anything of the sort was begun in 1817.

But the most convincing proof of the high moral as well as physical excellence of Mr. Holley, is the fidelity and reverence with which his now venerable daughters cherish his memory. We have already seen the cause of this in the letters already cited in the previous pages. His religion differed from that of most fathers in that it included what is good in all religions, grew from all sources, excluded none, conceived of God as simply a personification of all the abstract verities—eternally self-existent—a universal fatherhood—inseparable from the nature of things. There was in it, no total depravity, no original sin, no imputed righteousness, no atonement by blood, no miraculous conversion, no angry tyrant to be propitiated by the sacrifice of innocent enjoyments. No wonder then that his daughter Sallie should write of him—and her words will surely gain more credence than mine—"Nothing impressed me more, as I grew into young womanhood, than my father's earnest religious convictions, ever ardent, alive and all controlling. I never knew any soul who had such an unfaltering faith in immortality—more like sight than faith, a habitual anticipation of heaven, that transfigured all human life to him and dignified every act. He utterly repudiated the popular theology. He thought it unscriptural, irrational and demoralizing, and that it deplorably hindered the coming of the kingdom of heaven upon earth. So he, as I knew him, could not sanction going to the fashionable churches. I never in all my life saw him in a church. Instead he used to hold a simple service in our home parlor in Lyons, in which the family and the poorer neighbors joined. After his removal to Rochester he convened Sunday morning meetings at the Court House, where he preached regularly. There was no Unitarian or liberal preaching otherwise in the city. While he occupied the fine fruit and vegetable farm a few miles north of Rochester, at Carthage, his custom was to hold Sunday meetings in the poor old district school-house there. What a curious, odd audience used to gather to listen and look at him. Every rank in society was represented. There sat the elegant and courtly Judge E. B. Strong, with occasionally the ladies of his household. And the Episcopalian Hoopers, on Sundays too rainy to get to their St. Paul's in the city, came to this extraordinary kind of worship, where they met the poorest and most humble day-laborers, and even drunkards and outcasts did not feel themselves excluded from the all-embracing humanity of those ministrations."

"It was not an uncommon thing for families, too degraded by intemperance and vice to venture to ask a clergyman, to send for my father to officiate at their funerals. They saw in their daily intercourse with him, that his divine tenderness took them all in."

"This Carthage farm, which he named 'Rose Ridge' for the beautiful roses he used to grow there, yielded choice fruits and vegetables, that my father, in a light wagon, took himself up to the city to supply customers — mostly wealthy families, and one of the lively ladies used to declare that 'Mr. Holley sold early peas and potatoes, asparagus and tomatoes in the morning, with as much grace as he delivered Lyceum lectures in the evening.' The garden, the orchard and all out-door nature was a perpetual joy to him. The very trees and stars were significant and friendly to his pure heart."

"I was told this anecdote of those days. Dr. Whitehouse, the most exclusive and aristocratic Episcopal clergyman of Rochester, himself an

Englishman, had married a Bordentown lady of
the Joseph Bonaparte neighborhood, and brought
her to what she regarded as the outside barbarian
world. After a residence of some months, she
one day, in a fit of enthusiastic delight, ran up to
her husband's study, and broke in with, 'Why,
Doctor! I've just seen the only *gentleman* I have
yet met with in Rochester; and he was at our
basement door selling vegetables! how wonderful!
who is it? Who can it be?' 'O,' smiled the
Doctor, 'it must be Myron Holley.'"

In regard to the sin of selling vegetables that
Reverend Doctor could be more forgiving than in
regard to that of heresy. I have on the best
authority a fact characteristic of his profession and
of the age that is passing away. Mr. Holley's
son-in-law, Graham H. Chapin, was sent to Congress from Lyons by a combination of Democrats
and Masons, in the Anti-Masonic times. He was
a kind-hearted, unprogressive, college-bred, gen-
tlemanly man of the surface. Residing after his
return from Congress at Rochester, he regularly
attended the most fashionable church there, and
died in the odor of sanctity. Dr. Whitehouse
preached his funeral sermon, in which he praised
him for not accepting " the cold, frigid philosophy

of Unitarianism of Myron Holley," whom he did not hesitate to stigmatize as an "open infidel" — a phrase which had vastly more force then than now.

This pulpit anathema was ignorantly hurled at a man who had written the following beautiful form of prayer for his youngest daughter, **Grace.** I copy it from his own handwriting :

> " Father in Heaven, to thee I owe
>   The blessings which my days have **crown'd**;
> My parents kind, thou didst bestow,
>   And dearer, children never found;
> My sisters and my brothers too,
>   Thy goodness to my heart has giv'n;
> To thee, O may we all be true,
>   And find, in love, our path to heav'n."

No sane mortal ever objects to prayers devoid of superstition, and such were the sincere and unpretending prayers of Myron Holley. They were not pompous, pharisaic or dictatorial, and never asked for miracles. He would never have joined in any national teazing of the Infinite about the weather, or the healing of gun-shot wounds.

Is it to be wondered at, that a man who prayed in his family and taught his children **to pray,** should set his face resolutely against all religious fanaticism? About the time when revivalism broke out in a school in Lyons, as already related, a revival preacher, by the name of Littlejohn, came to that place and proposed to hold a " protracted meeting " of 42 days. Mr. Holley assembled the influential citizens in the Court House, and set before them the demoralizing effects of such meetings so vividly, that the project was abandoned. Happy would it be, wherever such extravagances threaten to become epidemic, if some enlightened and tenderly religious person would have the moral courage to do as he did.

As an employer of labor, we have already seen that Mr. Holley was eminently successful. It was his overruling sense of justice and warm sympathy with the laborer which pushed the great ditch through two hundred miles of forests, marshes and swamps. Shirking no hardship or danger, he inspired the digger and contractor alike with enthusiasm, which neither physical obstacles or popular clamor could daunt. Years after the canal was finished and he was living quietly in his five-acre garden in Lyons, or on his hundred and twenty acre farm in Carthage, some coarse-clad but grateful Irishman would call on him and remind him of the good old times of the digging. One said : " Commissioner, I was the man who carried the lantern," or recalled some other service; and he was seldom without the aid in his garden or on his farm, of one or more of these humble volunteers, happy to work for him without pay, weeks at a time; but whom he lodged, fed and dismissed with better clothes and a sense that in him they had a friend who would welcome them whenever they came. He had the strength of a giant, and did not abstain from using it in a combative sense on a fit occasion. When his eldest daughter was living in a house not far from his own at Lyons, with her first child in her arms, he became aware that she was in danger from a stout, unprincipled tramp who had called on her as a beggar and found her alone. Hastening to the house, without saying a word, he grasped the fellow around body and both arms, and carried him, bellowing for mercy, through the yard and into the middle of the street, where he set him down. Greatly relieved, the miserable wretch ran as if he had escaped from a lion.

He was an early riser, enjoyed his food, used neither intoxicating drinks nor tobacco. "Thank you, I smoke clear," he said, when invited to take a cigar. His evenings were always spent at home, when practicable. His daughters do not remember that he ever spoke a cross word in his family, or indulged in a selfish act, or showed anger under any provocation. He was refined without regard to conventionality. His patience was imperturbable and his self-command absolute. Such ability to govern his own spirit is to a good man and reformer as invaluable as it is rare.

His delight in little children was a conspicuous trait. They were never in his way. He loved to have them with him in his garden, teaching them how to sow seeds and pull up the weeds. When he came in, he would be carrying two or three of his little grand-children on his broad shoulders at once. He always carried in his pocket a little wooden folding comb which his own father had made for him, with his own hands, and once when he came in from his garden, after sowing pepper-grass, one of these little ones, who had been assisting, climbing up in a chair beside him, begged the privilege of using this comb on his head, which was granted. After she had proceeded a little in the operation, finding a bald spot on the top of his head, she excited a great laugh by saying, " Grandpa, why don't 'oo sow hair seed on here ? "

While he lived in Rochester, editing the " Freeman" for the abolitionists, he was resorted to from far and near, by entire strangers, for the settlement of disputes. They were ready to abide by his decision, for they said he was better than any of the city courts. "Grace Greenwood," who lived in Rochester at the time, says she well remembers "his grand and stately presence coming down the street, when the people would part in reverence and admiration on either side, like the waves of the sea, for him to pass through."

With all this dignity of demeanor there was never any austerity or arrogance. Once, in Lyons, when there was great excitement about the "sin of dancing," the ministers all preaching and praying against it, Mr. Holley quietly said: " It is as natural for young people to like to dance as for the apple-trees to blossom in the spring."

For the heart of a man we naturally look to the closing scene. One of his daughters gives me this account of it :

"The affection between my father - and his brothers and only sister was above anything I have ever known on earth. They never separated without tears and kisses, and to the latest hour of his life Salisbury was treasured with the fondest affection. The first person he expected to meet in heaven was his mother. His brain was clear and unclouded to the last moment of his life. I was with him most of the time during his last sickness. He again and again expressed his full faith in a glorious resurrection. He said, a few days before his death: 'I believe Jesus Christ was a man, and I believe in the final restoration of all mankind to happiness.' The day before he died he tenderly assured all of us, his family, that he 'should always love us and think of us in heaven.' 'I NEVER DECEIVED ANYBODY IN MY LIFE,' was one of his latest declarations. About the last thing from his lips was: 'I think I shall be dead in two hours. Let the funeral be plain. God bless my wife and children.' He died at 8 o'clock in the morning, on the 4th of March, 1841, while the Rochester bells were ringing and cannon firing, in honor of President Harrison's inauguration at Washington."

So much for his domestic character.

As to the public character of Myron Holley, no testimony can be more reliable than that of Col. William L. Stone, in his day the highly popular editor of the New York *Commercial Advertiser*. Col. Stone was well versed in the history of New York, was an outspoken anti-mason and a decided, if not bitter, anti-abolitionist. He was well acquainted with the Holley family, and personal characterization was his forte. In the following biographical sketch he makes some strange mistakes of facts — especially one, in saying the State allowed Mr. Holley "a commission upon the moneys he had disbursed" — and lets his pro-slavery prejudices appear in full force. The present generation will pity him for that, but it makes the praise he bestows on Mr. Holley all the stronger, — in fact, time has converted that part of his sketch into the highest eulogium. Take notice : Col. Stone supposed the State had paid Mr. Holley money which it still owes.

"DEATH OF MYRON HOLLEY. — The decease of this distinguished man was announced several days ago, during the absence of the present writer, or the event would have received a notice less sum-mary than it did. He was a native of the town of Salisbury, Connecticut, a brother of the late Rev. Dr. Horace Holley, President of the Transylvania University, and also of Orville Holley, the present Surveyor General of this state. There were seven brothers, distinguished alike for their talents and fine manly proportions, being all, or nearly all of them, larger than the ordinary size of man. Myron, the subject of this notice, began his collegiate life, we believe, at Williamstown, and completed it at Harvard.

"He was destined for the bar, and went through the usual preparatory course of legal reading ; but the drudgery of the profession was uncongenial to his habits, and his taste was better satisfied with the study of belles-lettres and the classics, than with the law. The consequence was, that he never entered upon the practice of his profession. At the age of about twenty-two he settled in the then infant and now beautiful town of Canandaigua, where he soon afterward married. In the year 1804 he went into the book-selling business there, and continued therein some five or six years, when he was appointed clerk of the county of Ontario.

"He was subsequently elected to the State Legislature, and was a member when the project of uniting the lakes with the ocean, by means of a canal, began to be discussed. He at once saw the importance of the subject. The grandeur of the enterprise suited well his expansive and vivid imagination, and he enlisted in the cause with all the talent and enthusiasm of his nature. He saw in the future a stream of gold from the great West, flowing into the lap of New York, and with all the energies of his mind he labored to induce the government of the State to cut a channel for the glittering wave. Side by side with De Witt Clinton during the sessions of 1816 and 1817, did he labor at Albany, to induce the Legislature to enter upon the mighty work; and on the passage of the act of 1817, authorizing its commencement, with Stephen Van Rensselaer, De Witt Clinton, and Samuel Young, Myron Holley was appointed one of the commissioners. He was charged as the acting commissioner of the Erie canal, and Colonel Young as that of the canal to unite the Hudson with Lake Champlain.

"Great apprehensions were entertained, in consequence of the magnitude of the undertaking, lest the people should be alarmed at the cost, or become discouraged at the slowness of the progress. Mr. Holley wisely counselled the construction of the middle section, from Utica to Syracuse, first, thus as it were, *compelling* the people East and West of that section to insist upon the completion of the whole with the utmost possible expedition. The result was unexampled in the annals of internal improvement. The ground was broken by the commissioners on the 4th of July. 1817, at Rome, and a boat from Lake Erie fell into the embrace of the ocean in October, 1825.

"Mr. Holley had never been remarkable for his attention to the minor details of business. In his own private affairs he oftener paid out his dollars and cents without counting them, than with it.* This easy trait in his character did not escape the subordinate agents employed to assist him in the disbursement of the public moneys along the line of the canal; and owing to his want of exactness in these matters, to probable losses, and possibly to the dishonesty of a bank teller through whose hands the bundles of bank notes were passed to him in Albany — a teller who afterward turned out to be a defaulter and a rascal — Mr. Holley's vouchers did not cover his apparent expenditures, and he became technically, a defaulter. The consequence was a resignation of. the post he had so ably filled. But he was not suspected of dishonesty; and by allowing him a commission upon the

---

* If this was so, Mr. Holley resembled Daniel Webster in that respect. But it is doubtful. Mr. Holley was not penurious, yet in the " minor details of business," his results and reports show that no man of his responsibilities was ever more careful and accurate.

moneys he had disbursed. his accounts were finally adjusted with the state.

"But with a soul alive to honor, his sensitive mind, wounded at the imputations cast upon him by the partizan papers of the day, rested ever afterward beneath a cloud. He settled at Lyons, a pleasant village upon the canal about twenty miles north of Geneva, where, in retirement, he devoted himself to horticultural pursuits for several years, with great success. His time was divided alternately between his library, his garden. and his private friends.

"After the abduction and murder of Morgan, Mr. Holley became actively engaged in the anti-masonic controversy. His feelings recoiled with horror from the dark tragedy * by which freemasonry killed itself as well as its victim, and he joined with spirit in the contest which ensued. Having labored with success in the cause in the West, he repaired to Connecticut and took the editorial charge of a newspaper devoted to it in Hartford. He edited this paper with ability for about a year, but the people of Connecticut saw little necessity

* That is true enough. But it was the fact that the authors of the tragedy were screened by an oath-bound fraternity, many of whose members sat on the bench of justice, that impelled Mr. Holly to action.

for fighting the battles of anti-masonry over again in that state, after the battle had been fought and won on the ground of the original excitement, and Mr. Holley returned to Western New York, and settled down upon a farm in the vicinity of Rochester, where he again turned horticulturist with as much taste and success as before.

"About three years ago another change came over him. He was ever a lover of 'the largest liberty,' and the idea of 'the oppressor's rod,' wherever or by whomsoever wielded, was abhorrent to the noble impulses of his nature. The exaggerated tales of human-suffering and woe among the sable sons of the South, as declared by the agents and ministers of the abolitionists, seized upon him with a degree of freshness and power which seemed to drive all other thoughts from his mind, and he at once entered upon this new field of labor with a zeal that would have done honor to Peter the Hermit. Disposing of his farm, he invested its proceeds in the establishment of an abolition press at Rochester. But it was too late. The abolition fires were fast burning out. Even his own acknowledged literary taste and talent could not sustain his paper; and having exhausted his means it died.

"Mr. Holley struggled onward by public lectures

to keep up the contest, but in vain.   .   .   .   .
Having ceased those exertions, all other earthly
labors have soon been ended, and he sleeps with
the dead.   He was a man of fine feelings and a
noble heart, of elegant person and accomplished
manners.   His mind was an ample store-house of
English and classical literature, and they were
poured forth in conversation with rich and eloquent
profusion.   As a colloquialist, it may be doubted
whether even Coleridge was more fascinating,
although he was more ambitious and profound.
His life, as we have seen, was full of vicissitudes.
In a pecuniary point of view it was never profitable to himself.   The middle portion of it was of
great advantage to the state.   His latter years
were by no means those of unclouded brightness;
and his sun has set in gloom!"

Mr. Holley was the last man in New York likely
to be carried into the abolition camp by "exaggerated tales," but Col. Stone, who did not remember
one of the "tales" in his own columns, ante, page
80, must somehow account for his old friend's
going over to the enemy.   It was not very long
after Mr. Holley's death that the heroic John
Quincy Adams, in his trial before the House of

Representatives, showed the slaveholders, out of their own mouths and newspapers, that these tales were by no means exaggerated.

Had Col. Stone lived till our day, he would have seen that Mr. Holley's founding the Liberty Party was the greatest success of his life, and really stands in the same relation to the present and, it is to be hoped, future unity and glory of our republic, as his canal success does to the prosperity and wealth of New York.

The State of New York, beyond dispute, saved $80,000 by throwing upon Mr. Holley a burden of responsibility, for which it paid him nothing — not even one per cent. on his disbursements. It ascertained his perfect honesty, and placed the fact on record. It then restored his small estate which he had placed in its possession, to secure it against an alleged default, at the same time exacting from him a voucher that he would not prosecute his righteous claim to any percentage whatever on his disbursements. This claim, at simple interest, must now amount to more than $100,000, which is as justly due to Mr. Holley's heirs, and as much needed by some of them, as any debt that was ever due in this world. It is impossible to predict when it will be paid. And it is equally impossible to see how the people of New York, made rich by Myron Holley's canal labors, can enjoy riding in their beautiful Central Park without seeing there a statue of Myron Holley, as well as one of De Witt Clinton.

The ROCHESTER DEMOCRAT of March 5, 1841, said of Myron Holley — and never were truer words uttered of the dead : —

"This eminent citizen, accomplished scholar and noble man, expired yesterday morning, at his residence on Johnson Street, in this city, at the age of sixty-two, carrying with him to the grave the love and regrets of all who knew him. The public services of Mr. Holley are engraved upon the state, as enduring as Lake Erie and the Hudson, while his private virtues and benevolence will live in the hearts of his friends and acquaintances until they cease to beat."